THE WICKED MARQUIS

When lovely young Orelia Stanyon returned home from the George and Dragon Inn, she found she could not forget the dark, sardonic stranger who had rescued her from two drunken fops. He was a man whose sudden and passionate kiss had stirred Orelia's deepest desires.

She was alone in the world. The only family she had was her cousin Caroline—a beautiful woman who lived a wild and impetuous existence. Hardly the proper guardian for Orelia.

But then, one day, Caroline announced her engagement. She was to wed the Marquis of Ryde. Handsome and irresistible, he was one of the wealthiest men in Regency England. Perhaps now the family would be secure.

But Orelia was in for a surprise when she met the Marquis. For she knew him as the dark, mysterious man who had secretly won her heart months before at the George and Dragon Inn . . .

**An enchanting new novel
of hidden passions by the world's best-loved
writer of romantic fiction.**

BARBARA CARTLAND

Books by BARBARA CARTLAND

Romantic Novels

The Fire of Love
The Unpredictable Bride
Love Holds the Cards
A Virgin in Paris
Love to the Rescue
Love Is Contraband
The Enchanting Evil
The Unknown Heart
The Secret Fear
The Reluctant Bride
The Pretty Horse-Breakers
The Audacious Adventuress
Lost Enchantment

Halo for the Devil
The Irresistible Buck
The Complacent Wife
The Odious Duke
The Daring Deception
No Darkness for Love
The Little Adventure
Lessons in Love
Journey to Paradise
The Bored Bridegroom
The Penniless Peer
The Dangerous Dandy
The Ruthless Rake
The Wicked Marquis

Autobiographical and Biographical

The Isthmus Years 1919–1939
The Years of Opportunity 1939–1945
I Search for Rainbows 1945–1966
We Danced All Night 1919–1929
Ronald Cartland
       (with a Foreword by Sir Winston Churchill)
Polly, My Wonderful Mother

Historical

Bewitching Women
The Outrageous Queen
       (The Story of Queen Christina of Sweden)
The Scandalous Life of King Carol
The Private Life of King Charles II
The Private Life of Elizabeth, Empress of Austria
Josephine, Empress of France
Diane de Poitiers
Metternich—the Passionate Diplomat

Sociology

You in the Home
The Fascinating Forties
Marriage for Moderns
Be Vivid, Be Vital
Love, Life and Sex
Look Lovely, Be Lovely
Vitamins for Vitality
Husbands and Wives

Etiquette
The Many Facets of Love
Sex and the Teenager
The Book of Charm
Living Together
Woman—The Enigma
The Youth Secret
The Magic of Honey

Barbara Cartland's Health Food Cookery Book
Barbara Cartland's Book of Beauty and Health
Barbara Cartland's Book of Useless Information

The Wicked Marquis
Barbara Cartland

BANTAM BOOKS
TORONTO · NEW YORK · LONDON

*This low-priced Bantam Book
has been completely reset in a type face
designed for easy reading, and was printed
from new plates. It contains the complete
text of the original hard-cover edition.*
NOT ONE WORD HAS BEEN OMITTED.

THE WICKED MARQUIS
A Bantam Book / published by arrangement with the author

PRINTING HISTORY
*Originally published by Hutchison & Co. in England 1973
Bantam edition published September 1974*

*Bantam Books are published by Bantam Books, Inc. Its trade-
mark, consisting of the words "Bantam Books" and the por-
trayal of a bantam, is registered in the United States Patent
Office and in other countries. Marca Registrada. Bantam
Books, Inc., 666 Fifth Avenue, New York, New York 10019.*

PRINTED IN THE UNITED STATES OF AMERICA

AUTHOR'S NOTE

The Bill of the Honourable Henry Grey Bennet to abolish the employment of Climbing boys was accepted by the House of Commons for the second time in 1819. But it was thrown out of the House of Lords after the Earl of Lauderdale made a facetious speech which kept his fellow Peers in roars of laughter.

Innumerable little boys suffered hell until "The Chimney-Sweeps Bill" in 1875 brought an end to their sufferings.

The Prince Regent's Chef—Carème produced a *Menu de 36 entrées* at a dinner party given on the 15th January, 1817.

1

The door of the 'George and Dragon' opened and a Gentleman stepped out into the crisp and frosty November air.

The sun was sinking low behind the trees, their leafless branches like skeleton fingers etched against the crimson and gold of the sky.

The noise and laughter from within the Inn was dimmed as the Gentleman closed the door.

Then, setting his high hat at a rakish angle on his dark hair, he looked to where across the Village Green a black and yellow Phaeton pulled by four perfectly matched chestnuts was waiting for him.

They were not the only fine piece of bloodstock on the Green: hunters, tired and muddy, were being ridden slowly home by their grooms, and the Phaetons, the curricles and the closed landaus of their owners, who had spent an exhausting day in the saddle, were waiting to convey their masters in comfort.

The Gentleman was just about to cross the narrow country road to his Phaeton when he heard a soft, musical, but slightly frightened voice say:

'I pray you, Sirs . . . to let me pass.'

'No, you have to choose! It must be one or the other of us!'

The Gentleman recognised the voice of a somewhat dissolute young Baronet, and glancing casually to the side of the Inn he saw, standing on the high step of a black and white thatched cottage, a girl wearing a long blue cloak trimmed with grey fur.

The hood was pulled over her head, but even at this

distance he could distinguish a small white face with
large dark eyes.

In front of her stood the Baronet and another young
man, both of them in mud-spattered white buckskin
breeches and pink hunting-coats with the green lapels
of the Morden Chase.

'Come along, make up your mind!' the Baronet insisted.

There was no doubt from the slight slur of his words
that the hot punch served in the 'George and Dragon'
had proved over-potent.

The Gentleman took another step towards his Phaeton. After all, it was none of his business, and if young
Haydon and his friend wished to bait a local maiden
he would not spoil their fun.

'Please . . . please let me proceed . . . I beg . . . of
you!'

It was the girl's voice which made the Gentleman
turn back. There was something so young, so defenceless about it, something which made him on an
impulse retrace his steps.

'I think I am the winner!'

It was the Baronet's friend who spoke. There was no
doubt that he was considerably foxed and that the
drink he had consumed had also made him aggressively
amorous.

'Come along, you entrancing little creature!' he said.

He moved forward and put out his arms as if he
would place them around the girl on the step.

She winced away from him, and as she did so the
Gentleman said drily:

'I think you heard the Lady say she wished to pass!'

He drawled the words with a slight note of amusement in his voice, but the Baronet turned to look at
him sharply and almost immediately there was a look of
apology on his face.

His friend, on the other hand, took longer to discover who had spoken.

'What the devil has it got . . . ?' he began, only, on
seeing who stood there, to appear confused, his aggres-
sion oozing away from him.

The Gentleman ignored them both. He merely bowed slightly ironically to the small figure on the doorstep.

'May I escort you, Madame, to your carriage—if you have one?'

She looked up at him. In the fast fading light he could see that she was very young and her eyes were indeed extraordinarily large.

'Thank . . . you,' she said breathlessly.

She moved down the step to stand beside him, ignoring the Baronet and his friend, who let her pass without saying anything further.

She was very small, her head hardly reaching to the top of the Gentleman's broad shoulders, but then he was unusually tall and there was, she thought, as she glanced up at him nervously, something almost overpowering about him.

It was less his looks than his presence, and she could understand why the men who had been harrying her as if she were a fox they had run to earth had been stricken into silence.

The Village Green extended to the right of the Inn and lay in front of some other black and white thatched cottages.

There were wooden stocks at the edge of it and on the other side the Duck Pond in which legend had it that more than a dozen witches had in one century or another met their deaths.

In the centre of the Green there was an old-fashioned gig and drawing it, or rather cropping the grass, was a large, fat piebald pony.

It was almost a ludicrous contrast with the elegant vehicles and the high-spirited horses of the Gentry clustered around the Inn.

The girl in the blue cloak moved towards the gig, walking quickly, and because she was so small she seemed to hurry while the Gentleman appeared merely to stroll and yet to keep pace with her.

They were away from the cottages and out of earshot of the two discomfited Hunting Bucks before she spoke again.

Then, in the soft little voice which had attracted the attention of the Gentleman in the first instance, she said:

'I am indeed grateful to you, Sir. It was my own fault—I had forgotten that the Hunt met here today.'

'It happens every year, I believe,' the Gentleman remarked.

'Yes, it does,' she replied. 'But it had slipped my memory.'

'Then I should be more careful next year.'

'I will.'

They had reached the gig by this time and he saw that the reins were neatly knotted and hitched to the dashboard.

'You have far to go?' he enquired.

She shook her head.

'A very short distance. And thank you once again.'

He looked down at her. The dying sun made a last effort and a ray of sunlight striking through the bare trees shone on her face. She was very lovely—surprisingly and unexpectedly lovely.

There was something ethereal about the small pointed face—a spiritual look—such as the Gentleman had not seen before, or at any rate not for a long time, on any woman.

It reminded him of a painting, although he could not for the moment recall the name of the artist.

He saw now that her eyes were blue—not the blue which might be expected to go with the very pale gold hair peeping from beneath her hood—but the deep tempestuous blue of a winter sea. And strangely enough the long lashes surrounding them were dark.

'Strange eyes,' he told himself. 'Eyes that hold a certain mystery about them!'

And he knew as he thought of it that the girl's eyes, looking up into his, were held as if spell-bound.

'You must take better care of yourself,' he said, and his voice was deep.

Then with a little twist to his lips he asked:

'Do I get my reward?'

'Reward?' she questioned.

She was still looking at him, thinking that never in her life had she imagined that a man could be so handsome, so incredibly goodlooking, and at the same time look so cynical, so sardonic, and . . . perhaps the right word was . . . raffish!

It was a face, she told herself, of a buccaneer. Then because the question confused her she dropped her eyes.

She put her hand on the gig as if for support.

'I have saved you,' the Gentleman said, 'and you must pay your debt. Do they not teach you in the country that a debt of honour must be honoured?'

She glanced up at him again bewildered, uncertain.

'I do not think . . . I know what you . . . mean,' she said hardly above a whisper.

'I think you do,' he replied, and lifting her chin with the fingers of his right hand he bent and kissed her lips.

For a long moment neither of them moved. She felt as if she had been turned into stone. The warm hard pressure of his mouth on hers was something she could not credit, could not realise was actually happening.

With his lips he captured and held her prisoner, and she knew in some obscure part of her mind that she should attempt to escape.

She must move, she must draw away! Yet she found she had no willpower, but was lost in a strange and breathless bewilderment in which she was mesmerised into immobility.

Then he raised his head and set her free.

'You will doubtless make some bovine young countryman extremely happy,' he said in a dry mocking voice, and walked away.

She stood very still watching him go. She could not believe what had taken place—a man she had never seen in her life before, a man she did not know, had kissed her!

Shamelessly, immodestly, unbelievably, she had not struggled against him or even fought to prevent it happening. She had just stood and let his lips hold hers.

It was a dream, it was something which could not have happened, and yet it had!

She climbed into the gig. The sun had gone and the tall, broad-shouldered figure walking away from her was lost in the dusk.

Anyway, she did not wish to look—she could not look—she only knew she must get away—she must return home and try and explain to herself, if she could, what had occurred.

The fat piebald pony moved slowly and with some reluctance onto the road. He was leaving behind the grass of the Green, but he knew he was going home and there would be a comfortable stall and fresh hay waiting for him.

He quickened his pace a little and after jogging along the road for barely a quarter of a mile, turned in through a stone-flanked gateway.

It was not a long drive, and as they emerged from the shade of the ancient oak trees, there was in front of them a beautiful red-brick Elizabethan mansion with its timbered roof, gabled windows, and studded-oak front door.

As the gig appeared a groom came hurrying from the side of the house where he had obviously been waiting.

'Ye be late, Miss Orelia,' he said with the reproachful familiarity of an old servant.

'I know, Abbey,' Orelia replied. 'But poor Sarah only passed away an hour ago.'

'She be dead then, Miss?'

Orelia nodded.

'Yes, Abbey, and we cannot be anything but glad. She has been in terrible pain these past months.'

'Aye, I knows, Miss, and her must have been glad to have had ye there.'

'I think she wanted me,' Orelia said simply as she stepped down from the gig.

As she did so the front door opened. Another old man, well into his seventies, stood waiting.

'You're back, Miss Orelia,' he said. 'I was just about to send Abbey for you.'

'Uncle Arthur?' Orelia asked quickly.

'The Doctor is with him, but I don't think there is much hope.'

'I will go up to him,' Orelia said.

She undid the clasp of her cloak and the Butler took it from her. She put up her hand to her hair. It was pale gold—so pale it reminded one of the sunshine in the very early spring.

Her dress was plain and slightly old-fashioned, but it could not conceal the thin, lithe grace of her young figure, and the soft curves of her breasts. Above them the long slim neck gave the tiny face with its fair hair a poise and at the same time a fairy-like beauty which made Orelia seem almost unearthly—a nymph or perhaps a very young goddess from Olympus.

She ran up the stairs, her slippers hardly seeming to touch the worn carpet.

Then on the landing she paused for a moment, her eyes dark with apprehension and anxiety before she opened the bedroom door.

It was the following day before Orelia had time to think again of the Gentleman who had rescued her from the undesirable attentions of two drunken young Hunting Fops, only to insult her himself.

And yet had it been such an insult? Had she not condoned his behaviour by not protesting or struggling against him? She knew he had thought her to be of no consequence. 'You will doubtless make some bovine young countryman extremely happy.'

She could hear his voice, with that dry, mocking note in it which told her all too clearly that he had not even thought of her as a fit wife for a Gentleman.

But of course no Lady of Breeding or Quality would drive unattended!

She longed to explain why she had taken the gig and fat Dapple to the village without a servant to escort her.

Abbey had had a bottle of medicine to collect from the physician's; the boy who assisted him in the stables was sick. If she was to visit old Sarah, who she knew to be dying, then she must go alone.

How could she have been so foolish as to forget the Meet of the Morden Chase at the 'George and Dragon'? And how could she have stood tongue-tied and motionless when the stranger had kissed her?

She thought perhaps she had been bemused into a state of stupidity by Sarah's death—dear old Sarah, whom she had known since she was a child, who had looked after her when she had first come to live with her Uncle Arthur at Morden, and who had for years been in fact the only mother-like figure in her life.

Yet now Sarah was gone, and Uncle Arthur too.

He died just before dawn, holding Orelia's hand, but talking of people long since dead or whom she had never known.

She had realised when he spoke of her father how deeply he had loved his brother. But there were other relations whom he must have known as a boy and who, to Orelia, were only names.

Then shortly before he had died he had asked:

'Caroline, where is Caroline?'

'She is abroad, Uncle Arthur,' Orelia answered. 'She would wish to be with you now if she knew that you needed her. But I am not even aware of her address.'

'Abroad! Always gadding about—never content to stay at home—always in trouble. You must help her, Orelia.'

'I am afraid Caroline will not listen to me, Uncle Arthur.'

'Yes she will,' he insisted.

Although his voice was weak there was a positive note in it that had not been there before.

'She would always listen to you. You were a good influence—a very good influence—on Caroline. You will stay with her—do not let her get into trouble—promise me!'

'I promise that I will try to do what you want,' Orelia replied.

'Promise!' he said again.

'I promise,' she answered.

She was not quite certain what she was promising

and yet she had the feeling that she had made a vow to a dying man that had some significance.

It was strange that his last coherent thought and words should have been of Caroline. In these past years she had meant very little in his life, and sometimes it seemed as if he had almost forgotten her and thought that Orelia was his daughter, because they shared so many interests in common.

Caroline could not be expected to be content with the poverty, the discomfort and the lack of amusement at Morden.

She was so beautiful, so gay, so alive, so eager to be amused by the social world, that it was not surprising that they heard little of her.

But now that her father was dead Orelia knew that somehow she must get in touch with Caroline, that she must come home; that she must claim what small inheritance was left to her.

In the months that followed Orelia felt that everything depended on Caroline's return.

She must do her best to carry on, to keep the Estate, such as it was, going until the daughter of the house and the heir came home.

The lawyers agreed to advance certain monies for the payment of the old servants and for the farming of the lands but they made it quite clear that they did it with reluctance, having really no authority to pay for anything without Lady Caroline's permission.

'I think she is in Rome,' Orelia told them, 'but I cannot be certain. A courier brought us a letter from her seven months ago. She told us she was travelling in Italy and intended to stay in Rome for some time. That is all I know. I have sent a letter by sea to the address from which she wrote, but of course she may have moved.'

'Then we must trust, Miss Stanyon, that you will be as economical as possible,' the lawyer said.

His precise, dusty voice, seemed to have no touch of humanity in it.

'I will do my best,' Orelia replied.

A few distant relatives had come to the funeral and when it was over the Will had been read. It was very simple.

The fifth Earl of Morden had left everything he possessed to his only child, Lady Caroline Stanyon. But in a codicil dated September 9th, 1817, he had added:

'I also leave to my Daughter the care and Guardianship of my niece, Orelia Stanyon, whose kindness and solicitude for Me During these Years has brought Me great Happiness. I enjoin my Daughter to allow her Cousin Orelia to make this house her Home and I ask Orelia in her turn to help my Daughter, Caroline, and to act as she has done in the past both as her Inspiration and her Conscience.'

Orelia felt a flush rise to her cheeks as the lawyer read out the strange request.

She had known that the elderly relations present had glanced at her curiously and at the same time that there was an expression of relief on their faces, thinking that she was provided for and they did not have to offer her any sort of hospitality.

It was only when they had all left and Orelia was alone in the house that she faced the future with apprehension.

What would Caroline think of her father's strange instructions? Would she be prepared to act as Guardian to a girl with whom she had been brought up but with whom she obviously now had very little in common?

It was one thing for Caroline to have had an affection for her younger cousin when they were children, to allow Orelia to run after her, to serve her, to obey her, to love her and to be proudly her confidante.

Orelia remembered how often she had sat perched on Caroline's bed, listening to the stories of her successes with men. Caroline had incited men to pursue her since she was thirteen, and, Orelia thought, it was not surprising.

There was no one more entrancing, more beguiling, or more flirtatious than Caroline.

With her dark, tumbled locks, her oval face, dancing black eyes and pouting red mouth, she was an irresistible bait for every young man within the vicinity of twenty miles of her home.

Then as she grew older she went off to stay in London with her Godmother, who was a distant relative, and came back elated with her success.

She was ready to talk from dusk to eve of the swains who had laid their hearts at her feet, had written odes to her eyebrows, and had toasted her the whole length and breadth of St. James's Street.

When she was seventeen Caroline fell in love.

It was then that she found Orelia indispensable, for Caroline had always to talk of her feelings, her heart-throbs, her future plans, and Orelia was only too happy to listen.

There were three years between the cousins and yet sometimes, at fourteen, Orelia had felt that she was older than Caroline.

Caroline was so impetuous, so irresponsible, so easily swayed by the excitement, the thrill of the moment, that she never gave herself time to think. She never stopped to consider before she acted.

'Oh, please Caroline, do not do that!' Orelia would plead, only to have Caroline reply:

'Why not? What am I waiting for? This is life! This is living! I want to enjoy myself every moment of it, Orelia! It is so easy to miss something and indeed I intend to miss nothing!'

Caroline did miss nothing—crazily impetuous, she married a Stanyon who was a distant cousin, a spendthrift, a gambler, a handsome young blade of no consequence, when she was eighteen.

It was reaction from her first love affair, as Orelia knew. It was a desperate gesture to prevent herself from being hurt, to pretend that her heart did not ache, that she did not miss the man she loved and who had gone away because he had loved her.

Left on his father's death with a multitude of debts and an impoverished estate, no other course was open to him.

'Yes, I am Lord Faringham,' he had said bitterly, 'a nobleman with a leaking roof and empty pockets! Of what value is my heart in such circumstances?'

There had been floods of tears from Caroline and wild incoherent utterances from the man who had worshipped her since she was in the nursery.

Then one morning he was no longer there.

'I will make my fortune, my darling,' he wrote. 'Wait for me—I love you, I love you!'

But Caroline would not wait! Denying her own unhappiness, running away from her own emotions, she allowed herself to be swept off her feet by an expertly plausible young libertine.

It was an idiotic marriage—a marriage that could never possibly have succeeded. But nothing Orelia might say would stop Caroline from marrying Harry Stanyon.

And within six months of the marriage Harry was dead. He died in the same crazy manner in which he had lived—riding blindfold in a race across country in which two other men were badly maimed and three horses had to be destroyed.

It was the sort of unnecessary tragedy which made people say that the roistering days of the Regency had gone too far—that the Regent was a degrading influence and set a bad example to the hot-blooded young Bucks who surrounded him; that Society should show more sense of propriety and that something would have to be done about it!

It was a nine-days' wonder—the gossips talked of little else; there were cartoons and scurrilous articles in the newspapers; but after it was quickly forgotten.

The fact remained that Harry Stanyon was dead and Caroline was a widow before she was nineteen.

It was then, when for the first time in her life Caroline was a little subdued and undoubtedly apprehensive of the future, that her Godmother came to the rescue.

Before the full effects of what had happened could be felt at Morden, before the Earl could realise with what a rake-hell set of Society his daughter had become involved, Caroline set off for Europe on the Grand Tour.

Only an occasional letter told her father and Orelia where she was and what was happening to her.

But even the few badly written lines she sent them told Orelia all too clearly that Caroline had not only recovered her spirits, but was enjoying herself inordinately.

Now, thinking of her cousin, Orelia gave a little sigh. Unless Caroline found another husband, what would she do on her return? That she would find Morden extremely dull was obvious.

As they were near London it would not be difficult to invite friends to stay and for Caroline to seek the Social world she so enjoyed.

Yet where was the money to come from? That was the real question, the real problem, the crux on which everything rested—money!

Orelia was tired of hearing about it—money needed for the land; money for the house; money for the wages —one thing was sure, although she never complained, there was never any money for herself!

Then Orelia began to think. She had plenty of time to do so for they were snowed in that Christmas.

Fortunately there was plenty of wood to keep the fires going in the house, and the old cook who had been at Morden for over fifty years had salted away game and fish so there was enough to eat, besides the hams hanging from the rafters in the kitchen and the doves which were plentiful in the dovecote.

But Orelia was not particularly concerned with what she ate.

A sudden idea had come to her as she tidied up her Uncle's papers—the papers on which he had been working up to the time of his death.

She had helped him with them, copying out his untidy manuscript in her beautiful, elegant handwriting; filing away the reference books so that he could consult them again at a moment's notice; keeping copious notes so that in the end she felt as if she knew as much about his subject as he did.

Papers would come from London and she would often read them first and then tell her Uncle the parts that were particularly applicable to the book he was compiling.

Copies of Hansard—the official daily report of the speeches in the Houses of Parliament—would arrive regularly and Orelia would look through them when her Uncle did not have time in case there was anything that had a bearing on what particularly concerned him.

But when he died his book was not completed. No more than half was done and Orelia knew that she could not finish it. There was, however, something else she could do.

The more she thought about it the more she was certain that it was within her powers.

All through December and after Christmas Orelia sat in her Uncle's Study working at his desk and at the end of January she packed up a parcel—not a very large one—and sent it to London.

When it had gone she felt curiously depleted—as if she had given so much of herself and now she was left with nothing more to give.

But life at Morden still had to carry on. It was not until the middle of May that unexpectedly and without any warning, Caroline returned.

One moment it seemed to Orelia the place was quiet and dark, and the next minute it was all noise, excitement and sunshine—Caroline was home!

She stepped out of an expensive carriage drawn by four sweating horses and for a moment Orelia found it was hard to recognise her.

Never had she looked so lovely or so elegant. Her driving-coat of red velvet trimmed with tiny bands of ermine was echoed by her bonnet trimmed with red ostrich feathers and tied under her chin with satin ribbons.

'Orelia, Orelia! I am home! My love, how divine to see you. I have so much to tell you.'

It was Caroline, there was no doubt about that.

She swept into the Hall, laughing, talking, smiling at the old servants, demanding refreshments, throwing her ermine muff on one chair, her bonnet on another.

Orelia felt as if life had come back to the house and that something within her own heart leapt to meet it.

'Dearest, what have you done to yourself?' Caroline exclaimed. 'But I know, of course, what it is! You have grown older. You have grown up, and I was still thinking of you as the little girl who sat on my bed and listened to my lurid adventures in love.'

'We cannot help growing older,' Orelia laughed. 'I am eighteen, Caroline, and you will be twenty-two in July!'

'Do not remind me,' Caroline begged. 'But you—you are lovely, Orelia. I had no idea you would grow into a beauty!'

'A very pale one beside you,' Orelia said quietly.

'Nonsense,' Caroline replied. 'We are a perfect foil for each other—as we always have been. You were always the good little angel and I was a naughty black devil—do you not remember?'

'I remember you were always beautiful and always the most exciting person I have ever known.'

Caroline laughed, obviously pleased with the compliment. 'Oh, I have so much to tell you,' she said.

Then looking round the room, she added:

'Heavens, how shabby it all is! Thank goodness we can get away from it! We are going to London, Orelia, and you are coming with me! I planned that I should take you as my companion, but now that I have seen you I know it is imperative that your beauty should no longer be hidden away in this dismally dull hole!'

She linked her arm in Orelia's.

'We will set the town on fire together. I wonder what they will call us? For everyone in the *Ton* has nicknames, as you well know!'

'I have heard that you are "The Incomparable of Incomparables",' Orelia said.

'That is but one of them,' Caroline replied. 'But what fun we will have! We will light the Social World with our looks and our brilliance, you and I! And how extraordinary it was of Papa to make me your Guardian—I shall be a very bad one—I expect you to guard me, Orelia!'

'You know about Uncle Arthur?' Orelia asked in a low voice.

'I found a letter from the lawyers waiting for me in my Godmother's house in London.'

'I wrote to Rome,' Orelia said.

'I had left, but a friend brought it to me in Paris,' Caroline replied, 'but you only told me that Papa was dead. When I returned last week I found with the lawyers' communication a copy of the Will.'

'I am afraid, Caroline, there is very little money,' Orelia said apologising. 'When you talk of our going to London I must ask how we can possibly afford it.'

Caroline threw back her head and laughed. She looked so pretty as she did so that Orelia felt she was like a gay bird of Paradise and that it would be impossible to explain to this glowing, glorious creature that none of the things she wanted would be possible because they could not pay for them.

'I have not told you my news,' Caroline said. 'Now, Orelia, hold your breath, for it really is stupendous! I am to be married!'

'Married!' Orelia ejaculated. 'But who to?'

'You would never guess, you would never guess in a thousand years!' Caroline said. 'It is so wonderful, so marvellous, so unbelievably exciting! But Orelia, the Marquis of Ryde has offered for me!'

'The Marquis of Ryde?' Orelia repeated. 'Should I know of him?'

'You do not know the Marquis of Ryde?' Caroline cried. 'Fie on you, Orelia—you really do live in the back of beyond if you have never heard of the Wicked Marquis!'

'The Wicked Marquis?' Orelia echoed rather stupidly. 'But surely, if that is what he is called, you cannot wish to marry him?'

'Not wish to marry the Marquis of Ryde!' Caroline exclaimed. 'But you must be nitwitted if you do not realise, Orelia, that I have landed the most elusive, the most sought after, the most stupendous matrimonial catch in the whole of Great Britain!'

She drew a deep breath.

'His Lordship is rich, he is of tremendous consequence, he has so many possessions I do not think he knows all of them himself; he is handsome, compelling, and, of course, wicked! He is irresistible!'

'And he loves you?' Orelia asked.

'I do not believe that the Marquis loves anyone but himself and never has,' Caroline replied. 'But he wants an heir and he wants a wife who will grace his table, his jewels and his position. Who better than I?'

Caroline spoke in her most gay and inconsequential voice, and then suddenly in a more confiding tone she said:

'I never believed, Orelia, that I would pull it off. We met in Paris and he said that he admired me. But you could never be sure with the Marquis—he is one of those men that make one feel that whatever he says he is only paying lip service and does not mean a word of it! And then, Orelia, I think he was in somewhat of a coil.'

'What do you mean by that?' Orelia enquired.

'Well, I heard rumours—vague rumours because the Marquis covers his tracks very skilfully—that he had become involved with some very important Lady and that her possessiveness might cause a political scandal!'

Caroline gave a little laugh.

'Anyway, suddenly, from being very pleasant but nothing more, he declared himself! Can you believe it, Orelia? I shall be the Marchioness of Ryde—the most important social figure apart from the Royal Family in the whole of England!'

Orelia moved away from her cousin.

'And what about George?' she asked quietly.

For a moment it seemed as if the whole room was still. Then in a very different voice from the one she had used before, Caroline replied:

'George? George must be dead! I have not heard from him for over a year. He was in India then or

some such outlandish place. It is no use thinking of
George, Orelia. Besides, how could you compare
George with the Marquis of Ryde?'

'You loved him,' Orelia said. 'You only married
Harry because you were so unhappy after George went
away. I thought perhaps now that Harry is dead you
would wait for him to return.'

'He will not return! He will never come back!'
Caroline said quickly. 'And besides, even if he did, I
expect our feelings have changed towards each other. I
was only seventeen, Orelia. What did I know of love,
and what did George know about it for that matter?'

'He went away because he loved you,' Orelia said.
'He loved you so desperately, Caroline, that he would
not ask you to share poverty and discomfort. He asked
you to wait until he could make his fortune!'

'And how long is that likely to be?' Caroline said.
'Do not be so nonsensical, Orelia! I have the most
splendid, the most glittering offer that any woman
could ever wish for—from the Marquis of Ryde! I am
to be his wife! No man in the world could offer me a
better social position.'

'The Wicked Marquis!' Orelia said reflectively. 'Why
is he wicked?'

Caroline shrugged her shoulders.

'It is the name he has been given because he is so
handsome; because every woman at whom he even
snaps his fingers runs behind him like a small dog begging for his favours!'

Caroline laughed, but Orelia did not smile.

'All the husbands are jealous of him,' she continued.
'Moreover, besides being so rich, His Lordship wins a
fortune every night at cards; his horses are successful
on the turf; the Regent consults him at every turn!

'So inevitably there are people ready to attribute to
him every sort of crime simply because they are consumed by envy!'

'Is that all?' Orelia asked.

'Of course not!' Caroline replied. 'In Rome he gave
orgies which were so outrageous that it is said that the
Pope threatened to excommunicate anyone who at-

tended them! In Venice a Princess tried to cut her throat when the Marquis was tired of her.'

'Did she die?' Orelia enquired.

'No, she was saved. In Paris His Lordship caused such a commotion in the gaming halls of the Palais Royal that he himself declared it was time he went home! He earns his nickname, I assure you!'

'And do you think he is really wicked . . . in himself?' Orelia asked.

Caroline made no pretence of not understanding Orelia's question. But again she shrugged her shoulders.

'I hope so,' she replied. 'At least he will not prove to be a dead bore like so many other men.'

'And do you believe,' Orelia persisted, 'that in time you will come to love him?'

'Love!' Caroline ejaculated. 'The Marquis does not wish for love! A clinging, maudlin wife would bore him to distraction. Dear, foolish Orelia, I really will have to educate you in the ways of the *Beau Ton!*

'His Lordship and I will deal well together—I shall supply him with the heir he needs and he will give me everything I want.'

'Everything?' Orelia asked.

There was a little pause and just for a moment Orelia thought Caroline's eyes went blank. Then defiantly, almost aggressively, she said loudly:

'Everything, Orelia, that I could possibly desire!'

2

All the way to London Caroline regaled Orelia with her adventures in Italy and France.

'The Comte was crazy about me,' she said, not once but a dozen times, of a young Frenchman she had met in Paris.

'But surely this must have been before you had become betrothed to the Marquis?' Orelia asked.

Caroline glanced at her mischievously out of the corner of her eyes.

'I am trying to teach you not to be rural, Orelia,' she smiled.

'Do you really mean to tell me,' Orelia enquired, 'that even after you had promised the Marquis you would marry him you were still flirting with the Comte?'

'But of course I was,' Caroline replied. 'You do not suppose that because I am to be married it means I must behave like a nun!'

'Perhaps not a nun,' Orelia conceded, 'but surely the Marquis will expect some degree of propriety?'

'I behaved with the utmost propriety,' Caroline replied. 'We only met at night in the garden of the *Château,* or if it was raining he crept into the house by the balcony!'

'Caroline!' Orelia exclaimed. 'You really are a disgrace! How can you be so naughty? Besides, what would have happened if the Marquis had discovered you?'

'I am quite certain His Lordship was still engaged

with his own flirts who are too numerous for me even
to know their names,' Caroline replied. 'He is pro-
digiously attractive, Orelia, and women flutter round
him in an infatuated manner which makes me laugh.'

'But Caroline, what will happen when you are married?' Orelia asked in a worried voice.

She was indeed very perturbed at Caroline's attitude
to her marriage. She knew that Caroline needed a husband who would not only adore her, but who would
master her!

Underneath her frivolity, her gaiety and her insatiable need for new excitement, Caroline had a very
warm-hearted nature. But being so beautiful she had
been spoilt all her life.

Now it seemed to Orelia that she was like an un-
broken horse ready to go to any lengths to get her own
way and in grave danger of sooner or later becoming as
irresponsible and as unrestrained as her husband had
been.

There was wild blood in the Stanyons: Harry had
been ruined by having too much money when he was
too young to exercise any restraint or control over himself.

Caroline, unless someone took a firm hand with her,
might go the same way since admiration and adula-
tion went to her head like wine.

'There was a Prince in Rome . . .' Caroline began,
and proceeded to tell Orelia of some intriguing adventure in love-making.

While it sounded exciting told in Caroline's gay, fascinating voice it was, as Orelia knew only too well, an
escapade which if it had been discovered would have
ruined Caroline's reputation irretrievably.

'But Caroline, did you love this man?' she asked as
Caroline told of kisses stolen during a Ball, of assigna-
tions to which they went disguised, of hours spent in
the moonlight by the side of a silver lake.

'I was crazy about him,' Caroline answered, her
voice deepening, her eyes half shut in a sudden ecstasy.

'Then why,' Orelia asked, 'if he loved you, did you
not marry him?'

'Because he was married already,' Caroline replied.

Orelia sat bolt-upright against the cushions of the landau.

'Caroline! How could you have behaved so improperly—and with a married man?'

'It sounds bad, does it not?' Caroline replied. 'But Orelia, he was so handsome, so compelling! I was far from home and it did not seem to matter what I did. Besides, I was unhappy about Harry's death—I needed consolation.'

'That is just fustian!' Orelia replied. 'You never cared a hoot about Harry. The only time you were ever unhappy, Caroline, was when George went away!'

'You cannot expect me to sport the willow for George all my life?' Caroline retorted with a sudden sharp note in her voice. 'Let me make it quite clear, Orelia, I am going to enjoy myself in the future.'

She put out her chin in an obstinate manner which Orelia knew only too well.

'The Marquis will not care what I do so long as I do not cause a scandal,' she continued, 'and I shall have all the money I want to spend and the most fabulous, outrageous clothes with which to stun all those fashionable females who up to now have looked down their noses at me!'

She gave a little laugh which was almost a sneer.

'They are going to look very stupid, I assure you, because they will have to be polite to the Marchioness of Ryde! They will have to fawn on her; they will have to admire her outwardly, however much their malicious hearts are eaten up with fury at having to do so!'

Orelia said nothing for a moment and then unexpectedly she reached out and took Caroline's hand in hers.

'Dearest Caroline, do not spoil yourself,' she begged. 'You have always been sweet and gentle inside. When you talk like that you are a stranger—someone I have never known.'

Her voice held a coaxing note as she continued:

'You have never been bitter about anything. You have been unhappy—which is something very different

—and I want above everything else in the world for you to find happiness—real happiness!'

Caroline's fingers tightened on Orelia's. Then she said very quietly, almost in a childish voice:

'I will try, Orelia, I will really. But I think somehow I have lost my heart. There is just an empty place where it once was. But I have no wish to cry about it. I want to laugh, I want to be gay!'

'Of course you do,' Orelia said. 'Only Caroline, do not let it alter the real you.'

'I will try not to let it,' Caroline said almost in a whisper.

Then, because she had been really moved by her cousin's words, she took her hand away and with one of those quick changes of mood which Orelia knew so well, she said:

'Clothes! That is what you and I have to concentrate on at the moment, Orelia.'

'Well, you will not be able to spend over much,' Orelia said, 'not even on your trousseau. You know what the lawyer said about there still being a mortgage to be paid off on the Estate.'

Caroline laughed.

'I certainly am not going to try to buy a trousseau out of the pittance Papa left me!'

'But how . . .' Orelia began, only to exclaim: 'You do not mean . . . you cannot mean, Caroline, that you are going to ask the Marquis for the money. You know, it would be vastly improper!'

'I am certainly not going to ask the Marquis to pay for my trousseau before I marry him,' Caroline replied. 'But naturally a husband must be expected to meet his wife's debts.'

'Caroline, you cannot do anything so crooked!' Orelia protested.

'I can and I will!' Caroline answered. 'The Marquis is so rich he would not even notice if I spent thousands of pounds on my wedding finery. And I am not going to the altar in a cheap tatty gown and have all the *Beau Ton* sniggering at me!'

'I am sure it is not the right thing to do,' Orelia said unhappily.

'Do not worry, my love,' Caroline admonished her. 'And incidentally, it will be to your advantage. You can have all my old clothes, and though they will want a lot of altering because you are so much smaller than I, you will look entrancing in them!

'As you look at the moment in that blue driving-coat of mine that I never liked! And that bonnet is quite ravishing!'

'They are both lovely,' Orelia said, 'and I am truly grateful, I am really, Caroline. I could not have gone to London in my old cape.'

'Indeed you could not,' Caroline replied. 'I do not wish to be ashamed of you. Besides, if you look shabby people will suspect that as you are my cousin I have no money either! And I have no desire publicly to play the beggar-maid to the Marquis's King Cophetua!'

'I can make myself some dresses,' Orelia said confidently. 'I really have not thought about my clothes for London until now.'

'I cannot imagine what you do think about!' Caroline exclaimed. 'But it is enough to turn anyone into a turnip-head living at Morden month after month with nothing to break the monotony except an occasional visit from the Parson!'

'It was not as bad as that, really,' Orelia replied. 'I assure you that Uncle Arthur kept me very busy!'

'On those deadly dull papers of his,' Caroline scoffed. 'Poor Papa! Who will ever read them? But never mind, dearest, I am determined that you shall be a success and however unworldly you may be, I assure you that clothes in the *Ton* are a necessity—not an extravagance!'

'Then I had best go straight back to the country,' Orelia smiled.

'Leave it to me,' Caroline said. 'I shall contrive something. In the meantime start altering those I have already given you, because I promise you I shall never wear them again!'

'Caroline! They are comparatively new!' Orelia expostulated.

'Of course they are,' Caroline replied, 'but you do not suppose that in my position I am going to wear anything more than a few times?'

Orelia did not answer, and she went on:

'Of course you are much shorter than I am, and I regret to say, much more slender, but luckily it is easier to take in than to let out! Until we can find you some really wonderful new gowns all of your own, Orelia, I know you will look very pretty in those I have given you.'

'I feel quite strange in them because the waist has changed,' Orelia said.

'Everyone in Paris is tight-lacing and you will see in a year all our straight gowns will be completely out of fashion,' Caroline predicted. 'So we shall start off by making people stare, you and I, when we appear in the French mode nipped in at the waist!'

'I do not think I really wish to be stared at,' Orelia said in a soft voice, but Caroline was not listening.

She was already chattering away about some compliment a French Beau had paid her when she appeared at a Ball at the Tuileries, wearing one of the gowns she had given to Orelia.

There was no doubt that both girls looked lovely enough to turn the head of any young Gentleman who encountered them.

Caroline in her red driving-coat trimmed with ermine, and Orelia in soft hyacinth blue, might have stepped straight out of the pages of the *Ladies' Journal*.

But while a man might be instantly attracted and beguiled by Caroline's somewhat flamboyant beauty, it was Orelia's ethereal loveliness and wide, rather worried eyes, which would remain in his memory.

It was, however, one thing for Orelia to say that she was not really interested in clothes, and quite another to arrive in London and be thankful that she looked at least reasonably smart as the carriage drew up at Ryde House in Park Lane.

Orelia had at first been surprised and apprehensive when Caroline had told her that they were to stay at the Marquis's Mansion.

'But surely that would not be correct, considering you are betrothed to His Lordship?' Orelia asked.

'The Marquis has invited his Grandmother, the Dowager Duchess of Wantage, to chaperone me,' Caroline answered, 'and besides, the house is so vast that there might be dozens of people staying in the place without one really being inconvenienced by them!'

'I was not thinking that you would inconvenience the Marquis,' Orelia said. 'It is just that it seems strange that you should live under his roof before you are married.'

'His Lordship is a law unto himself,' Caroline answered, 'and I cannot imagine anything more foolish than you and I taking a house together—which is an extravagance we can ill afford—just for a month!'

'For a month!' Orelia exclaimed.

Caroline laughed.

'Do not look so surprised, dearest. You must realise that the sooner I have the ring on my finger the more confident I shall be of my good luck and the fact that I have really captured the elusive Marquis of Ryde!'

'You are surely not suspecting His Lordship might back down?' Orelia asked in a shocked voice.

She knew that for a man to have become betrothed was to have given his word of honour—which was as sacrosanct and as binding as a gambling debt!

No Gentleman of Quality would jilt his fiancée, however much he might wish to do so in any circumstances whatsoever.

'No, of course, I am not afraid of the Marquis refusing to marry me after all he has said,' Caroline answered, 'and I expect the announcement is already in the *Gazette*. We shall see when we get to London. But at the same time something might happen to prevent it —an accident, a death—I do not know!'

She paused for a moment.

'I just have a creepy feeling, Orelia,' she continued,

'that my luck is too good to hold and I must make sure by clinging on to it while it is still there!'

'Fairy Gold, in fact!' Orelia said with a little smile.

She remembered how when she was young she had always searched for the elusive gold which the fairies were supposed to leave hidden in the woods to attract greedy and foolish travellers.

'Exactly!' Caroline agreed. 'But it is not to be Fairy Gold as far as I am concerned, which vanishes at the touch of human fingers. It is to be real gold, because that is what I want, Orelia, and that is what I intend to get!'

There was again that hard note in Caroline's voice which made Orelia sigh. But when she entered Ryde House she could in a way understand how Caroline longed to become the chatelaine of such a magnificent place.

The House, of grey stone enriched with turrets, was enormous—facing the green trees of Hyde Park in the front, and with a large garden at the back.

There was a glimpse of bright flower beds, purple and white lilac bushes, and golden laburnum trees as the Marquis's landau which had brought the cousins to London drew up at the huge porticoed front door.

The rooms in Ryde House were high, their ceilings ornamented with the finest plaster-work, the walls covered with pictures of great antiquity and value.

The furniture, handed down from generation to generation, was all worthy of being enshrined in a Museum.

There was a majesty and an atmosphere about the house which hushed even Caroline's chattering voice into silence as they were conducted through the marble Hall and shown into a large Salon which overlooked the garden at the back.

Here again everything was almost breathtakingly magnificent, but Orelia had eyes only for an elderly Lady who rose from the fireplace at their entrance.

She must have been getting on for eighty, but she still retained some of her legendary beauty. Her features had once been classical and her dead white hair arranged above an oval forehead was still luxuriant.

The Duchess had been an acclaimed beauty in her day and it seemed as if the aura of her triumphs still encircled her.

Dressed all in white, which Orelia was to find later was the Dowager's habitual custom, she wore row upon row of large pearls, a number of diamond bracelets, and two huge ruby rings which seemed almost too heavy for her thin and aged fingers.

At her side a small turbaned black boy wielded a huge fan made of peacock feathers.

As Caroline sank down in a curtsey the Duchess remembered in what seemed almost an amused tone:

'I hear, Caroline Stanyon, that I must offer you and my Grandson my best wishes for your happiness.'

'Thank you, Ma'am,' Caroline replied, 'and thank you for consenting to chaperone my cousin and me. It is more enjoyable and indeed far more comfortable to be staying at Ryde House than for us to have to rent inferior accommodation at this time of the year.'

'I am delighted to chaperone you,' the Dowager replied. 'I get exceeding bored, living as I do in the country and having nothing to enliven me but the chitter of cocks and hens!'

Caroline laughed.

'I cannot believe that, Ma'am, as His Lordship tells me you are constantly in London and always spend the Season with him.'

The Dowager's eyes twinkled.

'I see my Grandson has been telling tales about me; and now present your cousin.'

'This is Orelia, Ma'am,' Caroline said obediently. 'We were brought up together, and as you can see we are an obvious contrast to each other, not only in looks but also in character.'

Orelia was aware that the Duchess's eyes, which were bright and shrewd despite her age, appeared to take in every detail of her appearance. Then she said almost sharply:

'And what do you expect to find in London, child? A husband?'

Orelia, finding the question unexpected, felt herself blush.

'No indeed, Ma'am,' she answered. 'I am but happy to accompany my cousin, Caroline.'

'We should have no difficulty in finding an excellent *parti* for you,' the Duchess said. 'With your looks and indeed, as Caroline remarked, the intriguing contrast between the two of you, I can quite see that the house will be beseiged by importunate Beaux.'

Her eyes seemed to flicker over the two girls as she continued:

'At the same time I shall be very strict. No one ineligible will have his suit considered even for a moment. Your cousin also must make an enviable match.'

Caroline laughed.

'That is exactly what I have been saying, Ma'am. Orelia must be married. And with your help I am certain we can find her someone charming as well as eminently suitable.'

'As suitable as my Grandson?' the Duchess asked with a note of sarcasm in her tone.

'I doubt if anyone could be quite such a Nonpareil,' Caroline replied in a deliberately innocent voice. 'But then His Lordship is unique, is he not?'

'So I have always believed,' the Duchess replied, 'and as he has also told me so often himself—extremely elusive! I must congratulate you, Caroline. You have captured the citadel—where so many have failed to carry!'

'Perhaps I have been lucky!' Caroline replied. 'Or singularly well-armed!'

Orelia listened to this interchange between Caroline and the Duchess with a sense of bewilderment.

It seemed to her that the two women, one so old and one so young, fenced with each other, and that the touch of irony in their voices and the look of cynical sophistication in their eyes said far more than the words that were spoken by their tongues.

Then at that moment the door opened and a Gentleman entered the room.

Caroline gave a little cry of delight before she ran towards him, her hands outstretched, the feathers on her bonnet fluttering with the speed of her passage.

'So you have arrived safely,' a deep voice said.

Orelia felt as if her heart came to a sudden stop, and she was unable to breathe.

It could not be true—it was too fantastic! Too much of a coincidence! And yet she knew at the first glimpse of him before he had spoke, that she had seen him before, that once he had held her spell-bound.

She felt herself tremble; then drawing a deep breath she realised it would be unlikely that the Marquis would recognise her and that she must not betray herself.

She could hardly expect him, she told herself, to have thought of her for even a few minutes after he had left the village, and if he had, his memory would be of a girl in an old cloak, whom he had supposed to be some country nonentity quite unsuitable for the Quality.

He would not expect to find a village maiden whom he could kiss with a disdainful arrogance fashionably dressed in a French bonnet and a blue driving-coat from Paris in his own Salon in Park Lane.

With an almost superhuman effort, Orelia forced herself to appear calm and unagitated as moving slowly down the room, Caroline's arm linked in his, came the man she had never expected to see again.

Yet she had forgotten nothing about him.

That handsome face with its cynical sardonic expression was exactly as she had remembered: the faint twist to his lips, the lazy drooping of his eyelids, she had never forgotten!

And now he was close and the Marquis, taking the Dowager Duchess's hand, raised it to his lips before kissing her cheek.

'Forgive me, Grandmama,' he said. 'I should have been here to introduce you to Caroline, but I was detained.'

'A card, a horse or a woman?' the Duchess asked with a sparkle in her eyes.

'A question which undoubtedly deserves to be ignored,' the Marquis replied. 'But I will give you the answer—a horse! Are you disappointed?'

'It depends who was riding it,' the Duchess retorted and the Marquis laughed.

Then he turned towards Orelia. She tried to look at him but failed, and her eyelashes were dark against her pale cheeks as she sank down in a curtsey.

'This is my cousin, Orelia,' she heard Caroline say. 'I have told you about her, Darius, and how Papa left in his Will that she was to be my inspiration and my conscience.'

'She has undoubtedly taken on an extremely formidable task,' the Marquis said, and there was that mocking note in his voice which Orelia had heard before.

Then as she rose she glanced up at him and thought there was nothing unusual in his expression except a somewhat formal courtsey.

He had not recognised her and anyway, as she might have known, he had long forgotten the girl he had kissed on the Village Green. She was undoubtedly relieved but at the same time wondered why it was a trifle dispiriting.

They chattered about the journey and the plans the Marquis had made for Caroline that evening. Orelia was silent but she was acutely conscious of her host.

How could she have dreamt, she asked herself, that she would ever meet again the Gentleman who had been the first man ever to touch her lips?

She watched him surreptitiously from under her eyelashes, and then was thrown into confusion when unexpectedly he turned to her and said:

'I hope, Miss Stanyon, you will enjoy yourself in London. We must do our best to make your visit a memorable one, which indeed should be a very easy task.'

'Thank you . . . My Lord,' Orelia faltered.

But she felt he mocked her, as if his eyes penetrated the disguise of her fashionable clothes and saw—even if he did not remember meeting her before—that she was only an unfledged ignorant country girl of no consequence.

Caroline had undoubtedly spoken the truth, Orelia found during the next two days, when she said the house was so large that any number of guests could be entertained without inconveniencing the owners in any way whatsoever.

Orelia seldom saw the Marquis.

He took Caroline driving in the Park and the first two evenings after they arrived in London they were engaged to dine with relations—parties to which neither the Duchess nor Orelia were invited.

Most of the time was spent most enjoyably in visiting the shops.

Orelia had not believed, living quietly in the country, that London fashions could have changed so enormously or that gowns could be such fantastic creations of beauty, workmanship and expense.

She had imagined optimistically that she would be able to copy some of Caroline's dresses.

But after seeing the type of gown she was expected to wear she knew that it would be impossible, and was prepared to accept gracefully and without further protest those which Caroline insisted on giving her.

She did think, however, that she might make herself a few plain muslin gowns for the mornings.

Accordingly she refused to accompany the Duchess and Caroline on yet another shopping expedition, deciding to stay at home and try to cut out a new dress in the same shape as one of Caroline's simpler creations.

She took the roll of muslin she had bought into a sitting-room on the first floor which she and Caroline had been given as their special sanctum and where Caroline replied to her invitations and wrote her letters of thanks.

Orelia had everything ready to start work when she found that she had left her sewing-bag downstairs in the main Salon.

She had been showing the Duchess a piece of tapestry she had been stitching before she left home when she had intended to cover some of the dining-room chairs which were so old and worn that the pattern was almost obliterated.

The Duchess had exclaimed at her fine work, and then some visitors were announced and Orelia had hidden her bag behind the sofa and had forgotten to retrieve it.

She came down the staircase and as she did so saw one of the flunkeys open the front door and a young man enter the Hall.

Orelia could not help staring at him in surprise for his boots, his breeches and even his coat were splashed with mud.

His top hat was bashed in, perhaps by a fall from his horse, his crumpled, dirty cravat was untied, and he looked incredibly out-of-place in the grandeur of Ryde House.

Then as he stood just inside the door it seemed to Orelia as if he was swaying on his feet. The Butler came hurrying forward.

'Mr. Rupert!' he exclaimed. 'What has happened to you?'

'Where—is my—Uncle?' the young man demanded.

Orelia knew from his voice that he was decidedly tipsy.

'His Lordship is out at the moment,' the Butler replied.

'I have—to see him—do you understand—I have to see him—at once,' the young man insisted, slurring his words.

Then even as he said the last word he keeled over and fell onto the floor.

Orelia hurried down the stairs.

'He is ill!' she exclaimed to the Butler, who by this time was down on one knee by the fallen figure.

' 'Tis all right, Miss,' the Butler replied. 'I think that Mr. Rupert has just been indulging too freely. I'll get him upstairs.'

Orelia put her hand on the young man's forehead.

'It is more than that,' she said. 'He has a fever. It would be best to get him to bed. I have some herbal tea which will help him.'

'It looks as if Mr. Rupert has ridden from Oxford, Miss, if I'm not mistaken.'

'From Oxford!' Orelia exclaimed.

Two footmen carried the insensible young man up-stairs and Orelia went to her own room.

She had brought some herbs with her from Morden—herbs she had used for sick people in the village and which she had grown in the Herb Garden which had been first laid out in the reign of Henry VIII.

She had dried them herself and found they were in-valuable for treating fevers and ailments of all kinds and in all ages of persons.

She prepared the drink, adding two spoonfuls of honey, and took it along to the bedroom into which she had seen the footmen carry the young man.

She knew who he was because she had heard the Duchess speak of her Great-Grandson, Rupert Char-rington, who was the Marquis's ward and whose mother and father were both dead.

'Darius was exceedingly fond of his sister,' the Duchess had said to Orelia. 'But he finds his nephew both troublesome and an encumbrance.'

Orelia listened sympathetically as she had always listened to everything that was told her. She had not been particularly interested until now.

Looking down at the young man's pallid face and the dark lines under his eyes, she knew that this was not an occasional dissipation.

At the same time she felt sorry for him. He looked so young.

Now that the footman had undressed him and put him into bed there was something almost childlike about his tousled dark hair against the white pillows and the manner in which he stirred restlessly, muttering inco-herently to himself.

'I doubts if Mr. Rupert will drink that, Miss,' the Butler said in a low voice, seeing what Orelia held in her hand.

'Let us try to make him do so,' Orelia replied. 'It will sober him and he will feel so much better afterwards.'

'Very good, Miss,' the Butler replied.

Orelia knew he was not convinced, but he put his

arms round the young man and drew him up into a sitting position.

'Now come along, Mr. Rupert,' he said. 'This kind young Lady has brought you something that'll make you feel well again.'

'I want to see—my Uncle!'

'As soon as His Lordship returns I'll tell him you're here, Sir,' the Butler said soothingly. 'You'll find it easier to talk when you've something inside you.'

'That's it! I am hungry—damned hungry!' Rupert Charrington exclaimed.

'Please drink this first,' Orelia begged.

'I could do with—a drink,' Rupert replied almost rudely.

He took the cup she held out to him and drank it down without even tasting the liquid. Then he gave a little laugh.

'I was hoping for something—stronger than that—filth!'

'I think you have had enough strong liquor for the moment,' Orelia said gently. 'Try and sleep and when you wake up, if the fever has gone, you can have something to eat.'

She put her hand on his forehead as he snuggled down amongst the pillows.

'Have it your—own way,' he said hoarsely. 'I am too damned tired to—argue.'

'Then just go to sleep,' she said softly.

An hour later she went back to the room to find Rupert Charrington just opening his eyes, having slept soundly as she had expected him to do.

'What the devil am I doing in bed?' he asked when he saw her.

'You collapsed when you arrived,' she answered. 'Had you been riding all night?'

'Riding and drinking,' he replied.

'I thought so,' she answered. 'If you are wise you will stay here for the rest of the day.'

He had sobered up and was talking quite sensibly but he looked incredibly ill. His face was very pale, his eyes deep-set and lustreless.

'What have you been doing to yourself, you foolish boy?' Orelia asked.

She felt for a moment he was one of the village children she had nursed so often when they were ill, and forgot that an Undergraduate would consider himself a Gentleman of Fashion and entitled to be spoken to with far more respect.

But Rupert did not seem to resent her words. On the contrary he reached out his hand to take hers.

'I have to see my Uncle,' he said. 'I have to convince him that I cannot go on any longer!'

'Go on where?' Orelia enquired.

'At Oxford,' he replied, 'I cannot stand it! It is ghastly, I tell you, and they made me go with them last night! I did not want to—I refused—but they came to my lodgings and held me down while they tipped a bottle of wine down my throat! I knew it would be terrible! I knew it!'

'What was terrible?' Orelia asked.

She saw that something had upset him, something which had shaken him off his balance. He was speaking in a feverish, agitated manner and his fingers clutching hers were hard and hot.

She knew that for the moment for him she was not a young woman or for that matter any woman. She was just someone to talk to, someone to whom he could unburden himself!

It was the best thing he could do, she thought, to talk and let his grievance, whatever it might be, expend itself.

At the same time she was aware that he was still not quite sober, otherwise he would not have been so expansive to a stranger.

The worst effects of the drink had worn away but it had loosened his tongue, and after a sleep he was in the relaxed state when he was willing to confide in anyone who would listen.

'What is it that has upset you?' Orelia asked in her soft, sympathetic voice which had already brought her in her short life hundreds of confidences from all sorts of different people.

'It was the horse,' Rupert replied. 'That was what made me realise that I could go on no longer! Charles impaled it! He impaled it on the iron railings of the Churchyard. It screamed! Have you ever heard a horse scream?'

'No, and I hope I never shall!' Orelia answered.

'It was horrible,' he said, moving his head from side to side and shutting his eyes. 'I can see it now—poor beast!'

He shuddered before he continued.

'It was Garvin who insisted that we should ride through all the Churchyards—all of them—leaping the tombstones, forcing our way through the gates or jumping the walls and railings if they were locked! I said it was a damned silly idea, but no one would listen to me!'

His hand clutched Orelia's even more convulsively.

'I think Charles was killed,' he said. 'He fell off when his horse was impaled on the railings. He fell on his head and I am sure he is dead!'

'Do not think about him,' Orelia begged. 'You will be able to find out for certain later on.'

'I cannot go back!' he cried. 'I turned and galloped away. I do not know where I went at first—I stopped and had a drink, several drinks, at an Inn. It was then that I decided to come to London.'

'To see your Uncle?' she asked.

'To tell Uncle Darius that I cannot stay at Oxford. He said it would make me into a man but I do not want to be that sort of man!'

'Have you spoken to the Marquis about this before?' Orelia asked.

'He would not listen to me! He said I had to stay there. I told him that I couldn't do so. Then they forced me to join the Club!'

'What Club?' Orelia enquired.

'It is called "The Magpies". We have to do a lot of cursed stupid things—like—knocking over the Watch. The last time we did it the poor old man was left unconscious with a cut on his cheek at least four inches long!'

'How senseless!' Orelia exclaimed.

'Senseless and cruel,' Rupert answered. 'And all because they drink so much! Three bottles is the minimum. If you are a sporting blade like Garvin you drink four or five!'

He gave a deep sigh.

'I never was a good drinker. I get sick. I do not feel gay and I am so damned ill the next day.'

'Can you not resign from the Club?' Orelia asked.

'That is what I want to do, but they will not let me. I tried to stay at home last night but they came and fetched me out. I hate it, I tell you! I hate it!'

He was silent for a moment and then he said:

'There was a girl—she screamed too! She was not much more than a child.'

'Do not think about it,' Orelia urged. 'Try to forget it.'

'How can I?' he demanded. 'But if Uncle Darius makes me go back I swear I will kill myself! I cannot go on any longer! I hate them! I hate the cruel, senseless things we do! I have always hated Oxford!'

'What would you like to do?' Orelia asked.

'I want to go into the Army—into my father's Regiment. That is where I belong. If he had not been killed at Waterloo he would have let me do what I wanted to do. It is only Uncle Darius who has other ideas, and because he thinks he is God Almighty I have to obey them!'

'Have you spoken to your Uncle about this?' Orelia enquired.

'I tried to talk to him last vacation but he would not listen! But you know what he is like—aloof, uninterested, unapproachable. I hate him!'

He paused and then he said:

'I am not going back! I will not go back! Charles is dead and Charles was the best of them. I shall never get the sound of that horse out of my ears! Help me—please help me!'

He was almost delirious and Orelia knew the fever was mounting. She felt his forehead and was sure he had a high temperature.

'Try to go to sleep,' she said. 'I will send for a Physician.'

Rupert murmured something, but he was too tired to say any more. She knew as she looked at him that she had to help him.

No one had ever appealed to Orelia in vain. But she thought that she had never been set a more difficult task!

How could she face the Marquis? How could she presume to discuss his plans for his nephew, to challenge his decision? But Rupert had turned to her in his trouble and whatever the cost to herself she could not refuse him.

She went from the room and as she closed the door she saw the Butler coming down the corridor.

'Is Mr. Rupert awake, Miss?' he asked before Orelia could speak.

'He has been but I think he will go to sleep again. He has a temperature and it would be wise to send for a Physician.'

'I will do that, Miss, but I was just going to tell Mr. Rupert that His Lordship has returned.'

'Is he downstairs?' Orelia asked.

'Yes, Miss. In the Library. And it's none too pleased, he is, at Mr. Rupert arriving here unexpected from Oxford.'

'I will go and speak with His Lordship,' Orelia said. 'Perhaps you will show me the way to the Library and then send for a Physician.'

'Very good, Miss,' the Butler answered.

He was far too well-trained to show his feelings but as he walked ahead of her Orelia was aware that his whole bearing was eloquent of his disapproval.

Young Ladies staying at Ryde House did not take it upon themselves to give orders, or take over the nursing of someone like Mr. Rupert, who should be at Oxford instead of upsetting His Lordship by making an unwelcome appearance and in such a state of inebriation.

What was more, Orelia committed another solecism in the Butler's eyes, when, on crossing the Hall so that she was aware where the Library lay, she said:

'There is no need to announce me, thank you.'

The Butler therefore threw open the door but was silent as Orelia walked into the Library alone.

He did not realise she was fighting her shyness and her fears, and felt she must creep into the room without ceremony.

There were three long French windows opening on to the garden in a room that was otherwise lined from floor to ceiling with books. In the centre of the room there was a large flat-topped desk, at which the Marquis was writing.

He looked exceedingly elegant in a coat of superfine grey cloth over pantaloons of a very pale shade of yellow. His snowy cravat was tied in the most intricate folds and his boots, polished with blacking mixed with champagne, glinted in the sunshine.

Glancing up, he raised his eyebrows as if in surprise, and then seeing Orelia in the doorway he rose slowly to his feet.

'May I have a word with Your Lordship?' she asked.

'But of course,' he replied courteously.

He walked towards the fireplace and indicated a high wing-backed armchair in red velvet. She seated herself on the edge of it, looking up at him a little apprehensively, the pale gold hair framed her small face, her large eyes were dark and anxious as she said hesitantly:

'I think, My Lord, you have already learnt that your nephew is not well.'

A frown appeared between the Marquis's eyes.

'My nephew?' he said. 'Is that the reason you wish to see me?'

'I saw him arrive and collapse,' Orelia replied. 'He has slept for an hour but he is running a fever and I have asked your Butler to send for a Physician.'

'I should have thought that was quite unnecessary,' the Marquis replied.

There was a sharpness in his voice which made her almost wince. He was so tall and over-powering as he stood looking down at her and as she had thought the first time she had met him, it was not only his obvious good looks that were so disturbing.

It was a sense of consequence which seemed to emanate from him—something about his very presence which made her realise why Rupert was frightened of him.

And since he was so frightened, she knew that it had in fact been an act of bravery on his part to come to London.

Undoubtedly he had drunk to give himself courage during the journey, besides all he had been forced to imbibe in Oxford, and this was in some part the reason for his collapse. But nevertheless it had been a brave act.

Orelia clasped her hands together.

'Please,' she said in a very small voice, 'there is something I wish to say to Your Lordship—could you not sit down? You are so very tall and what I desire to tell you is difficult to put into words.'

The Marquis looked at her in a strange manner. Then unexpectedly he smiled.

'I have no desire to frighten you, Miss Stanyon. Do you consider me a frightening person?'

'Yes, very!' Orelia answered frankly. 'And your nephew is frightened of you too. That is why it was brave of him to ride all the way from Oxford to see you.'

'To see me?' the Marquis queried.

'To tell you that he cannot stay any longer,' Orelia said, stumbling a little on the words. 'He is distraught, terrified, disgusted, and he wants your sympathy!'

The Marquis seated himself on the other side of the hearth. He looked very much at ease and relaxed with his legs crossed, as he leant back against the velvet of the armchair.

Then his voice was hard as he replied:

'Rupert is a weakling and a fool! He has no right to trouble you with such nonsense!'

'It is not nonsense to him!' Orelia answered. 'He is desperate!'

'Rupert will return the moment he is on his feet,' the Marquis said. 'I cannot credit that anyone so poor-spirited can be any relative of mine!'

'It is not cowardice to realise that one cannot com-
bat the forces of evil single-handed,' Orelia said. 'It is
often best to acknowledge that some things are so evil
they are best left alone!'

'You are talking about an idiotic, brainless boy who
has not the strength of character to look after himself,'
the Marquis sneered.

'He may be all that,' Orelia admitted. 'But he has
come to London to ask your help, to plead with you, to
beg you to give him consideration and understanding.
Are you determined not to hear him?'

The Marquis's lips tightened.

'I am not being rude in saying that it is no business
of yours, Miss Stanyon,' he said. 'And I deeply regret
that you should have become involved in my private
affairs. But if you want an answer to your question I
will give it to you—my nephew will go back to Oxford.'

There was something in the unremitting harshness of
his tone which swept away Orelia's shyness and fear
and made her angry. No wonder Rupert had said that
his uncle thought himself God Almighty!

'If you do that Your Lordship may drive him too far,'
Orelia protested. 'He has already threatened to take his
life rather than continue to take part in the bestiality
and the degradation into which he had been forced by
his contemporaries in a Club called "The Magpies".'

The Marquis raised his eyebrows.

'So that is the company the young fool has chosen!
Only an idiot would join anything so reprehensible!'

'Whether or not he was foolish in joining or not,'
Orelia answered, 'the fact remains that he is a member
and that they now force him to do things which he has
no wish to do. Last night his friend—someone called
Charles—impaled his horse on the railings of a Churchyard. He thinks Charles is dead!'

She paused but as the Marquis did not speak she continued.

'It was some nonsensical ride through the Churchyards of Oxford. But they have done worse things and

Rupert can no longer go on. You have to help him. He has no one to turn to but you!'

Her voice was soft again but the Marquis replied:

'As I have already told you, Rupert will return to his studies. And before he goes I shall tell him exactly what my opinion is of the type of young man who bleats to a woman.'

The scathing tone in which the Marquis spoke made Orelia's eyes flash and she was surprised at her own daring in defying the Marquis.

'Very well,' she said, rising to her feet. 'If that is your last word, My Lord, there is nothing I can do about it. I can only say that I think you are aptly nick-named . . . for it is wicked, truly wicked to destroy someone young and helpless.'

She drew a deep breath because her heart was thumping so violently.

'He may be a weak character,' she continued. 'Is that his fault? He may not have your strength, your self-assurance, your contempt for the world and for other people. That again may not be his fault. But with you to teach him he may learn in time to be as hard and as cruel as you!'

She drew a deep breath.

'Then of course he can be proud of being a man! But he may not live long enough to achieve such a desirable state. He might in his weakness take his life as he threatens to do!

'That to you may be a matter of utter indifference but his death will be entirely and absolutely your fault!'

Orelia felt her voice break on the last word and there were tears of anger in her eyes as she walked towards the door. Only as she reached it did she hear the Marquis say:

'Stop!'

She turned back to look mistily through her tears at him standing on the hearth rug.

'Do you always fight so passionately for what you desire?' he asked in a different voice from the one he had used before.

'I am not fighting for myself,' she replied, 'but against injustice.'

She told herself she hated him! He was hard and brutal. Yes, she hated him!

'You have already used some very hard words to me —and now you tell me I am unjust,' the Marquis remarked.

'Perhaps it could all be summed up in the word cruel,' Orelia retorted. 'There is no one more cruel than one who is insensitive, who has no understanding of the weakness of others.'

She paused to catch her breath.

'It is easy to be strong and steadfast when you are made that way—far more difficult to stand up to anything when you are naturally weak; when you feel pain more acutely than other people.'

'You are championing my nephew, whom you have never met before and about whom you know very little,' the Marquis said, and Orelia could hear the cynicism in his voice.

'He is still a human being,' she replied. 'He is still young and defenceless—little more than a boy.'

She felt she could not reach him, and made a last desperate effort.

'Your Grandmother told me you were fond of your sister. What do you think she would feel if you send Rupert back now, if not to his death . . . to a degradation that no woman . . . whoever she might be . . . would want for her son?'

Again Orelia heard her voice break and felt the tears start to her eyes. She had failed! There was nothing more she could do. She turned her back on the Marquis and reached out for the door-handle.

'Very well,' the Marquis said quietly. 'You have won the battle.'

She turned round incredulously, hardly believing she had heard correctly. She could not see him clearly.

'Go and tell that young Jackanapes,' he said, 'if he is capable of listening, that his Uncle has been defeated by a very formidable adversary.'

'Do you mean that?' Orelia hardly breathed the words.

'I mean it,' he answered. 'What does the boy want? A Cavalry Regiment?'

'You know that is what he wants! He wants to follow in his father's footsteps.'

'Very well,' the Marquis said. 'I will see to it. But remember, he will be your responsibility from now on. If he fails again you will only have yourself to blame.'

For a moment Orelia could not speak and almost without thinking she walked across the room to the Marquis until she stood beside him. Then she looked up into his face.

'Thank you,' she said softly. 'Thank you. That is a good thing to do.'

'Are you really thinking you can white-wash me so quickly?' the Marquis asked sarcastically. 'As you have so clearly reminded me—my nick-name is apt!'

'Not at the moment!' Orelia answered. 'Not at the moment!'

He looked down at her and their eyes met. There was something in his which made her feel strangely breathless—the same feeling she had felt once before.

Rupert was forgotten. She was suddenly overwhelmingly conscious of the Marquis, of his presence, of the fact that he was a man—a man such as she had never known.

'Forgive me . . . for being rude . . .' she whispered.

Then her eyes dropped before his and she sped towards the door.

3

After three day Rupert was better and Orelia at last found time to return to the roll of muslin.

It was still waiting to be cut out in the Sitting-room which she and Caroline used when they were not otherwise engaged.

This was seldom; for Caroline was increasingly being entertained now that her engagement to the Marquis had been announced, and Orelia had spent all her time in attempting to restore Rupert to health.

This was not difficult after he received the news that he was not to return to Oxford but was to go into the Army.

He was at first incredulous, then was overcome with excitement and exuberance which contributed immediately to his recovery.

'How did you manage it, Miss Stanyon?' Rupert asked. 'How could you possibly have persuaded the Wicked Marquis to change his mind?'

He saw the surprise in Orelia's face and said quickly: 'I thought you must know that is what everyone calls my Uncle.'

Orelia did not speak, and he added rather shamefaced:

'I suppose it was bad *ton* of me to say that, especially now he has agreed that I should join my father's Regiment. But I know that his generous gesture is your doing! How did you contrive it?'

Orelia smiled.

'I think His Lordship realised it was a reasonable request.'

'Reasonable!' Rupert exclaimed. 'He has never been reasonable where I am concerned. No, you must have some magic power over him! Can it be that he is in love with you?'

'That is impertinent!'

Orelia had drawn herself up proudly and her eyes were flashing. Rupert capitulated.

'I apologise, please do not be angry with me, Miss Stanyon. I am just bewildered and of course excited beyond words! And anyway, since you are so lovely, who could blame him!'

Although Orelia tried to look severe, it was hard to be incensed with this ingenuous and beguiling young man, who was in fact still far from well.

The months, if not years, of dissipation had taken their toll, and Orelia realised that it was necessary for him to build up his strength before he could face anything so strenuous as life in the Army.

She was not particularly impressed by the Physician, whose only idea of treating any patient was to cup them!

After three blood-lettings Rupert's fever undoubtedly abated, but at the same time he was so weak that Orelia returned to giving him her herbs and trying to tempt his appetite with nourishing dishes.

She was also convinced that sleep was a better healer than anything the Physician could prescribe.

This morning Rupert had woken in unusually good spirits and eaten quite a reasonable breakfast. But after a while he ceased to chatter about what he would do in the Army and his eyelids closed.

Orelia had crept from the room knowing that he would sleep now until later in the day.

It was with almost a sense of relief that she realised that at last she had time to think about herself. She was sadly in need of new clothes.

Although Caroline had promised her a number of gowns, those she had chosen for her trousseau had not been delivered, and with so many social engagements she really needed for her own use everything she owned.

Orelia knelt down on the carpet and spread out the muslin, at the same time studying one of Caroline's Paris gowns which she had draped over a chair as a model.

She was so intent on her task that she did not hear the door open and started when a familiar voice behind her said:

'Would it be impertinent to enquire what you are doing?'

Orelia sat back on her heels and looked up at the Marquis. As usual she was overwhelmingly conscious of how smart he appeared, of the snowy whiteness of his cravat and of the cynical twist to his lips as he looked down at her under his drooping eyelids.

'I am attempting to make myself a dress, My Lord,' she replied, 'and not very successfully!'

'Make yourself a dress!' the Marquis repeated, an incredulous note in his voice. 'Is that something you do often?'

'I have always made my own clothes,' Orelia replied simply.

She had as she spoke a desire to laugh, knowing that the Marquis with his great wealth and living in the rich and fashionable *Beau Ton* would never before have come into contact with anyone so poor as she was herself.

The Marquis made no further comment but after a moment said:

'I have just learnt from my secretary that you have refused to accompany us to the Ball given by the Duchess of Devonshire tonight. May I ask the reason?'

'It is quite simple,' Orelia smiled, 'all women complain that they have nothing to wear, but in my case it is true!'

'I do not understand,' the Marquis said.

'Well let me explain,' she answered. 'I have only one ball-gown which Caroline most kindly gave me, but unfortunately one of the servants last night knocked a cup of coffee over it. It is irreparable!

'Caroline has very sweetly given me another, but I

have not yet had time to alter it. Therefore, My Lord, I cannot go to the Ball!'

'So it was Caroline's gown you were wearing,' the Marquis said reflectively. 'I did not think the colour of it became you.'

'No indeed,' Orelia agreed. 'But there is an ancient adage, My Lord, which has never been applicable in your life. It is "Beggars cannot be choosers!" '

'Are you really so poor?' the Marquis enquired.

'I am completely penniless,' Orelia replied.

Then she continued.

'Pray do not look so surprised! I know Your Lordship is unlikely to have come into personal contact with the poor and needy, yet I assure you they do exist! But not usually, I must admit, inside Ryde House!'

She spoke lightly and there was laughter in her eyes. But she saw that the Marquis was not smiling and there was a frown on his forehead.

'This is nonsensical,' he said. 'I am sure you will allow me . . .'

'. . . No, of course not!' Orelia interrupted quickly. 'And pray do not say what I suspect is trembling on your lips. It is kind of Your Lordship and very generous, but you know as well as I do that I could not accept anything of that sort from you.'

'But why?' he asked. 'Are you afraid that in doing you a favour I might claim my reward?'

For a moment Orelia was absolutely still, her eyes looking up at him, wide and startled. Then involuntarily, without choosing her words, she exclaimed:

'So you did remember!'

'Do you imagine that I could ever forget such a moment of enchantment?' he asked quietly.

His eyes, dark and penetrating, looked down into hers and she felt the blood rising like a crimson flood on her pale cheeks.

Then, as she was unable to take her eyes from his, the colour ebbed away leaving her paler than she had been before.

'A moment of utter and complete enchantment,' he said, almost beneath his breath.

Without speaking again he turned and walked from the room leaving her curiously shaken and for a long time unable to move.

Orelia had done very little work before Caroline returned.

'The Marquis and I are lunching with one of his innumerable relations,' she announced. 'You and the Duchess will be alone. Do not look so frightened, Orelia, Her Ladyship will not eat you!'

'I admit she scares me,' Orelia said. 'She is so aloof and so worldly-wise that I feel as if she lives in a different world to mine.'

'She forgets she is old!' Caroline exclaimed scornfully. 'Her Grace thinks she can order everyone about as she did when she was at the height of her beauty!'

Orelia's heart was touched.

'It must be sad for anyone who has been so beautiful to grow old,' she said.

'Oh, do not be sorry for the Dowager,' Caroline begged, 'or she will bully you unmercifully. I had a "battle royal" with her this very morning over some tiresome Assembly she wished me to attend. But I won by sheer perseverance!'

Caroline kissed her cousin.

'There are lots of things I want to tell you,' she said, 'but Darius is waiting and he gets exceedingly irritated if people are unpunctual.'

'Then go to him at once,' Orelia cried. 'I would not wish you to incense the Marquis.'

'It would do him good as it happens,' Caroline retorted. 'He is far too fond of getting his own way!'

Orelia went downstairs rather apprehensively. Caroline had been right when she had accused her of being afraid of the Duchess.

There was something about the Marquis's Grandmother that was extremely awe-inspiring and Orelia found her in the Salon, dressed in white as usual, and glittering with a fantastic collection of jewels.

'Come along, child,' she said sharply as Orelia appeared. 'You and I cannot linger over our meal; we have much to do this afternoon and I have ordered the carriage for half after one of the clock.'

'The carriage?' Orelia questioned. 'Are we driving anywhere particular, Ma'am?'

'We are going shopping,' the Duchess answered. 'I have learnt that you are desperately in need of new gowns and I intend to provide you with quite a small trousseau. Not as extensive as Caroline's, but nevertheless all that a young Lady of Fashion will require for her first Season in London.'

Orelia drew in a deep breath.

'I am sorry, Ma'am, but I cannot accept such generosity,' she said. 'I have an idea who has told you of my need and although I am extremely grateful for such kindness, the answer is "no".'

'Indeed,' the Duchess answered. 'And is there any reason why Caroline should not have informed me that you had no gown to wear for this evening's Ball?'

'C . . Caroline . . . told you?' Orelia questioned.

'But of course,' the Duchess replied, 'who else?'

There was no answer to this and Orelia could only feel confused.

'And I thought,' the Duchess continued, 'that you would be pleased and perhaps a little grateful to me for a present of which you are quite obviously very greatly in need!'

'You . . . . Ma'am, are making me a . . . gift of the g . . gowns?' Orelia stammered.

'That was my intention,' the Duchess answered. 'You really cannot expect me to introduce to the *Beau Ton* a country wench who is not elegantly attired!'

'But Ma'am . . .' Orelia began—only to realise there was nothing she could say.

She was quite convinced that the Marquis had told his Grandmother to purchase some clothes for her. She was sure that he would receive the accounts for them, yet how could she say so openly?

She looked into the Duchess's face and saw what she thought was a look of contempt on those once beautiful features. But there was nothing she could do, but to accept with gratitude the Duchess's declared generosity.

'Thank you . . . Ma'am, it is indeed . . . very kind of . . . you,' she managed to falter.

Three hours later she returned to Ryde House with her head in a turmoil.

Never had she believed for a moment that she would possess such entrancing, such ravishing, such a breathtaking collection of gowns, coats, pelisses and underwear.

The Duchess had been determined that she should have everything, choosing even reticules to match the gowns and wraps trimmed with swansdown to wear in the evening in case the air was chill.

There were embroidered slippers and nightgowns so transparent they could have passed through the proverbial wedding-ring!

There were gloves of every length and even embroidred wreaths of flowers and feathers to match the sparkling diamanté on the gowns themselves.

'No! No, please! No more!' Orelia pleaded not once but a dozen times.

But the Duchess had paid no attention, buying and buying until Orelia felt she could not even remember what had been purchased. Bonnets, shawls and sunshades—the Duchess was insatiable.

When finally they set off for home in the open carriage Orelia could only gasp:

'How . . . Ma'am, can I ever . . . thank you?'

'You can do that by making a brilliant marriage,' the Duchess replied. 'I am sure now there will be no doubt of it. Indeed, although I thought you a pretty girl, I had no idea until I saw you wearing white and the soft shades of the blue and green which suit your fair hair, that you were in fact a beauty.'

She paused for a moment before continuing:

'Surely you must have had the taste to realise that the gowns which Caroline has given you were the wrong colour.'

Orelia did not answer. What was the point, she wondered, of trying to explain to these rich people that it was a case of either wearing Caroline's cast-offs or going naked?

How could the Duchess or her Grandson, with all their wealth and circumstance, even begin to understand what it was like to be poor?

When she and Caroline were alone, Orelia asked: 'Is the Duchess very rich?'

'Good Heavens, no!' Caroline replied. 'She is eternally leaning on Darius for everything she requires. Only last month he bought her a new carriage and two exceedingly expensive bloodstock to draw it."

Orelia took a deep breath. She had suspected who was to pay for the extravagant wardrobe with which she had been presented during the afternoon, but now her suspicion was a certainty.

She felt herself tremble with anger. How dare he do this to her? How dare the Marquis behave in such an outrageous manner? Yet, if she were to say anything to him, she was quite certain he would pretend not to understand why she should be annoyed and would doubtless be prepared to swear that the gift came from his Grandmother and from no one else.

'How dare he! How dare he!' Orelia said to herself over and over again.

And yet when she was ready for dinner in her new ball-gown she could not help being thrilled by her appearance.

The Duchess had chosen a dress from the most expensive French couturière in the whole of Bond Street. It became Orelia more than anything she had ever worn.

Of white gauze embroidered with tiny diamonds which glittered and sparkled with every movement, she looked with her fair hair and white skin as if she were a creature from another world.

There was something so ethereal, so fairylike, about her that she herself felt as if she floated rather than walked. And that she might at any moment fly away into the translucence of the evening sky rather than move prosaically down the staircase to the Salon where they were to assemble before dinner.

As she walked into the Salon she knew that the Marquis's eyes were on her.

She told herself she was angry with him and that if she were cold and distant he would realise why she was incensed.

She kept her eyes down-cast as she moved across the Salon towards the crowd of guests who had been invited to dine and who were chatting with their host.

Then feeling almost as if a tidal wave swept her to the Marquis's side and that his will mastered her, she found herself looking up into his face.

'That is how I wished to see you,' he said very softly so that no one else could hear.

Before she could attempt to reply he had turned away to attend to his other guests and he did not speak to her again.

It was very different, Orelia found, going to a Ball or a party in clothes that were not particularly becoming and arriving garbed like a Princess which made her look so lovely that she excited admiration from all who looked at her.

She was besieged by partners asking her to dance. Face succeeded face, and she found herself making the same conversation with the same type of Beau over and over again.

She could not formulate even to herself any particular impression: she was only bemused with the grandeur of Devonshire House!

The beauty of the statues, the pictures, the furniture and the kaleidoscope of Ladies with their glittering jewels, of Gentlemen sporting decorations, all sparkling in the candle-light from the crystal candelabra, left her no time to think of anything else.

It was then she realised that she was dancing for the second time with a Gentleman to whom the Duchess had presented her early in the evening—the Earl of Rotherton.

'It is cursed hot in here,' he said after they had made only one turn of the Ball-room. 'Shall we seek a little air outside?'

'I think that would be very pleasant, My Lord,' Orelia replied.

They went down the stone staircase which led from the balcony of the Ball-room into the garden.

Here there were twinkling lights to illuminate the edges of the paths and glitter amongst the flowers, while Chinese lanterns hung from the boughs of the trees.

There seemed to be as many people in the garden as there were in the Ball-room, but the Earl guided Orelia to a seat set beneath a great shady willow tree whose leaves half obscured them from the perambulating crowds.

The light from a golden Chinese lantern shone on Orelia's pale hair and sparkled on the tiny diamond stars Caroline had lent her to wear amongst her curls.

'You are very lovely!' the Earl said.

Orelia turned her head to look at him. He was a man getting on for forty, dark-haired with already a little grey at the temples; hard over-bold eyes, with obvious lines of dissipation beneath them, and a thick mouth which somehow as she looked at it seemed vaguely repulsive.

Yet most women would consider him handsome, and she remembered that the Duchess when introducing them had said that he was a particular friend of the Marquis.

'This is the first big Ball I have ever attended,' Orelia said in a conventional tone.

She hoped that he would not notice that she had blushed at the compliment he paid her.

'You are unspoilt, very sweet and very beautiful,' the Earl replied.

She felt his hand on her naked shoulder and moved further away from him.

'I think . . . perhaps you do not know me well enough to say . . . such things,' she said uneasily.

'That is easily remedied,' he replied. 'We will get to know one another better—very much better.'

There was something in his voice which made her tremble.

'I think . . . perhaps I should be going back to . . . the

Ball-room,' Orelia said nervously. 'I am engaged for the next dance.'

She made as if she would rise but the Earl put out his hand and laid it on her arm.

'There is no hurry,' he said. 'I wish to talk with you.'

'What about?' Orelia enquired.

'Yourself,' he replied. 'When I first saw you here to-night I knew we must become acquainted. Where have you come from? How can you have suddenly appeared in the Social Firmament and no one be aware of you until now?'

'I live in the country,' Orelia answered, 'and I have only come to London to be with my cousin Caroline until she marries the Marquis of Ryde.'

'So that is the explanation,' the Earl said. 'And you? Are you betrothed? Or can it be possible that you are single and your heart is unengaged?'

'I am both single and heart-free,' Orelia said, striving to speak lightly and with an air of unconcern.

But she was conscious that the Earl's hand was still on her arm and that he seemed in some inexplicable way to draw closer to her. It was stupid, she knew, and yet she had a feeling of danger.

'Look at me!' the Earl commanded.

Obediently she turned her head, and found his face was very near to hers, his dark eyes staring at her in what she felt was an impertinent, over-familiar manner.

'I must return . . . to the Ball-room,' she said in a frightened voice and sprang to her feet.

'We will go back together,' he answered, 'because I wish to hold you in my arms. Besides, there is much more I wish to say to you.'

'I am . . . engaged for this . . . dance,' Orelia faltered.

'You can leave everything to me,' the Earl replied.

She tried to protest, but somehow when they arrived back at the Ball-room she found herself dancing with him again and when the dance was over she found it was impossible to escape from him.

He took her into one of the Ante-rooms and insisted that they sit on a sofa in a dark corner.

'Do you believe in love at first sight, Orelia?' he asked.

'I have not given you permission to call me by my Christian name,' Orelia retorted, 'and I am sure the Duchess would not approve.'

She was trying to speak severely, but she only sounded breathless and very young.

'Her Grace will approve of anything I do,' the Earl smiled, 'especially where you are concerned.'

'What do you mean?' Orelia asked.

'I think you know what I mean,' he answered. 'Elderly women are inveterate match-makers and Her Grace is no exception.'

Orelia felt herself blush.

'I do not understand . . . what you are . . . saying,' she said quickly.

She heard the Earl laugh softly and knew he was not deceived by her pretence.

'Do you, Sweet Innocent, believe in love at first sight?' he asked again.

'No, no of course not!' she answered.

'So vehement,' he smiled. 'I think perhaps you do not listen to the beatings of your own heart.'

There was something about him, Orelia thought, which made her feel as if he was reaching out towards her, holding her, drawing her nearer to him, suffocating her utterance, making her feel that he was crushing her resistance even before she could express it aloud.

'Shall I tell you something?' the Earl was saying, and there was something silky and seductive in his voice that made her feel even more afraid.

'What is it?' Orelia asked.

'I believe in fate,' he replied. 'It was fate that brought me here tonight. It was fate that brought you to London so that we could meet. It is, I believe, my lovely one, fate that we should mean a great deal to each other!'

'No! No! My Lord . . . that is not . . . true!' Orelia cried. 'You are mistaken . . . very mistaken.'

He smiled and she felt as if she were a small bird in a net, in which she could only flutter helplessly without a hope of escape.

'You are adorable,' he said suddenly. 'And I want more than I have wanted anything for many years to feel your lips beneath mine.'

'You have no right to say such . . . things,' Orelia protested.

'Then give me the right!' he urged, a compelling almost mesmeric note in his voice.

She glanced at him and the expression in his eyes—bold, possessive and somehow menacing—made her start to her feet.

This time, before he could prevent her, she had turned and run from the sofa on which they had been seated, across the Ante-room and back into the crowd of people moving down the corridor towards the Ballroom.

She crossed the floor, moving between the dancers, searching as she did so amongst the Dowagers lining the sides of the room to see if she could find the Duchess. But there was no sign of her.

Then, as she went out of the Ball-room onto the top of the stairs, she saw the Marquis standing alone and looking down into the well of the Hall as if in search of someone. Without thinking she sped to his side.

She did not speak but only felt in some strange manner that she was safe because she had reached him.

He turned his head to look at her, seeing the fear in her face and the tumultuous rise and fall of her breasts beneath the soft gauze of her gown.

'What has happened?' he asked.

'I could not . . . find your . . . Grandmother,' Orelia stammered. 'But I saw you and now . . . now it is all . . . right.'

'What has frightened you?'

'Nothing! I was just . . . foolish. Is it not time to go home?'

The Marquis raised his eyebrows.

'Most young women would be horrified at the idea of leaving Devonshire House at such an early hour. But if you really wish it, I will find my Grandmother and tell her you desire to retire.'

'No, no, she would think it ungrateful of me,' Orelia

said. 'But can I . . . stay with . . . you until I find
. . . her?'

She glanced apprehensively over her shoulder as she
spoke, dreading to see the Earl coming from the Ball-
room in search of her.

'If there is no hurry for you to depart,' the Marquis
said, 'let me suggest that as it is a long time since dinner
we repair to the Supper Room.'

'Can we . . . do that?' Orelia asked a little breathlessly, and added: 'Thank you, My Lord, I would like it
very much.'

They went downstairs to where supper was laid out
in a huge Dining-Room. Small tables for four were lit
with candelabra and the Marquis found one which was
unoccupied at the far end of the room.

As Orelia sat down she felt some of her agitation
subside. It was unlikely that the Earl would find her
here and anyway she was with the Marquis.

The Earl would not dare to speak to her in such a way
—would not make love to her—when someone else was
present.

Then she remembered she was in fact incensed with
the Marquis. She saw his eyes flicker over her gown as
if he knew what she was thinking and impetuously she
said:

'It was extremely kind of Your Lordship, but wrong,
very wrong . . . as you well know!'

He did not pretend to misunderstand her.

'If you saw a beautiful picture lying neglected in a
dark corner of a room,' he asked, 'would you not wish
to frame it and place it where it could give pleasure to
all who saw it?'

'You have an answer to everything, have you not?'
Orelia asked shyly, her eyelashes dark against her
cheeks.

'Botticelli!' the Marquis exclaimed unexpectedly.

She looked up at him enquiringly and he went on:

'It has been tantalising me ever since we met—
the very first time—of what you reminded me. Now I
know! The pictures I saw in Florence when I was
there the winter before last—pictures by Botticelli.'

He paused.

'They are what you are like: a Venus rising from waves, a Goddess in Primavera! He drew with such delicacy, such beauty, that I never thought I could find one of those exquisite creatures living in this world.'

Orelia looked down. She did not understand why, but when the Marquis spoke like that it sent a little thrill through her as if the flame of a tiny candle burnt within her breast.

'You are . . . teasing me, My Lord,' she said at length because she could not think of anything else to say.

'Do you really suppose that?' the Marquis asked in his deep voice. 'I am speaking the truth.'

Orelia felt as if his words took her breath away.

Then when she would have replied she saw Caroline advancing towards them escorted by an elegant Buck with such high points to his collar and such an intricately tied cravat round his throat that it was almost impossible for him to move his head.

'Oh, here you are, Darius!' Caroline exclaimed. 'I have been looking for you everywhere. And Orelia— Lord Rotherton is asking everyone why you have vanished. He swears that your real name is Cinderella and like her you were forced to disappear at midnight!'

'Who is Cinderella?' Caroline's escort enquired curiously.

'She is the little cinder-girl in Perrault's *Cendrillon*,' Orelia explained, and added—'And her fairy Godmother gave her a gown so that she could go to the Ball.'

As she spoke she glanced mischievously from under her eyelids at the Marquis.

'I prefer the tale of the Princess who fell asleep for a hundred years,' he said in a low voice.

He turned his head towards Orelia as he spoke so that the others busily seating themselves at the table did not hear him.

Orelia met his eyes, surprised that he should have read the mythical folklore which she enjoyed. Then she remembered that the Princess had been awakened by a kiss! She felt the colour rising in her cheeks.

Caroline was studying the Supper Menu.

'I cannot imagine!' she said after a moment, 'why Orelia should wish to vanish when she is being such a success. Lord Rotherton is quite distraught!'

She looked across the table at her cousin.

'Should you not go back to the Ball-room and dance with him?'

'I . . . I am tired,' Orelia said quickly. 'I have been trying to find Her Grace to say that I am ready to go home.'

Caroline laughed.

'You will not drag the Duchess from the card table! Not when she is winning, as I saw she was doing just now. But perhaps by the time we have finished supper she may change her mind!'

'I hope so,' Orelia said in a small voice.

She had, however, to wait until after two o'clock before the Duchess could be persuaded to return home, and then only because Caroline also said she was tired, as this was the fifth consecutive night she had been to a party.

The Marquis did not accompany them, but after escorting them to their carriage he said goodnight. As they drove away from Devonshire House Caroline remarked:

'I suspect His Lordship has an engagement at White's Club. I am sure if he wins much more there will soon be no one left who will agree to game with him!'

'He has been winning a lot?' the Duchess asked with what seemed to Orelia an envious note in her voice.

'His Lordship always wins,' Caroline replied confidently.

'Be careful!' the Duchess warned her, and there was a touch of spite in her tone. 'Lucky at cards, unlucky in love!'

'Darius is the exception to every rule,' Caroline answered confidently, 'so he will be lucky in both!'

The Duchess did not reply, but as the carriage proceeded towards Park Lane she said to Orelia:

'You were a great success tonight, my child. I flatter myself that no one could have found a gown which becomes you better!'

'No indeed,' Caroline interposed before Orelia could speak. 'And you have made a very notable conquest, Orelia! The Earl of Rotherton is extremely eligible, is he not, Ma'am?'

'He is indeed,' the Duchess answered. 'And I have always wondered why he has never married again.'

'He has been married before?' Orelia asked.

'Yes, his wife died when she was but twenty—of a stillborn child. It was a tragedy because of course His Lordship, being both wealthy and of an ancient family, needs an heir.'

'Why do you think he has remained unwed?' Caroline enquired.

The Duchess shrugged her shoulders.

'His Lordship has had many *chères amies,* as you can imagine. One in particular was a Lady of Great Consequence whom he could not marry and who has now left England to live in France. I think that is why His Lordship is now seriously considering the enviable state of matrimony. And what better bride could he find than our sweet little Orelia?'

A note of sarcasm might have been expected in the Duchess's voice as she praised Orelia, but there was no doubt that she was speaking in all sincerity.

'No!' Orelia said quickly. 'No! No! I am sure His Lordship is not considering any such thing as far as I am concerned. But I would not marry him, even if he asked me!'

'Do not be so nonsensical, child,' the Duchess said sharply. 'You would jump at the opportunity, as would every other unmarried girl in that Ball-room tonight if she got the chance!'

The following week it seemed to Orelia as if she had walked into a nightmare. Huge baskets of flowers arrived from the Earl the morning after the Ball almost before she was awake. There was also an invitation to take her driving in the Park.

Orelia would have refused, but she found that he had been clever enough to invite Caroline as well.

Although her cousin would have cried off, when she found that Orelia was adamant about not going alone, she insisted that they should both accept the Earl's invitation.

This was the first of a flood of invitations from him to which Caroline dragged an unwilling Orelia.

Fortunately once they met Caroline chattered away in her usual animated and inconsequential manner and Orelia needed to say little.

But she was acutely conscious that the Earl was watching her, that he took every opportunity of being close to her, that his hand held hers unnecessarily long and that every nerve in her body shrank from him!

She became more and more convinced that as far as she was concerned he was dangerous. She was being pursued, hunted and there seemed no way of escape from the trap which awaited her.

Once while Caroline was talking to someone else in the Park the Earl said in a low voice:

'You shall be mine—no power on earth shall keep you from me!'

She looked at him in astonishment, thinking she had not heard him aright, then she saw the fire in his eyes, and the hunger on his lips and turned away speechless with terror. She knew he would not let her go!

'What is the matter with you, Orelia?' Caroline asked three days later. 'His Lordship is infatuated—one can see that at a glance! And dearest, he is so rich! He is everything I ever wanted for you!'

'He is too . . . old and a . . . widower!' Orelia protested.

'He has a magnificent Estate near Guildford,' Caroline said. 'He has some of the best race-horses in the country. His house in London is nearly as grand as this, and the Prince Regent honours him with his friendship. Surely, Orelia, you cannot be so birdwitted as to expect you will find a better suitor?'

'I do not want a suitor!' Orelia declared frantically. 'I have no wish to be married!'

'Fustian!' Caroline exclaimed. 'At times, Orelia, I could slap you! Of course you want to be married. What do you think will happen to you otherwise? Of course there will always be room in my house for you, dearest, but you know as well as I do that that is not the same as having a house and a husband of one's own. Inevitably, whether you like it or not, whether I love you or not, you will be relegated into the position of the poor relation! It is unavoidable!'

Caroline paused to let her words sink in. Then she said:

'Stop being obstinate, Orelia, and indeed a turnip-head, which I have called you before. You will never get a better catch than His Lordship. From the way he was looking at you today you have merely to smile at him and he will declare himself.'

'No! No! I cannot bear it!' Orelia cried.

But not much later she was to realise that the Earl was far too experienced to put himself into the position of being refused by a young woman whom he sensed was so shy and inexperienced as to be frightened by his attentions.

It was Caroline who broke the news.

'He has declared himself!' she cried theatrically, bursting into the Salon where Orelia was sitting with the Duchess waiting for tea to be served.

'Who has?' the Duchess asked before Orelia could speak.

'The Right Honourable the Earl of Rotherton has requested my permission,' Caroline replied, 'to pay his addresses to my ward, Miss Orelia Stanyon!'

Orelia went very pale. The Duchess gave a little laugh.

'So he has come up to scratch,' she said. 'I thought that he intended to be formal in his proposal when he asked me who was Orelia's Guardian. Well, my child, I congratulate you! I could not have done better if I had been in your shoes, and that is a compliment.'

Orelia drew a deep breath.

'His Lordship has addressed you formally,' she said to Caroline. 'Then will you please convey my reply.

It is—"While deeply aware of His Lordship's condescension, I am unable to accept his proposal. My answer is no."'

'Orelia, you cannot mean it! You must be demented!' Caroline exclaimed. 'And let me tell you once and for all that I have no intention of conveying such a message to His Lordship. I shall tell him that your answer is yes.'

'But it will not be true!' Orelia cried.

'It will be,' Caroline said confidently.

'Of course it will,' the Duchess interposed. 'You are unsophisticated and overwhelmed that anyone so important should desire you. But you will accept His Lordship thankfully.'

'I will not!' Orelia retorted.

'Oh yes you will,' the Duchess insisted. 'A little hesitation is very becoming nowadays when girls are bold and husband-hunt so openly. I know His Lordship—who is a connoisseur—will appreciate that you are not springing at him as if you were a hungry salmon!'

She laughed.

'You may not be up to scratch, but you certainly know how to make a man extremely ardent. Every man wishes to do his own hunting.'

'Of course!' Caroline said with relief. 'Now I see that Orelia is being clever. Let him think you are reluctant, dearest. I shall not hesitate to tell him so—it will be good for him to have a slight set down.' She smiled. 'It is quite obvious that he has been spoilt by far too many women running hot-foot in the race to capture his affections!'

'Please . . . will you understand that I do not intend ever to marry His Lordship,' Orelia said.

She knew even as she spoke they were not listening to her. Soon it seemed as if the Duchess and Caroline entered into a conspiracy.

Orelia found that she was never left alone with the Earl so that she could tell him firmly and categorically that she had no intention of becoming his wife.

When he called at Ryde House she was always

chaperoned in his presence, and every time she tried to convey to him her positive decision that no marriage would take place, her words were swept away before she could utter them.

She felt that he ought to be as frustrated as she was, and yet she was almost sure by the look in his eyes that he was well aware of her feelings and was deliberately ignoring them.

Determined that the Earl should know the truth she sat down and wrote him a letter.

She sealed it and gave it to the Butler requesting him to have it delivered to Rotherton House by one of the footmen. But it seemed certain, although she could not confirm her suspicion, that it was never taken there.

The Butler, she thought later, would have asked the Duchess if he should obey such an order. And it was quite obvious what the answer would have been.

In the meantime Orelia received flowers, notes of affection, and the Duchess and Caroline talked of her marriage, planned her trousseau, even discussing her honeymoon, until Orelia felt she must scream.

Finally it seemed to her that there was only one thing she could do—she must run away!

She found that any protest she made was so ineffectual, any argument she put forward was dismissed so peremptorily that she had a sudden terror that she would wake up one morning to find herself being taken forcibly to Church and married to the Earl before there was anything she could do about it.

She told herself over and over again that she was being ridiculous—she only had to see His Lordship, to tell him firmly that she would not marry him.

But when finally she asked if she might see the Earl alone, she was told by the Duchess that it was quite unnecessary and certainly unconventional.

'Perhaps,' the Dowager added, 'it will be possible after the engagement is sent to the *Gazette*. His Lordship is considering doing that next week.'

'But I will not marry him! I have told you I will not marry him,' Orelia protested.

'In my day,' the Duchess retorted sharply, 'girls who behaved in such a monstrously stupid manner were given a good whipping and shut up in their bedrooms with nothing to eat but bread and water until they came to their senses.'

Orelia did not speak, and the Dowager added scornfully:

'Have you never thought how embarrassing it would be for Caroline and my Grandson to have you for ever hanging round their necks? You say yourself you have no money. Surely your pride if nothing else will prevent your being a permanent encumbrance on them.'

The Dowager's voice was sharp and her words seemed to Orelia like daggers that she aimed at the heart.

It was true! That was exactly what she would be—an encumbrance, not only to Caroline, but to the Marquis.

She thought now that the reason he had given her all her beautiful clothes was that he desired her to get married. She had hardly seen him since that night at Devonshire House and he had not spoken to her alone.

Perhaps he was deliberately keeping away from her because he too thought her foolish and nonsensical not to accept his friend—the Earl of Rotherton!

Orelia went up to bed feeling as if a fog, dark and impenetrable, encompassed her. She knew that she was afraid of the Earl and that there was something about him that repelled her. She thought of his thick lips and shuddered.

Yet how could she escape from him? What alternative was there to marrying him?

And he was so sure that she would in fact be his!

Only that afternoon at a Reception the Duchess was giving a few of her intimate friends Orelia had found the Earl by her side as she went to the far end of the big Salon to fetch a cushion to place at the feet of an elderly guest.

'Do you know how entrancing you look?' he asked. His eyes flickering from her face to soft curves of her breast beneath the fine silk of her gown made her feel as if he undressed her.

'I am busy, My Lord,' she murmured.

'I, too, will be busy telling you of my love,' he replied. 'And once you are mine, my Sweet Innocent, you will have no time for anything or anyone else.'

It was not what he said but the lust in his voice which unsophisticated as she was she sensed and feared.

This was the opportunity to tell the Earl that she would never marry him, but even as she parted her lips to speak his hand, greedily possessive, had clutched hers.

It was as if she had been touched by a reptile— snatching up the cushion she turned and ran from him speechless with a terror she could not control!

She must be free of him, she must!

Now like a light in the darkness an idea came to her. She jumped out of bed and going to the cupboard collected some clothes together and put them into a canvas hold-all which fortunately had been put in a cupboard just outside her bedroom.

It was a bag she could carry herself and into it she packed the few garments she had owned before she came to London.

She left hanging in the wardrobe the elegant, glittering gowns that the Duchess had bought for her in Bond Street; she left behind the transparent fragility of the underclothes which so elegant and seductive could only have come from Paris.

Searching at the very back of the cupboard she found her old blue cape trimmed with fur which she had made herself and which she had worn for so many years.

She looked at her clock and saw it had not yet struck the hour of two. She must wait, she thought, until dawn. Then she would creep downstairs before the household was on duty.

She would take a hackney carriage to the 'Bull and Mouth' in Regent's Circus where she knew she could board a Stage Coach which would take her within two miles of Morden.

Fortunately she had just enough money for her journey.

It was her own, she thought thankfully, because she had a few pounds saved before she left the country and had spent nothing since she had come to London.

She had meant to tip the servants with it after she had stayed at Ryde House for three weeks. But now she must expend it on running away—on returning home.

Once safe in familiar surroundings she could write to the Earl and tell him firmly that she would not marry him.

What was more she felt that her action in leaving Ryde House would convince the Duchess and Caroline that she was serious in her intention of refusing His Lordship's suit.

She dressed herself and lay down on her bed, thinking of the problems that lay ahead. Somehow she had to manage to live!

Unless Caroline provided for her, she could not even pay for her food at Morden! But that difficulty would be overcome later. At the moment she could only think of how she must get away.

Finally she heard the clock strike four and knew it was time to go. At five o'clock the servants would be rising.

Already the dawn was creeping up over the rooftops —the pale fingers of the sun seeping slowly almost reluctantly into the sable darkness of the night.

Orelia put on her cloak, pulling the hood low over her forehead as if she would disguise herself, and picked up her bag. Slowly, moving so softly so that it would have been impossible for anyone to hear her, she crept down the staircase and into the Hall.

As she had expected, the candles had guttered low in their silver sconces so that they hardly gave any light, and there was no footman on duty.

She moved towards the front door, and turning back

the heavy key in the lock she used both hands to release the lower bolt. It was when she tried to move
the bolt at the top of the door that she ran into difficulties.

She was so small that she could only reach it with
the tips of her fingers, and as it was stiff she knew she
would really need all her strength to move it even a
fraction.

Then as she struggled she heard a voice behind her
ask:

'Can I perhaps be of assistance?'

It was so unexpected that she turned round with a
little cry!

There standing watching her, immaculate in his evening clothes, a grim expression on his face, was the
Marquis!

4

For a moment Orelia was too frightened to move or speak; she could only stand, her face very pale, staring at the Marquis with wide, frightened eyes.

'May I enquire,' the Marquis said with that sarcastic note in his voice which Orelia knew meant he was incensed, 'the name of the gallant who has captured your heart and who, too cowardly to call in daylight, is waiting for you outside?'

'There . . . is no . . . one,' Orelia managed to stammer in a low voice.

'You can hardly expect me to believe that!'

'It is the . . . truth.'

He stared at her in the dim light, as if he would look penetratingly down into her heart to see if she lied. Then he said in a different tone:

'Perhaps it would be wisest if we go somewhere where our conversation will not awake the household. May I suggest that you step into the Library?'

Obediently Orelia preceded him across the Hall. She would not bow her head and carried her chin high, but she felt as if she were going to the guillotine and her heart was thumping suffocatingly in her breast.

She reached the Library and saw a red velvet wing-backed armchair was drawn up in front of the fire. A table stood beside it on which there was a decanter and a half-empty glass of wine.

She wondered what had drawn the Marquis to the Hall.

Had his ears been so acute that he had heard any

small noise that she might have made or had some instinct told him something untoward was happening?

But there was no time for speculation. The Marquis shut the Library doors behind him and crossed the floor to where she stood irresolute, the hood of her cape with its grey fur framing her small white face, her fingers twisting themselves together in nervousness.

'Where were you going?' he asked.

'A .. away.'

'That was obvious,' he replied. 'May I, as your host, to whom you somewhat ungraciously omitted to say farewell, enquire your destination?'

'I was going . . . home.'

'Why?'

The question was sharp and it seemed to Orelia as if it reverberated round the room. For a moment she did not reply, and then the Marquis, his voice hard and compelling, said:

'I insist on knowing the reason, Orelia.'

'It is because . . . I w . . . will not . . . I c . . . cannot . . . m . . . marry Lord Rotherton!'

Orelia's voice was very low as she stammered over the words. She felt the Marquis would be angry, perhaps infuriated with her because she was determined to refuse his friend.

She knew that it would make her seem foolish and indeed childish in his eyes, that she should run away from a man who had offered her nothing more terrible than his hand in marriage.

Why could she not have faced up to the Earl? Why could she not have contrived to send him away without resorting to such drastic measures?

There was silence after her words, a silence in which Orelia could hear her heart beating. She dared not look at the Marquis.

Then unexpectedly he said, in a strange tone which she had not heard from him before:

'Perhaps you would explain to me a little further, and could we not sit down? Give me your cloak, it is warm in here.'

His words were so unexpected that Orelia felt the

colour come back into her face and she ceased to tremble.

She undid her cloak with fingers that fumbled a little at the clasp, and the Marquis taking it from her walked across the room to lay it on a chair by the door.

As he moved back towards her she knew he was no longer angry with her.

She felt however he would note and be offended that she was wearing not one of the glamorous expensive gowns that he had given her, but a plain white muslin she had made herself.

She did not realise that it made her look very young and very vulnerable, but she thought there was a sudden gentleness in his voice as he said:

'Will you not be seated, Orelia?'

She obeyed him, but not by seating herself on the chair opposite the one he had previously occupied.

Instead she sank down on the fur rug in front of the hearth, her skirts billowing out around her, the flames from the fire glinting on her fair hair and illuminating her small unhappy face.

The Marquis seated himself in the red velvet arm-chair, crossed his legs and leaned back at his ease. There was silence for a few moments and then at length he said, almost beguilingly:

'Will you not tell me about it?'

'I am . . . ashamed at being so . . . foolish,' Orelia answered in a low voice, 'but I cannot make anyone understand that I have no . . . wish to marry the . . . Earl.'

'By "anyone" I presume you mean my Grandmother and Rotherton himself?' the Marquis said.

'I have tried to tell His Lordship,' Orelia replied, 'but I am never allowed to be . . . alone with him, and when . . . I wrote him a letter I am . . . convinced he did not receive it.'

'And you have told my Grandmother that you wish to refuse this suitor?'

'I have told Her Grace, but she will not listen,' Orelia answered. 'She and Caroline do not . . . understand. They think I should be . . . pleased to marry anyone so wealthy and important. But I cannot . . . I cannot do it!'

'Why?'

Again that simple question—and yet because it was so direct, so unvarnished, it seemed to Orelia as if it were a weapon pointed at her menacingly.

She dropped her head a little lower so that the Marquis could not see her face.

'I do not . . . love him,' she said, and the words were almost inaudible.

Even as she spoke she thought how nonsensical a reason it would seem to him. He would undoubtedly treat such an explanation with the same contempt that his Grandmother and Caroline had shown.

Then, as she waited for him to laugh or perhaps mock her stupidity, he said very quietly:

'You believe that love is essential to marriage?'

Before she spoke she saw at once how easily she could insult him. Caroline had told her that there was no love between herself and the Marquis—it would be purely a marriage of convenience.

How could she possibly make him understand that she was different from Caroline—that she could not give herself to a man, any man, unless she loved him?

At last, because she knew the Marquis was waiting for her answer, she managed to say:

'It is . . . My Lord, as far as I am . . . concerned.'

'And because you do not love Rotherton you intend to refuse him?'

'Yes,' Orelia said briefly.

'I had understood that the match met with your approval,' the Marquis said slowly. 'Rotherton, it is true, is slightly old in relation to you, but he is exceedingly wealthy. He has a place of importance in Society, his possessions are often envied.'

Orelia did not speak, and after a moment he continued:

'He has undoubtedly lived a somewhat gay existence since he was widowed, but that might be said of any man in the *Beau Ton*. His reputation is certainly more respectable than mine! But if he loves you, as I am told he does, you will undoubtedly be able to reform him.'

'I know . . . all this,' Orelia said. 'Your Grandmama has pointed out to me very clearly the advantages I should gain in becoming His Lordship's . . . wife.'

'And you still wish to refuse him?' the Marquis asked.

'They will not give me an opportunity to do so,' Orelia replied. 'They will not listen to anything I have to say! But I thought that if I went home I could write to His Lordship. I could then tell him that while I am honoured by his proposal I cannot accept it, and then perhaps Caroline and Her Grace will . . . understand.'

She paused for a moment, then raised her eyes, dark with distress, towards the Marquis.

'I will not be an encumbrance upon . . . you and Caroline—that I promise you! I will find employment of some sort so that I can support myself. You must believe that that is my intention!'

The Marquis moved impatiently.

'You cannot really think that has any bearing on the situation?' he asked.

'But of course it has,' Orelia retorted. 'Her Grace has pointed out to me what an encumbrance I should become to you unless I married, and Caroline is afraid that I may have to be treated as a poor relation! But I would not stay . . . here, My Lord, that I would never . . . do!'

'Let me say one thing first,' the Marquis said in a deep voice. 'You are always welcome in my house, not as an encumbrance, not as a poor relation, but as someone I respect and honour.'

His words brought a flush to Orelia's cheeks.

'Thank you, My Lord,' she said. 'It is very kind of you to say so, even though I know that it could not remain true after a little while.'

She gave a little sigh. 'Caroline is right, I should indeed be a poor relation; and besides you will want to be alone together. You will not want me or anyone else with you!'

'You talk as if you were planning your life for ever,' the Marquis said. 'If you do not marry Rotherton, there will be other men. Good God, child, have you not looked in the mirror? Do you not realise there will always be men—men who will desire you, men who will wish to possess you?'

It seemed to Orelia that his voice was unnecessarily harsh, and she said quickly:

'Perhaps you are right, My Lord, perhaps one day I shall find someone I love; but until I do I will not marry Lord Rotherton or any other man.'

'And if you do not find such a man,' the Marquis asked, 'what will become of you?'

'I have plans for the future,' Orelia replied. 'But if Your Lordship will excuse me, I would rather not speak of them at the moment. All that I now wish to do is to go home and extricate myself from the present tangle in which I have become involved. Have I your permission to leave?'

'Do you really credit,' the Marquis asked, 'that I would let you go alone, unprotected, into the streets at this hour of night?'

'I was only going to take the Stage Coach from the Inn at Piccadilly,' Orelia said.

'There is something you have to promise me,' he said.

'What is it?'

'That never again will you attempt anything so fool-hardy,' he replied. 'If you are in trouble, if anything goes wrong with you, if you are frightened—come to me, I swear to you that I will protect you!'

She looked up at him in astonishment, not only because of his words, but because of the depth and sincerity which she heard for the first time in his voice.

He was not mocking her, he was not being sarcastic or cynical. He was speaking, it seemed to her, from his heart.

He had bent forward in his chair and his face was not far from hers. And as their eyes met something happened. Something strange and completely inexplicable passed between them.

It was as if he held her captive, and that she wanted to be held. There was something mesmeric, compelling, in his eyes which made it impossible for her to look away from him.

In some strange and extraordinary manner it seemed as if her whole being had become very quiet, very still, and he stole her soul from her body.

Then a coal dropped in the grate and the sound released the spell that bound them.

Orelia turned her face away from the Marquis, but even as she did so she felt that it required almost a superhuman effort, though why she could not understand.

'Give me your promise,' the Marquis said in a voice she had not heard from him before.

'I . . . promise,' she answered.

'You will stay here,' he said authoritatively. 'I will speak to Rotherton. He will trouble you no more. And I will tell my Grandmother what has been decided. Try to enjoy yourself, Orelia. Already the Social World is talking of your beauty, your charm and sweetness.'

'Talking of me? she asked in surprise.

'Are you really so modest?' he asked, the old mocking tone back in his voice.

'I did not . . . think that anyone had . . . noticed . . . me.'

There was a faint smile on his lips as he looked down at her—at her curls shining in the firelight, at the colour that had come back into her cheeks, at her eyes—not so dark and frightened as they had been when she first came into the room but still uneasy and a little bewildered.

'You are very beautiful, Orelia,' he said slowly. 'Have you not realised that yet?'

'Do you mean that?' she asked a little breathlessly.

'I mean it,' he replied.

Again she would have looked at him but suddenly she was too shy. Her eyelashes fluttered dark against her cheeks and she turned her face towards the fire.

There was silence until the Marquis said: 'I have something to tell you. Today I had a letter from Ru-

pert—the happiest and most enthusiastic letter I have
ever had from him. He enjoys being in the Regiment
and already he has been commended by his Com-
manding Officer.'

'Oh, I am glad, so glad!' Orelia exclaimed. 'I felt
sure that if he could once have what he wanted in life
he would find himself and would no longer be lost and
unhappy.'

'You sound as if you were mothering him,' the Marquis said, 'and that is in fact what you did. It is somewhat difficult to realise that you—so small, so young
and unsophisticated—know how to deal with a dissolute young man and were, let me say it, completely
right in your diagnosis of his needs.'

'It was you who gave him his dearest wish,' Orelia
said softly.

'On your insistence,' the Marquis said. 'You are a
very formidable adversary, Orelia.'

'Now you are teasing me!' she protested. 'I only
fought for Rupert because I could not bear to see anyone so desperately unhappy, so entangled, perhaps
through no fault of his own, in a coil which could ruin
his whole life.'

'You will find a great number of people in the world
in the same kind of situation,' the Marquis said, 'and
usually through their own sheer stupidity!'

'I do not think that is true,' Orelia replied. 'For most
people unhappiness comes because they have no one to
talk to, no one to help them. Everyone needs love and
guidance.'

'A very sweeping statement,' the Marquis said with a
touch of cynicism in his voice. 'And just because you
have solved Rupert's problem, it does not follow that
you can solve other people's in the same manner!'

'No, of course not,' Orelia agreed. 'Everyone is different. At the same time the general principle which
makes a man turn to crime and a woman miserably
unhappy is that their lives are empty of those special
factors which bring contentment to the human race.'

'Which in one word is—money,' the Marquis said.

'Do you really believe that?' Orelia cried. 'Oh, I

know some people will steal and even kill for money, but there is much more in human needs than money.'

She paused before she continued. 'I have known families, on the verge of starvation, who nevertheless because they are together, because of their closeness between the parents and the children and the love which binds them, have been what one could call really happy!'

'How do you know these things?' the Marquis asked.

'I have been in contact with quite a number of people who were suffering in one way or another,' Orelia answered.

'In Morden Green?' he enquired. 'I cannot believe, Orelia, that one small village can have given you much experience!'

She said nothing and after a moment he continued:

'But if you have a panacea for all ills, what about mine? Do you believe that had you known me earlier, perhaps when I was Rupert's age, you could have saved me from myself, from becoming the notorious Wicked Marquis?'

Orelia knew he was mocking her, but she glanced at him and her face was serious:

'Who loved you . . . really loved you . . .' she began.

Then she saw his lips twist and added quickly:

'. . . I mean . . . when you were young . . . a child.'

The Marquis stared at her for a moment, the firelight deepening the sardonic lines on his face. Then he replied, it seemed to her almost defiantly:

'No one! Does that give you the cue you need to dissect me more accurately?'

'No one?' she asked.

'My mother died when I was born,' the Marquis answered. 'My father never forgave me for being instrumental—although inadvertently—in causing her death. My sister went to live with an Aunt where I believe she was happy, and I was brought up at Ryde and in this house.'

'Your father was not fond of you?' Orelia questioned.

'I think he hated me,' the Marquis replied. 'At the

same time I was his heir and he was determined to discipline me. In fact I think the only times I saw him were when he sent for me so that he could punish me!'

'But there must have been other people who were fond of you?' Orelia asked. 'Your Nurse, perhaps.'

'My father had an uncontrollable temper,' the Marquis replied, 'that became progressively worse as he grew older. He vented it on his son and on his staff. I, unfortunately, could not give notice or be sacked, so I survived. But the servants changed as frequently as the seasons of the year.'

There was so much bitterness in his voice that Orelia knew that as a child he must have clung first to one Nurse and then to another, only to have them snatched away from him.

'I suppose all only children, or all children who are brought up without brothers and sisters, are lonely,' the Marquis went on.

It was almost as if he were talking to himself rather than to Orelia.

'But I discovered very early in life that it was not the loneliness I minded, but being ignored! I wished to assert myself, Orelia, and so I did so, even though it meant I was punished for bringing myself to the notice of adults who were not interested in me.'

Orelia turned her head to look up at him.

For the first time she was seeing him not as an important personage, but as a lonely, little boy wandering round this vast house alone, unwanted, uncared for, except materially, by a band of servants who disliked their master.

'Was it better when you went to school?' she asked.

'Better?' the Marquis queried. 'I suppose so—I had learnt my lesson by that time. When I went to Eton I soon found that to be aggressive, and if possible a rebel, would always attract other malcontents. There was always someone more humble, more crushed than myself, who would follow where I led.'

It was inevitable, Orelia thought, that he should crave the attention he had been denied during the first twelve years of his life, and like Rupert he must have so easily drifted into the wrong set.

He would have so little in common with the boys who had come from happy, warmhearted homes, who knew the love of a mother and counted the days until they could return to the warmth of a family circle.

'What did you do in the holidays?' she asked.

'I took some of my friends to stay at Ryde,' the Marquis replied, 'and I soon found at Eton, and later at Oxford, that there were always people willing to invite the son of a wealthy and powerful aristocrat to stay in the hope that the invitation would be returned.'

He paused and laughed.

'You have inveigled me into telling you my life story! Well, now you have heard it, what is your verdict? Am I condemned out of my own mouth?'

'Not condemned,' Orelia answered. 'Now I understand so many things that I did not before.'

'From just a few sentences?' the Marquis enquired. 'I am suspicious of you, Orelia, I think you are a quack —not a true physician.'

'I have never pretended to be anything,' Orelia answered, 'but sometimes I can help people.'

'And can you help me?'

She looked at him for a moment before she dropped her eyes.

'I do not think you need my help, My Lord,' she answered, 'for you yourself are clever enough to know what is wrong.'

'Who said anything is wrong?' the Marquis answered almost violently.

She did not reply and at that moment the clock on the mantelpiece chimed the half-hour. Slowly Orelia rose to her feet.

'I must go,' she said. 'The clothes I was taking away with me are in the Hall; if someone should see my bag they would know I intended to leave.'

'Yes, you must go,' the Marquis repeated, and she thought that there was a note of regret in his voice.

'Perhaps . . . some time . . . we could . . . talk again,' Orelia hesitated.

The Marquis had also risen to his feet, and now he looked down at her, a strange enigmatic look on his face.

'Do you think that wise?' he asked.

'Wise?' she enquired. 'I do not understand, My Lord.'

'I think you do,' he answered. 'But at least I can look at you.'

He turned abruptly and walked across the room to open the door for her. She hesitated for a moment and then she followed him. He picked up her cloak and placed it over her arm. As he did so his hand touched her bare skin.

It was only a touch yet she felt as if a flash of lightning struck her whole body. She drew in her breath swiftly and looked up at him. Again their eyes met.

They stood looking at each other. She felt as if their hearts said what their lips dare not utter, what their minds dare not think. Abruptly the Marquis turned away, opening the door wide.

'Goodnight, Orelia.'

'Goodnight . . . My Lord,' she whispered, her voice somehow constricted in her throat. 'And . . . thank you.'

The Hall was almost in darkness, for the candles had finally guttered and gone out. But the dawn was coming through the windows and by its light Orelia could see her bag at the foot of the stairs.

She picked it up and started up the stairway. Only when she had taken half a dozen steps did she turn to glance back at the Library door.

She thought he would be watching her, but the door was closed.

Orelia was woken by Caroline coming noisily into her bedroom.

'Are you awake, sleepy-head?' she asked.

Orelia sat up against the pillows.

'What time is it?'

'Nearly eleven o'clock. You are becoming very fashionable! When we first came to London you rose at eight!'

'Eleven o'clock!' Orelia ejaculated, and then remembered she had not gone to bed until.five.

Although she had expected to lie awake thinking of her conversation with the Marquis, she had in fact fallen asleep as soon as her head had touched the pillow.

'Yes, eleven o'clock!' Caroline said, 'and it will surprise you to know that I have been up for over half an hour. His Lordship sent for me. Oh, Orelia, why did you not tell me?'

'Tell you what?' Orelia enquired.

'That you were unhappy—that you disliked Lord Rotherton.'

'But I did tell you, at least I tried to,' Orelia said.

'I did not believe you,' Caroline answered, 'but Darius has now explained it to me, and I am sorry, Orelia. You know that I would never try to force you into marriage with anyone you did not like.'

'What did the Marquis say?' Orelia asked in a low voice.

'He spoke so warmly and so kindly about you, Orelia,' Caroline replied, 'that I really felt quite fond of him!'

Orelia's eyes were wide open as she sat bolt upright with a start.

'Caroline!' she ejaculated, 'what do you mean?'

'What I say,' Caroline answered, walking restlessly about the room. 'When Darius is like that—sincere and pleasant—I find I have a positive affection for him!'

'But, Caroline, surely you are fond of His Lordship, you are . . . going to marry him!'

'I have told you before, Orelia, that Darius is the most splendid suitor that any woman could expect to find—he has so much to offer! But when, as so often, he is cynical, disagreeable, and sarcastic, I assure you I find him a dead bore!'

'Caroline!' Orelia ejaculated again.

'But when he speaks as he did this morning about you,' Caroline said, 'then I find that underneath all the trappings of wealth and rank he is almost human. To tell the truth I was quite surprised!'

'You do not know what you are saying,' Orelia cried. 'Caroline, dearest, you cannot marry a man unless you have a true affection for him, unless you also respect and admire him!'

'Oh, I admire Darius all right,' Caroline replied, 'he always gets everything he wants! I admire anyone who can do that! And I wager you, Orelia, that he will make mince-meat of his Grandmama! She is in the Library with him now!'

'Talking about me?' Orelia asked in horror.

'Who else? The noble Marquis is concentrating on you this morning.'

Caroline was laughing, but Orelia looked upset.

'Her Grace will be furious with me.'

'Oh, no, she will not,' Caroline answered. 'Darius is far too clever for that! He will just tell her, as he has told me, that you are not going to marry Lord Rotherton and that we are not to plague you or try to make you do anything you do not want to do!'

She gave a little laugh and went on:

'He said you were different from all the nitwitted Society wenches who had only one idea in their heads and that was to get themselves a titled and wealthy husband!

'He said you were an idealist and that is the way he wished you to be treated in his house. And he would not have you forced to associate with anyone you did not like!'

Caroline laughed again.

'How I wish I could see the Dowager's face while she is listening to him!'

'I do not at all wish to see it,' Orelia retorted. 'Let me go home, Caroline. I will be quite all right there. And later I will find some employment so that I can support myself.'

Caroline ran across the room to sit on the edge of the bed and put her arms around Orelia.

'Darius told me you were thinking of going away and I did not believe him! Oh, my dearest, do you think I could really manage without you? I want you here. It makes all the difference having you with me. You are not to leave me—I could not bear it!'

'Do you really want me?' Orelia asked in surprise.

'Of course I want you,' Caroline answered. 'Can you not understand, Orelia, that it means everything to me for us to be together—to know that you understand?'

'Understand what?' Orelia asked.

Caroline took her arms from Orelia's shoulders.

'I do not know, Orelia,' she answered. 'I do not know what I feel!'

'Caroline, are you not happy?' Orelia demanded.

'Of course I am happy!' Caroline replied. 'I have everything in the world that anyone could want, have I not? And yet I do not understand the Marquis. I do not pretend that I do.'

'Then why are you determined to marry him?' Orelia enquired.

'Now we are back to the same old question,' Caroline answered. 'I intend to marry him because of all he can give me, because of the position I shall hold as his wife. But he is a strange man—I never know what he thinks or what he feels—and I am not certain that I particularly want to do so!'

She paused.

'He always gives the impression of criticising me, of summing me up and not being particularly pleased with the total!'

'Caroline, I am sure that is not true! His Lordship is proud of your beauty and I am sure, yes, I am sure he must . . . love you.'

Her voice sounded unconvincing even to herself.

Caroline laughed.

'This conversation started about you, if you remember,' she said. 'Darius has chosen to champion you, and he is quite right! I am ashamed that I let that horrible old witch, his Grandmother, persuade me not to listen to you when you tried to tell me you did not want to marry Lord Rotherton.'

'You must not talk about the Dowager like that,' Orelia said in shocked tones.

'Why not?' Caroline asked. 'It is true enough. She is horrible, as hard as nails and, from all I hear, always has been! She led her husband a fine dance, and I do not believe she cares a snap of her fingers for Darius except for the money he gives her. That is something she cares for very much indeed!'

Orelia remembered how the Marquis had said last night that no one had loved him. Would not any normal Grandmother care for a grandson left alone when he was so young?

She must have known what his father was like! She must have deliberately been indifferent to the needs of a child!

Caroline was right—the Dowager was hard—and perhaps she was typical of the rest of the Marquis's relations, grasping greedily at his pocket without love, without affection, taking but never giving anything in return. No wonder he was cynical!

And what about his wife? What would his wife give him?

Even as she thought of it, Orelia realised that she was thinking not of Caroline's happiness—Caroline, who was her cousin and who had been her friend all her life—but of the Marquis.

'Caroline,' she said urgently, 'have you ever thought what a miserable life the Marquis must have had as a child? His mother died when he was born and knowing his Grandmother you can realise that she offered little consolation to a lonely little boy brought up by a difficult father.'

Caroline shrugged her shoulders.

'I expect Darius soon managed to assert himself,' she said. 'His cousins still talk of how naughty he was when he was small and the pranks he got up to. If he was in trouble it was his own fault. From what I hear punishments did him no good whatsoever!'

'When children are naughty there is usually a reason for it,' Orelia said.

'I will try to remember that when I have half a dozen of my own,' Caroline smiled. 'If they are going to be anything like Darius they will certainly be a handful. You will have to help me look after them, Orelia. I am sure they will find you far more sympathetic than I shall ever be!'

She paused for a moment and then said:

'Did I say half a dozen? I must be to-let-in-the-attic! I have no fondness for children. As soon as there is an heir, there will be no more, I assure you.'

'Caroline, do not talk like that,' Orelia pleaded. 'You will love your own children.'

'Not if they all turn out like Darius—difficult, unpredictable, ready to sneer at their mother!'

'Who has been sneering at you?' Orelia asked.

'Who do you think?' Caroline retorted. 'Who is cynical, sarcastic, disdainful, aloof, unapproachable? Heavens! I cannot help feeling sometimes that in many ways I am getting a poor deal when I remember the success I was in Rome and in Paris!'

'You cannot expect Englishmen to pay you such pretty compliments as foreigners manage to do,' Orelia said practically. 'It is just not in their nature!'

'I know,' Caroline answered, 'but that is just what I like! It is so romantic, Orelia, to walk in the moonlight with a man who declares he loves one to the edge of madness, and to know by the expression in his eyes, by the hunger on his lips, that he wants one unbearably.'

She gave a little sigh. 'That is what I enjoy! That is what I want out of life—to be loved—loved—loved—by attractive, handsome men who can express themselves, who can tell me how beautiful I am, and whose hearts beat quicker because I am near to them!'

Orelia felt there was nothing to say. There was a throb of pain in Caroline's voice which told her all too clearly that she was speaking the truth.

That was indeed what she wanted—love—as everyone else wanted it; but it was a romanticised, unreal, transitory love, that Orelia knew could never bring her real happiness.

That sort of emotional desire, a glamorous lust,

could never give Caroline the security which every woman needs in her life, not only in her youth, but especially in her old age.

'Oh Caroline! Caroline!' she murmured, 'how can I help you?'

'You cannot,' Caroline replied, 'and make no mistake, Orelia, I know very well I am being nonsensical! However I am going to marry the Marquis of Ryde, and I am the most fortunate, the most envied woman in the whole of the *Beau Ton!* He has everything, and after all, he is very handsome and is what old Sarah would have called "very presentable".'

Orelia smiled. It was in fact exactly what old Sarah would have said.

Then she wondered with a strange pain in her heart what that lonely little boy who had been brought up without even a Sarah in his life would find in his marriage as a compensation for love!

5

Orelia and Caroline came down the Grand Staircase arm in arm.

Caroline was chattering away about a party that she had enjoyed the night before, and they had almost reached the Hall before they realised that the Marquis, having just come in from riding, was waiting for them.

Orelia felt the colour rise in her face and she felt shy and a little embarrassed, remembering what had happened the previous night. But Caroline ran towards her fiancé eagerly, saying:

'Good-morning, My Lord, I hope you have not forgotten that you promised to take me driving in the Park this morning!'

'I remembered,' the Marquis replied, 'and I have this moment ordered my High Perch Phaeton because I know you think that it shows your new bonnet off to the best advantage.'

'Only my bonnet?' Caroline asked coquettishly. 'Shame on you, Darius, that is not a very effusive compliment!'

As they were speaking the Butler approached Orelia with a small parcel on a silver salver.

'This has just arrived by hand, Miss.'

Orelia looked at it in surprise, and Caroline exclaimed:

'A parcel for you, Orelia! What can it be? Can some lovesick Beau have sent you a present? It looks to be too large to contain a jewel! And as we all know, the best parcels are always the smallest!'

She laughed at her own joke but Orelia, taking the parcel from the silver salver, said quickly:

'I think it is . . . something I was . . . expecting.'

Without further explanation she started to reascend the stairs. Caroline looked after her in surprise, but her attention was diverted from her cousin because at that moment the Duchess came from the Salon and re-marked:

'Good-morning, Caroline, and Darius—many happy returns of the day. I have just recalled that it is your birthday!'

'Your birthday!' Caroline exclaimed to the Marquis in astonishment. 'Why did you not tell me?'

'I feel it is a milestone in one's life which should be forgotten,' the Marquis replied indifferently.

Orelia, who had now reached the top of the staircase, looked down for a moment at the little group below her.

How typical, she thought, that the Duchess should remember her Grandson's birthday only at the last moment, and apparently had no present for him.

She wondered if he had received birthday presents when he was a boy and thought that it was unlikely.

Then she reflected how during the past years when, after Caroline's marriage, she had been living alone with her Uncle, he had never remembered her birthday.

Often she had felt hurt and absurdly alone because the anniversary had passed without anyone being aware of it!

She ran down the passage to her bedroom, and when she reached it she shut the door and with fingers that trembled with impatience tore open the parcel.

There were four small leather-bound books inside it and a letter. She touched the books almost as if she caressed them, and opened the letter.

It was from a well-known firm of publishers, and spreading out the thick paper she read:

"Madam,

We have the Honour to Enclose Four Volumes of your Book of Poems which is published Today. We have been extremely Gratified by the initial Response from the Booksellers and we Enclose a Cheque in advance Royalties for the sum of Fifty Pounds.

We anticipate that your Work, Madam, will Command a great deal of Attention and we would be Grateful if in the very near Future you would Discuss with us the Possibility of Publishing a further Volume of your Poems or, if you prefer, a Book of Prose.

We remain, Madam, your most Obedient Servants,

Watkins and *Rufus.*"

Orelia gave a little gasp and stared at the cheque as if she could not believe it was real. Fifty pounds! It seemed to her an incredible sum of money.

Then she picked up one of the books, staring at it as if she could hardly credit that the words to which she had given so much time and thought, were actually in print!

The volumes were elegant and engraved on the green leather was the title—*London* by *The Watcher*. There was no other clue as to the identity of the author and Orelia gave a little sigh of relief that no one would guess who *The Watcher* might be.

It was when she was alone after her Uncle had died that the idea had come to her to try to express in her own way what he had taken so many years to write in a book that was only half finished.

She had indeed not expected that her work would be accepted, but she had received almost by return of post a letter of appreciation and indeed enthusiasm from Watkins and Rufus after they had read the manuscript.

Even now she did not set much store by the fact that they expected the book to sell well. Who was likely to be interested in a book written by an anknown and anonymous author?

Although, owing to Lord Byron, verse had become fashionable, her lines were, she felt, not worthy to be called poetry and would therefore, whatever Watkins and Rufus might think, command very little attention.

At the same time fifty pounds seemed an enormous

sum to have earned. Then, as she looked at the cheque, an idea came to her. She could repay the Marquis for his kindness.

Not by giving him back the monies expended by him on her gowns—that would be impossible—and indeed she was not foolish enough to believe that they had not cost much more that fifty pounds would be but a drop in the ocean towards repaying him.

But she could give him a present, and there would indeed be nothing strange in making it a birthday present for him to receive today.

Excited at the idea, Orelia put on her bonnet and driving-coat and ran downstairs, the cheque securely hidden in her reticule.

The Marquis and Caroline must have already left on their drive for they were not to be seen. But the Duchess was in the Salon entertaining an elderly friend who obviously had just arrived to call on her.

'Excuse me, Ma'am,' Orelia said, curtseying politely, 'but would it be possible for me to go to the shops? There is something I need urgently.'

The Duchess looked up with a bored expression on her face and a resentful glint in her eyes, which told Orelia all too clearly that Her Grace had resented her Grandson's intervention on her behalf.

'Ask one of the maids to accompany you,' she said briefly, and turned again to her friend.

Orelia slipped from the room, feeling a sudden elation at being free to go where she wished. She asked the Butler to order her the town landau which was always at Caroline's disposal, and went upstairs to find the housekeeper.

Mrs. Mayhew, an elderly woman who had been in the Marquis's service for over thirty years, was perfectly agreeable to release one of the house-maids to accompany Orelia.

'You had best take Emma, Miss,' she said. 'The girl's been looking a trifle peaked lately and the fresh air will do her good. She's from the country and I often thinks, Miss, that country girls find the London climate oppressive. They also lack the exercise they get when they're working at His Lordship's other houses.'

'I would like to have Emma,' Orelia said.

Emma frequently maided her when the lady's-maid who was allotted to Caroline and herself found it difficult to dress two young ladies at the same time.

Emma, with her rosy cheeks, her bright eyes and soft Hertfordshire accent, was, Orelia felt, just the companion she would have chosen at this particular moment.

It was a lovely day and the sun shone as they drove down Piccadilly towards their destination, which was Mr. Coutts' Bank in the Strand.

Emma, with her coarse straw bonnet tied with black ribbons under her chin, sat opposite Orelia with her back to the horses.

She watched everything with an interest which would have told Orelia all too clearly, even if she had not known already, that up till now the girl who was little more than seventeen had seen very little of the city.

'Ooh, Miss, look at that monkey with the red coat on top of th' hurdy-gurdy!' she exclaimed.

And later:

'A dancing bear! I've heard of such things, Miss, but I never believed I'd see one with me own eyes!'

'The streets are full of such excitements,' Orelia smiled. 'I remember being astonished the first time I visited London—it must have been nearly five years ago —and then I came again in 1817, soon after my seventeenth birthday. I thought then how many strange and extraordinary things there were to be seen even just driving along as we are now!'

' 'Tis an awful big place,' Emma said in awe-struck tones.

Orelia cashed her cheque at Coutts' Bank at No. 59 Strand, being helped and looked after from the moment she entered its impressive porticoed entrance.

Then, back in the carriage again, she directed the coachman to drive to Bond Street.

She had seen in a shop near where the Duchess had

bought her gowns a snuff-box which she had admired
and which she knew now was a present particularly
suitable for the Marquis.

She did not know why, but the box had made her
think of him when she had first seen it, and what he
had told her last night made it seem exactly the right
gift for his birthday.

Of Chelsea enamel in lovely hues of deep blue and
dark red, the top of the snuff-box was painted skilfully.
It portrayed the figure of a man, or perhaps a god, sitting high above the world on the stone steps of a ruined
temple and looking over a great vista beneath him.

There was something omnipotent but at the same
time lonely about the single figure.

'It is a very fine box, Madam,' the Shopkeeper informed her, 'and the artist is making a name for himself.'

'Is it very expensive?' Orelia asked nervously.

She knew that the Dandies and Bucks often paid
astronomical sums for their snuff-boxes and she was
afraid that after all her careful planning the money she
had in her reticule would not be enough for the Marquis's birthday gift.

The Shopkeeper hesitated for a moment.

'As I should wish to have your continued patronage,
Madam,' he said, 'I will make you a special price—
twenty-five guineas. I assure you I am hardly making a
profit for myself on the box, but I should like to number
you, Madam, amongst my customers.'

Orelia gave a little laugh.

'I am afraid I shall not have the money to patronise
you very often but I would very much like to buy this
box, and I have twenty-five guineas with me.'

She drew the money from her reticule as the Shop-
man packed up the snuff-box. What money she had
left, Orelia thought, would go towards the wedding
present she intended to buy for Caroline.

She was already trying to think of what she could
give her cousin, who seemed to have everything that
any young woman could desire.

But Orelia was certain that sooner or later she would

find something that Caroline really needed and which would be a fitting memento of their friendship and affection for each other.

She was bowed from the shop impressively and stepped back into the carriage.

'We can go home now,' she said to the footman, who closed the door and climbed up on the box as the Coachman started the horses.

'Have we a finished, Miss?' Emma asked wistfully.

'For today,' Orelia answered, 'but I must arrange to take you out again. I can see you have enjoyed the drive.'

'And I have, Miss,' Emma answered. 'It's been just wonderful. I've never driven in a carriage before, though I've always a wanted to.'

'Then you must certainly come with me another time.'

A shadow seemed to pass over Emma's face and then to Orelia's surprise tears gathered in the girl's eyes as she said:

'I wish that'd be possible, Miss, but I won't be here!'

'You will not be at Ryde House?' Orelia asked. 'Why? Are you returning home or moving to one of His Lordship's other houses?'

'Neither, Miss. But I shouldn't be a speaking of it, please forgive I. 'Tis only that I've been that happy with you this morning, Miss, I forgot!'

'Forgot what?' Orelia enquired.

She could see something was troubling Emma, who was wiping the tears fiercely from her cheeks with the back of her hand.

'I shouldn't have said anything, Miss,' she muttered.

'There is something wrong,' Orelia said. 'Do tell me what it is. You know you can trust me!'

'I daren't, Miss. I daren't! But I've got to go away, and soon!'

'But why?' Orelia insisted.

'I can't tell you, Miss. I can't!' Emma murmured, twisting her fingers together in her cheap black cotton gloves.

'Emma, if you are in any trouble,' Orelia said in her

soft voice, 'you know I will try to help you. Just trust me. Tell me what is wrong!'

For a moment she thought that Emma would refuse. Then, as if the words burst from her lips, the girl said:

'It weren't me fault, Miss! I swear to you, it weren't! I tried to get away from him, I tried with all me strength, but he was too strong for me. He pushed me down on th' bed, put his hand over me mouth and says: "If you scream I shall say you made yourself objectionable and you'll be sent away tonight without a reference." '

Emma gave a little sob.

'I didn't scream, Miss, as I knows he meant it! But I fought against him, I did really, Miss. But it weren't no use. And when it 're over he throws a guinea at me and says: "Keep your mouth shut and there'll be no harm done." '

Emma shut her eyes but the tears were pouring down her cheeks.

'But th' harm were done, Miss. I prayed and prayed that nothing'd come of it, but God don't listen to them sort of prayers. And now I be two months gone!'

'You are having a baby?' Orelia exclaimed, hardly breathing the words.

Emma nodded her head.

'Yes, Miss. And what's to become of me? I daren't go home. My father'd kill me. He's been respectable all his life—Head Game-keeper, he be, to His Lordship, and a proud man!'

The words died away miserably and Orelia, her face very pale, hardly able to utter the words, asked:

'Who did . . . this to . . . you? Who was . . . it, Emma?'

There was a pause.

' 'Twere Sir Mortimer Wrotham, Miss.'

For a moment Orelia felt almost faint with relief, and then she hated herself for even the momentary suspicion that it could have been someone else.

How could she imagine that the person she had suspected, with his pride, his presence, whatever his reputation, would stoop to anything so bestial?

'Who is Sir Mortimer Wrotham?' she asked.

'Th' Gentleman be a friend of His Lordship's. There were a big party at th' house and he stays th' night because, as Mr. Willand, the Butler, says, it be too much trouble to get th' Gentry home after a party of that sort!'

'And this happened during the party?' Orelia asked.

'No, no, Miss! 'Twere before! He comes up to change for dinner. I'd gone along to his room to see if th' fire were burning properly. 'Twere early and his valet was not there.

'I were bending down over the fire when he comes in. When I gets to my feet and curtsies, he shuts th' door behind him and locked it! I knew then what he were about, Miss. I were real frightened!'

Emma sobbed pathetically.

'What can you do?' Orelia asked. 'Could you tell Sir Mortimer? Would he help you in any way?'

Emma shook her head.

'Oh no, Miss! He'd just deny it! Nobody'd take my word against a Gentleman's.'

'That is true,' Orelia murmured. 'But if you cannot go home, where can you go?'

'Jim'd a help me if he had th' money,' Emma replied. 'We was a walking out together. I've known Jim all me life and 'twere always understood that we'd get married some time. He'd marry me now and treat th' child as his, but not if I had to go home.'

Emma gave a sob.

'There'd be too many people that'd know, and his father be as proud as mine! Head Groom, he be, to His Lordship in th' country!'

'Jim would marry you,' Orelia said slowly, 'and how much money would you need to go away somewhere where you would not be known?'

'Jim had thought that one day he might open a Livery Stable somewhere in th' North of England,' Emma replied. 'We were a going to save for it. He be good with horses, Jim be, and he like the North. He has a brother who has done well for himself—near

York I think he lives. But we haven't th' money! We've nawt but a few pounds between us!'

'But what would a Livery Stable cost?' Orelia enquired. 'Suppose Jim could set one up or buy one?'

'Oh, an awful lot, Miss. We were a talking about it once and Jim's brother, that's the one who's done well, said he started with seven hundred pounds! Seven hundred pounds! That be a fortune!'

Emma gave a deep sigh, then wiped her eyes again.

'I thinks, Miss, the best thing for th' likes of I w'd be th' river!'

'Emma! You must not say anything so wicked, so wrong!' Orelia cried.

'I knows, Miss, t'would be bad,' Emma answered, 'but what else can I do? I'll get no employment, for nobody'll take me into a decent house. Besides, it'll be showing soon and then everyone'll know of me shame!'

'It is not your shame,' Orelia said furiously. 'That man—he should be made to pay for what he has done!'

Even as she spoke her eyes widened. An idea had come to her!

'Listen, Emma . . .' she began.

Then she looked round, and realised they were approaching Park Lane. Orelia leant forward and put her hand on Emma's.

'Listen, Emma,' she repeated. 'I am going to try and help you. Do nothing. Do not worry too much until I speak to you again. Promise me?'

'How can you help me, Miss?' Emma asked, but there was a glimmer of hope in her eyes.

'I will try, I promise you I will try,' Orelia replied.

'You won't tell His Lordship?' Emma asked hesitantly.

'Perhaps that would be the best thing to do,' Orelia said slowly.

'No! No, Miss,' Emma cried. 'Even if he wished to be kind His Lordship could do nothing! Th' others would have to know—Mrs. Mayhew, Mr. Willand, and all th' other servants! They'd have me out within a few hours.'

She sobbed again.

'There's been cases like mine afore and they've shown no mercy for th' woman! 'Tis always th' man who gets away with it!'

'I am sure that is true,' Orelia agreed. 'I will say nothing, Emma, to His Lordship, but I will still try and help you.'

'Oh, thank you, Miss, thank you more than I can say! And Jim'll thank you too. He be a good man and he wouldn't hold it against th' child that'll be born through no fault of its own!'

The carriage drew up with a sweep at the front door of Ryde House. Orelia stepped out and moved through the line of flunkeys into the marble Hall. Emma scuttled away to the back entrance.

'Has Lady Caroline returned?' Orelia asked the Butler.

'Her Ladyship is upstairs.'

'And His Lordship?'

'His Lordship is in the Library.'

'Alone?' Orelia asked.

'Alone, Miss.'

Resolutely Orelia crossed the Hall. A footman opened the Library door and she went in.

The Marquis was seated at his desk writing. He looked up in surprise when he saw her and then setting down the big white quill pen he had been using, rose to his feet.

'Where have you been, Orelia?' he asked. 'Shopping?'

She crossed the room towards him and holding out the small package which contained the snuff-box she said:

'Many happy returns of the day, My Lord. I have bought you a present.'

The Marquis looked astonished. Then he took the small parcel and undid it. The paper fell aside and he looked down at the snuff-box, staring at it as he placed it on the palm of his hand.

Then Orelia remembered she had told him she was penniless.

'I bought it with my own money,' she said hastily.

'Your own money?' he questioned.

'I sold . . . something,' she answered, which, she thought, was in fact the truth.

'A present for me!' he said quietly. 'Why?'

'Because you gave me all these wonderful clothes,' Orelia answered, 'and because I thought you ought to have a present on your birthday. It is a day when we all . . . want to be . . . remembered.'

'It is a very beautiful box,' he said. 'Was it for any particular reason that you chose it as a gift for me?'

She thought it was perhaps typical that he should be perceptive enough to understand that the snuff-box might have a special significance.

'I thought . . .' she said hesitatingly, the color rising in her cheeks, 'that the man sitting . . . alone with the world at his feet was somehow . . . like you.'

'Like me?'

'In the way you sometimes seem to be aloof . . . watching what is happening around you but not taking part in it . . . almost as if you . . . deliberately stood aside from . . . life.'

He looked at her in surprise.

'How do you know this?'

'I do not know,' Orelia answered. 'I just felt it was true.'

'It is true,' he replied, 'but I did not think that anyone knew it!'

He looked into her eyes for a moment and then down at the box in his hands.

'I do not have to tell you, Orelia,' he said in his deep voice, 'that I shall treasure this. It is not only the first birthday present I have received for many years, but it is something which means more to me than I can possibly put into words.'

'I am . . . glad,' she said a little breathlessly, wondering why she was finding it difficult to speak.

Taking her hand in his the Marquis raised it to his lips.

She felt the pressure of his mouth on her bare skin and then with a sudden shyness which left her completely speechless, she turned and ran from the room, leaving him staring after her, the snuff-box held tightly in his fingers.

There was a large number of guests for luncheon and the Marquis was at the other end of the table from Orelia.

When the meal was over, the Duchess took Caroline and Orelia out in her carriage to call on various acquaintances. They left cards, they visited several hostesses who were entertaining that afternoon, and returned to Ryde House about five o'clock.

'I intend to rest,' the Duchess announced, 'and I advise you girls to do the same. It will be a very grand occasion tonight at Carlton House and I wish you both to look your best.'

'I shall certainly rest,' Caroline answered, 'and you must do the same, Orelia. This is the night when we will see all the *Beau Ton* squeezed together in one place and it is very difficult to make oneself shine amongst such a host of social meteors!'

'You will shine,' Orelia smiled, 'and I will watch you.'

'We will shine together,' Caroline replied firmly. 'You must wear the silver gown, dearest, which becomes you greatly. And I will wear my red gauze with the pigeon-blood rubies from the Ryde collection.'

'You will look wonderful,' Orelia cried in all sincerity.

'I hope so,' Caroline said with a sigh.

They had reached her bedroom by this time, and as Caroline pulled the bell for her maid Orelia said:

'Tell me, Caroline, what do you know of Sir Mortimer Wrotham?'

'Has he attracted your fancy?' Caroline asked.

'No, indeed,' Orelia answered. 'I have not met him, but I heard someone talk of him.'

'Oh! He is very smooth, very plausible, and personally I think he is so conceited that when he pays me

a compliment I always feel he really expects one himself!'

'Is he married?' Orelia asked.

'Indeed, he is,' Caroline replied, 'and it is said that
he is frightened of his wife who is very strait-laced,
and blue-blooded! She lives in the country and Sir
Mortimer enjoys—and this is the right word—a bache-
lor existence in London.'

'Is he a very close friend of His Lordship?' Orelia
enquired.

'He certainly comes to the parties Darius gives,' Caroline answered, 'so you will meet him sooner or later
as you are so curious. But we will not see him tonight at Carlton House.

'Sir Mortimer fancies himself as a courtier and has
attached himself not to the Regent, but the Queen at
Buckingham Palace. He is a Gold-stick-in-waiting or
something, and makes the very most of it, I can assure
you!'

'I have the feeling you do not like him,' Orelia said.

'Oh, he is not one of my flirts!' Caroline replied,
'and I advise you, Orelia, not to let him become one
of yours!'

'That he will never be!' Orelia said in a hard voice.

She left Caroline undressing and told her that she too
intended to rest.

But when she went to her own room she put on her
bonnet and driving-coat again and took from one of
the drawers in her bedroom a large white swansdown
muff which the Duchess had chosen. It was the very
latest fashion, but Orelia had not yet carried it.

Then she went downstairs, hoping that she would
not encounter the Marquis.

She knew that at this time of the evening he usually
went either to his Club or to the Boxing Parlour in
Bond Street, where Caroline had told her he was most
proficient as an amateur pugilist.

'I have warned Darius that if he is not careful he
will get his aristocratic nose broken!' Caroline had said,
'but His Lordship just laughs and says he enjoys the
exercise.'

There seemed to be nobody about except two footmen on duty in the Hall. Having asked one of them to order a carriage for her, Orelia went into the Morning Room. She had seen on a side-table a box which she had guessed contained a pair of duelling pistols.

They were something which were to be found in most gentlemen's houses, and when they were particularly ornate, as were those belonging to the Marquis, they were usually placed on display.

Inlaid with ivory and skilfully chased, the pistols were both valuable and beautiful. They were, also, Orelia ascertained, well balanced and ready for use.

She found the bullets underneath the velvet on which they rested and having primed a pistol as her Uncle had taught her to do, she slipped it into her muff.

She had hardly done so before the door opened and the footman announced:

'The carriage is at the door, Miss.'

She moved across the room a little self-consciously but felt certain the man was not suspicious of what she carried.

Willand, the Butler, was waiting in the Hall, and seeing Orelia alone said with a note of surprise in his voice:

'Would you wish a Maidservant to accompany you, Miss?'

'I am only going a few streets away,' Orelia said. 'And I have a note to leave at Sir Mortimer Wrotham's residence. Will you give the Coachman the address.'

Again there was a flicker of surprise on Willand's usually impassive face but she heard him tell the Coachman to drive to twenty-five, Half Moon Street.

Orelia stepped into the closed carriage and it did not take long to reach Half Moon Street. She descended onto the pavement while the footman was still ringing the bell.

'Is Sir Mortimer at home?' she asked the manservant.

'Yes, Ma'am, but I do not think he is expecting visitors,' the man replied.

'He will see me,' she answered.

Sir Mortimer's rooms were on the first floor. Orelia climbed the staircase, her heart thumping a little as she realised how daring and unconventional it was of her to visit a man's lodgings.

'What name, Miss?' the manservant asked.

There was an insolent note in his voice, and Orelia knew that he had no respect for the type of Lady who would visit his master unexpected and unattended.

'Miss Orelia Stanyon,' she replied.

The man threw open the door of the Sitting-Room.

'Miss Stanyon, Sir Mortimer,' he announced.

Sir Mortimer was lying back at his ease in an armchair, a glass of brandy in his hand. He was a goodlooking man getting on towards middle age with a figure which was just beginning to thicken through too soft living.

His astonishment at seeing Orelia was almost ludicrous, but after a moment's pause he put down his glass and rose to his feet.

'Forgive my surprise, Ma'am,' he said, 'but I do not think I have had the pleasure of your acquaintance.'

'I am Orelia Stanyon,' Orelia replied, 'and my cousin, Caroline, is to marry the Marquis of Ryde. You are, I think, a friend of His Lordship.'

'I am indeed,' Sir Mortimer answered, 'and on my honour, Miss Stanyon, I was not expecting to receive anyone so beautiful and so attractive as yourself at this hour!'

'I hoped to find you alone, Sir Mortimer,' Orelia answered, 'because I have something of import to say to you.'

'You intrigue me,' Sir Mortimer smiled. 'Will you not sit down and tell me what is your business. And may I say what a pleasure it is to see you in my lodgings, even though I fear that if it were known that you had come here alone it might set the tongues of the gossips wagging!'

'I am not concerned about what is said about me,' Orelia replied. 'I have come, Sir Mortimer, on behalf of a girl called Emma Higson!'

'Emma Higson?'

There was no doubt that Sir Mortimer was ignorant of the name.

'Emma Higson?' he repeated. 'Forgive me, Miss Stanyon, but I have no knowledge of such a female!'

'Apparently you omitted to ask her name,' Orelia said, her voice icy with contempt. 'But, having taken your pleasure of her, you gave her a guinea—hardly I should think very adequate compensation for someone dwelling at Ryde House!'

She knew by the sudden narrowing of his eyes and the way the colour rose in his cheeks that Sir Mortimer realised of whom she was speaking.

'I have not the slightest idea, Miss Stanyon,' he said in a lofty tone, 'to what you refer. In fact I think it would be best for you to leave my rooms and return to Ryde House, if that is where you are staying.

'There is no reason for us to discuss such matters, which indeed is not a fit subject for a Lady such as yourself!'

'You would prefer that I discuss it with someone else?'

'I do not know what you are talking about,' Sir Mortimer said angrily, 'or indeed, what you want of me. Emma Higson indeed! I have never heard of the woman!'

'I will tell you what I want of you, Sir Mortimer. Emma Higson is having your child. To get her away from London, to marry her to a decent young man who will treat the child as his own, I require the sum of one thousand pounds.'

'One thousand pounds!' Sir Mortimer ejaculated. 'Are you demented? Do you really think I would hand over such a sum to you because of those assertions, which I assure you are completely untrue?'

'They are the truth and you know it! You ravished this girl in a bedroom at Ryde House. Somewhat, I should have thought, abusing the hospitality of your host.'

'If the girl says that I behaved in such a manner she lies!' Sir Mortimer retorted. 'How can you believe such

an accusation from some gutter-snipe who will say anything to excuse her own immorality?'

'I cannot believe that your friend, the Marquis of
Ryde, would employ a gutter-snipe as a housemaid,'
Orelia said slowly. 'In fact, the girl is the daughter of
His Lordship's Head keeper. She is a decent girl, or
was, until you misused her, and the only way to save
a scandal, Sir, is for you to give me the money I ask
of you!'

'Save a scandal!' Sir Mortimer exclaimed furiously,
walking backwards and forwards across the room in his
agitation. 'What scandal can such a girl as that cause?
Do you imagine that her word would be believed
against mine?'

'That remains to be seen,' Orelia replied, 'because if
you do not give me the money, Sir Mortimer, I shall
take her to your wife, and if your wife will not listen,
I will take the girl to the Queen! I believe Her Majesty
is a very understanding woman and would at least give
me a hearing!'

'You would do what?' Sir Mortimer shouted in a
fury. 'How dare you threaten me?'

'I am not threatening you. I am merely informing
you what I shall do unless you give me a thousand
pounds to help Emma Higson and the man she will
marry to start a new life!'

'It is preposterous!' Sir Mortimer raged.

Then suddenly he stopped still and looked at Orelia.

'How do I know that you are who you say you are?'
he asked. 'You come along here demanding a thousand
pounds! Perhaps you are as generous in your favours as
little Emma Higson whom you are so busy championing!'

He paused.

'Suppose we come to an arrangement, my dear. I
could very much begrudge giving a thousand pounds
to Emma Higson, but you are a very different proposi-
tion. It might be worth a thousand pounds to make
love to you!'

He moved towards Orelia as he spoke, a smile on his

lips, and a look in his eyes which she had seen before in Lord Rotherton's. Slowly Orelia drew the pistol from her muff.

She did not say anything, she just looked steadily at Sir Mortimer. He stopped dead in his tracks and began to bluster.

'You are mad! That is what you are—mad! I shall ring for my servant and have you thrown out, for that is what you deserve!'

'Throw me out and I go straight to your wife,' Orelia warned him.

For a moment he defied her and then he capitulated.

'Very well, you shall have the money. I know only too well the trouble a little vixen like you can cause. My wife would not believe you, but at the same time I am all for a quiet life. How do you want such a vast sum?'

'As much in cash as possible,' Orelia replied.

Sir Mortimer pulled open the drawer of his desk.

'There is two hundred pounds here,' he said, 'which I won last night at cards. I will write you a cheque for five hundred.'

'Eight hundred, if you please, and make it out not to me, as I am well aware it might be traced, but to Emma Higson. I will get it cashed for her and I promise she will not trouble you again.'

Sir Mortimer wrote the cheque, muttering oaths under his breath. Then he placed it on top of the notes and held it out to Orelia.

She took it from him and placed it in her muff which lay in her lap, her other hand still holding the pistol.

'Just in case you were thinking of stopping the cheque, Sir Mortimer,' she said, 'remember that my threat to tell your wife remains valid until the money is actually in Emma's hands.'

'You have what you want! Now get out, damn you!' Sir Mortimer replied.

'You cannot think that I wish to stay,' Orelia said. 'I assure you, Sir Mortimer, that you make me feel physically sick. The fact that you have given me one

thousand pounds may have assuaged your conscience,
but I hope sometimes you will think of the child you
have fathered.'

She drew in her breath.

'A child who, except for my intervention, would
have been nameless and brought up in a foundling
hospital, or might, with its mother, have ended up in
the river. I hate and despise you for the loathsome
animal that you are!'

Orelia turned as she spoke and walked from the
room. She shut the door sharply behind her and walked
slowly downstairs.

The manservant opened the door to the street, she
crossed the pavement, stepped into the landau, and told
the footman that she wished to return to Ryde House.

She did not realise that a Phaeton coming down the
street had stopped behind the landau to let another
vehicle pass.

She did not know that it then followed her carriage
all the way back to Park Lane.

Orelia walked into the Hall at Ryde House and
thought that the first thing she must do was to return
the duelling pistol.

She went into the Morning-Room, shut the door, and
crossed the floor towards the polished case where the
pistols were displayed.

Even as she did so she heard the door open behind
her and turned her head. Then her heart gave a frightened leap, for it was the Marquis who had entered the
room.

He stood looking at her for a moment and she realised
she had never seen a man in such a blazing fury.

His lips were set in a hard line, his chin was square,
and his eyes seemed to be flashing fire as he crossed
the room towards her.

'What were you doing in Wrotham's lodgings?' he
asked, and his voice sounded like a whip.

Orelia looked up at him with wide eyes.

'I saw you come from there,' the Marquis said. 'I
thought I must be dreaming! I could not believe it
true! What were you doing? What possible inducement

could he have offered to take you to his rooms in broad daylight when you might be seen? And why did you go to him? Will you tell me that?'

Orelia tried to speak but in the face of the Marquis's fury she felt as if her voice died in her throat.

'Answer me!' he shouted. 'What does Wrotham mean to you—that lecher, that pursuer of virgins—Can he really have captured your heart? I believed you were different—I would have staked my life you were not as other women—and yet I see I was mistaken!'

His voice sharpened. 'What did he offer you! A married man! A man with a reputation where young women are concerned that stinks!'

He glared down at her, and then looking at her white face and trembling lips he suddenly lost control. Putting out his hands he grasped her shoulders and started to shake her.

'Answer me, damn you! Answer me! Tell me the truth! Tell me what happened there in secret with a man who is a notorious rapist! Tell me and let me know how low you have sunk! Tell me!'

He shook Orelia backwards and forwards so violently that her bonnet fell from her head and was held only by the ribbons which were tied round her neck.

And then as she tried to put out her hands in protest against him, the ferocity of his action shook the notes from her muff so that they fluttered onto the floor and were followed by a crash as the duelling pistol followed them.

The noise checked the Marquis and made him look down to see what had fallen. His eyes took in the notes, the cheque, the pistol, and then he looked again at Orelia.

She saw that there was a white line around his mouth and his expression was that of a man stricken by a nameless horror.

'Is that how you got your—money?' he asked, and his voice almost seemed to snarl the words.

6

'How dare you . . . think . . . such things of . . . me!'

Orelia's voice was breathless from the shaking the Marquis had given her, but she was also exceedingly angry. She stared up at him, her eyes dark and stormy and she was trembling with rage.

The Marquis had dropped his hands from her shoulders, but he was still standing close to her, the pistol and the notes lying on the floor between them.

'What do you expect me to think?' he asked roughly.

'I do not expect anything from you . . . My Lord,' Orelia said bitterly.

'Nevertheless,' he retorted, 'you will tell me why you went to Wrotham's lodgings, and you will tell me the truth if I have to beat it out of you!'

He made a movement with his hands and thinking he was about to shake her again she stepped back instinctively.

Then with an anger that was as fierce as his, save that she kept her voice low, she answered:

'Very well . . . I will tell you the . . . truth! I went to visit this . . . friend of yours because he had . . . ravished a young girl . . . here in this house and given . . . her a . . . child!'

For a moment the Marquis did not move or speak, and then furiously, his eyes still fiery with rage, he stormed:

'And what the devil is that to do with you? If what

you say is true, my Housekeeper can deal with such matters!'

'And what do you suppose she would do about it?' Orelia demanded, 'except to turn the girl into the streets or send her back to your Estate in the country where her shame would be known to everyone!'

'What else could be done with her?' the Marquis enquired.

'She herself had a solution,' Orelia answered. 'She was ready to throw herself into the river and destroy the . . . b . . . bastard fathered by your friend!'

'For God's sake! Do not go on saying "your friend",' the Marquis exclaimed in an exasperated tone. 'You speak as if you thought that I had countenanced Wrotham's behaviour.'

'Nevertheless, you accept it!' Orelia said accusingly.

'I am not denying that occasionally men behave in such a manner,' the Marquis replied. 'What I deeply regret is that anything of such an unsavoury nature should have occurred in my own house. But the girl could surely have contrived to look after herself?'

'You really believe that?' Orelia said. 'You really credit that a frightened country-girl, little more than a child, could hold her own against a man of Sir Mortimer's calibre?

'I can assure Your Lordship that the only way she could have retained her purity was to have armed herself as I did before coming into proximity with him!'

'Are you insinuating that he made overtures to you?' the Marquis asked incredulously.

'As it happens, he did!' Orelia answered sharply.

'God damn him!' the Marquis swore. 'I will kill the swine for this!'

'You seem annoyed that he should have approached me,' Orelia said bitterly, 'but it is of little consequence that he should rape a girl who was also under your protection, even if you do not concern yourself with her. I can only think, My Lord, that your moral standards are very much the same as Sir Mortimer's!'

'Damnit! I will not be spoken to in such a manner!'

the Marquis retorted. 'I would have you know, Orelia, that I have never taken a woman who was not willing, and I do not amuse myself with servants—either my own or other people's!'

'Then let us hope,' Orelia said, 'that in future Sir Mortimer will not be invited so freely to stay in any establishment you own, where he will come into contact with decent girls, whatever the class to which they belong!'

'You can be certain of that!' the Marquis asserted. 'But let me say again, Orelia, you should not have concerned yourself personally in this. Ladies should leave such matters to be dealt with by people of experience.'

'And who may they be?' Orelia asked. 'Upper servants, who are exceedingly censorious of their own kind.'

She paused.

'No, what you are inferring, My Lord, is that Ladies of Quality should remain remote from such unsavoury incidents. Is that not what you are trying to say?'

'Exactly!' the Marquis agreed.

'Then let me tell you,' Orelia said angrily, 'that I am not a Lady of Quality and I think it is time that women, into whatever position they may be born, should be aware of the filth, the vice, and the crime that is taking place around them.'

Her eyes flashed as she went on, her voice vibrant with feeling:

'Apparently the Gentlemen of Quality do not concern themselves with such matters unless it proves a passing amusement.'

Her voice was sharp.

'But their wives could at least show some compassion for girls like Emma, and censure an Administration which permits the abomination of Flash Houses to flourish but a short distance from the homes they think so sacrosanct!'

'What can you know of Flash Houses?' the Marquis asked, in what seemed to Orelia almost a contemptuous manner.

'I know there is one not five minutes' drive from here,' she answered, 'and any Lady who is not blind can see as she drives to Carlton House or any other of the grand mansions where the Quality congregate the pathetic little prostitutes, trained in the Flash Houses, soliciting in the shadows of Piccadilly!'

'You should not speak of such things!' the Marquis exclaimed.

'What shall I do—shut my eyes?—when I see those pitiful creatures, sometimes little more than ten years of age hoping that some drunken Buck will acquiesce in their invitations?' Orelia asked scornfully. 'And shall I forget that there are four hundred inhabitants in the Flash House at St. Giles,' she went on, 'the boys taught to be delinquents from their earliest years, sent out to thieve and pick pockets, the girls forced into prostitution—for there is not other employment available for them!'

'How do you know this?' the Marquis asked.

'Do you suppose living in London I only see the glitter of jewels, or the clink of champagne glasses?' Orelia inquired sarcastically. 'And do you also believe that anyone who reads a newspaper or follows the debates in Parliament, is unaware of the horrors that are taking place in others parts of the country?'

Her voice was low as she said:

'How can I help thinking of women naked to the waist and dragging coal-trucks through the dark putrid air of the mines; or of children, sometimes not more than five years old, working fourteen hours in the mills and being thrashed to keep them awake!'

Her voice had a note of horror in it as she added:

'And if that does not prevent me sleeping at nights I can always listen for the cries of the climbing boys as the Sweep lights fires under their bare feet to force them up your Lordship's . . . chimneys!'

Her voice broke on the words, and turning away from the Marquis so that he should not see the tears in her eyes, she walked across the room to stare blindly out of the window.

Her anger made her small breasts rise tumultuously

beneath the soft silk of her driving-coat, and for the first time she realised that her bonnet was hanging down her back, still held to her neck by the ribbons that had been tied under her chin.

Hardly aware what she did she threw her muff down on a table and untied the ribbon at her throat, letting the bonnet fall to the ground.

The evening sun came through the window and turned her hair to shining gold.

But Orelia saw none of the glory of it, she only felt as if she stood alone in a darkness which was impenetrable, in which every light had been extinguished.

Then in a very different tone and in a voice quiet, and for the Marquis, almost humble, he said:

'Forgive me, Orelia.'

'No . . . No,' she answered, but despite her resolution to be firm, her voice trembled. 'No, I will never . . . forgive you for what y . . . you . . . thought of . . . me!'

She turned back and crossing the room, her eyes downcast, she picked up the scattered notes.

Her hands were shaking as she stacked them together, aware as she did so that the Marquis, standing still in the same spot, watched her.

She placed the notes in her muff but left the pistol lying on the floor. Still with a composure that was but superficial, her face very pale, her eyelashes wet against her cheeks, Orelia picked up her bonnet and turned towards the door.

Only as she reached it did the Marquis speak again.

'Orelia,' he said, and this time there was no doubt of the appeal in his voice. 'Let me help you in this matter.'

'I have no need of your help, My Lord,' Orelia replied coldly. 'I do not trust you.'

'If you mean to hurt me by that remark,' the Marquis said bitterly, 'you have succeeded.'

Just for a moment Orelia hesitated, then she said:

'There is . . . nothing more to be . . . said, My Lord.'

The Marquis did not reply and she went from the room, closing the door quietly behind her.

When she reached her bedroom she rang for Emma. The girl was at first incredulous when Orelia told her that she had the money for her to go North with the man she loved and start a Livery Stable as they had planned. Then she burst into tears.

'Oh, Miss, I didn't believe there was so much goodness left in th' world,' she said. 'How can I ever thank you, Miss?'

'By getting in touch with Jim as soon as possible,' Orelia answered. 'I suggest that you tell Mrs. Mayhew and the other servants that Jim has had the offer of a Livery Stable in the North, and if he is to buy it he must leave at once.'

Orelia thought for a moment, then continued:

'You can say that he is taking you to his brother's and that you will be married from there. They may think that the plan is somewhat hasty, but there is no reason for them to be suspicious that there is any other motive.'

She showed Emma the notes, drawing them from her muff.

'There are two hundred pounds here. I will arrange for the Bank to transfer the rest of the money to Jim as soon as he is able to open an account in his own name.'

'Oh, Miss! Miss! 'Tis more . . . wonderful than I'd ever . . . dares to hope,' Emma sobbed.

'Then stop crying or people will think you are going to a funeral rather than a wedding,' Orelia admonished her. 'I will hide the notes in the drawer of this chest, Emma. It is best for you not to have them in your own bedroom.'

'Yes, indeed, Miss,' Emma replied, 'for th' other housemaids might see them.'

'And as soon as I have gone out to dinner, try and talk to Jim,' Orelia said. 'But now, if you do not help me, Emma, I shall be late, and as we are dining at Carlton House, Her Grace will be extremely incensed with me!'

As Orelia hurried over her bath and into her clothes, she wished that she need not go to the dinner-party. She longed to send the Duchess a message to say she was indisposed, but she knew this would cause a comment.

She had been well enough when the Dowager and Caroline had left her to rest; they would think it extremely strange that any indisposition should have come upon her so swiftly and for no apparent reason!

There was also the chance that if they were to probe too deeply, they would discover that she had been out of the house.

Then however skilfully she tried to hide what had occurred, they might by some quirk of fate, discover poor Emma's guilty secret, and then all that she had done on the girl's behalf would be rendered useless.

'No,' Orelia thought firmly, 'I must disguise my feelings and go to Carlton House. I only hope that I do not have to speak to the Marquis, because . . . I hate . . . him!'

But a reaction from the violence of her anger had set in and the words sounded flat and lacking in the fire she had shown during her quarrel with the Marquis.

Orelia took one last glance at herself in the mirror before she left the bedroom.

The silver gown that Caroline had suggested she should wear was very lovely. It made her look as if she were part of the moonlight shimmering on the waters of a smooth lake.

But her cheeks were very pale, and her eyes seemed enormous and filled with a deep unhappiness that she could not explain to herself.

Nevertheless, when Orelia met Caroline at the top of the stairs, her cousin had no idea of any disturbance to her emotions.

'You look lovely, dearest!' Caroline exclaimed.

'And you are a vision of beauty,' Orelia managed to reply.

It was in fact true. Caroline's dark hair, white skin and red seductive mouth were set off to the best advantage by the pigeon-blood gauze of her Paris gown. Caught in tightly at the waist as was Orelia's, and ornamented around the neck and the puff sleeves with ruchings of tulle scattered with imitation rubies.

But the jewels round her neck were real enough and so magnificent that if Caroline had not been a widow they would have been considered far too ornate for anyone so young.

Her thin wrists were weighed down with heavy bracelets, also set in rubies and diamonds, and on her engagement finger, instead of the diamond that the Marquis had given her on their betrothal, she wore an enormous ruby which seemed to reflect mysterious, fiery lights in its crimson depths.

Caroline swept down the Grand Staircase to where the Marquis was waiting for them in the Hall.

The Duchess was beside him, festooned in diamonds with a huge tiara of diamonds and sapphires on her head.

Only Orelia wore no jewellery. She came down the stairs looking very young and very ethereal, and her eyes avoided the Marquis's as he said:

'I think, Grandmama, if we do not wish to spoil the elegant gowns you Ladies are all wearing tonight, it would be best to travel to Carlton House in two carriages. I will take Caroline with me and you bring Orelia.'

'A sensible idea, Darius,' the Duchess agreed. 'You go ahead, Orelia and I will be just behind you.'

'We will wait for you inside the Hall if you are at all delayed,' the Marquis promised.

As he turned towards the door, following Caroline to the carriage waiting outside, Orelia stole a glance at him. Angry and disgusted as she might be, she could not help realising that she had never seen him look so impressive.

His coat, which fitted his broad shoulders superbly, was covered in decorations. There was the blue ribbon of the Order of the Garter over his shoulder, and the Insignia glittered against his white satin knee-breeches.

'I hate him!' she thought beneath her breath.

Yet there was a strange pain in her heart at the
thought that he could even for a moment have believed
her capable of such behaviour.

But because she felt humiliated at the thought, she
carried her chin high as she stepped into the carriage
after the Duchess.

They drove for a little while in silence—then the
Dowager, her voice distinctly spiteful, said:

'I hope as you are so particular, Orelia, that you will
find some of the Beaux at Carlton House congenial to
you.'

Orelia had no answer ready, and the Duchess continued:

'I am afraid that with such high-flown romantic ideas
no ordinary English Gentleman will take your fancy
—but then some females were born to be old maids.'

Orelia felt too wretched to try to defend herself.
Perhaps, she thought, the Dowager was right and she
was romantic to the point of absurdity.

'What sort of man do I want?' she asked herself but
could find no answer.

The Dowager went on talking, maliciously trying to
humiliate her, but she only succeeded in calling up
Orelia's pride to her rescue.

She managed to walk a little taller than she really
was as they entered the brightly lighted portals of
Carlton House.

Orelia had heard so much about Carlton House that
at any other time she would have been thrilled to see
what it was like, and would have enjoyed inspecting
the rooms with their ornate gilded splendour and priceless ornamentation.

But now, because she was so depressed and upset
within herself, the Yellow Chinese Room left her cold;
the Dining-Room walled in silver supported by
columns of red and yellow granite seemed almost dull.

The pictures, the statues, the porcelain, the innumerable *objets de virtu* collected by the Regent, and which
had caused him to plunge, ever since he was young,
deeper and deeper into debt, were mere inanimate fur-
nishings which did not excite her.

She knew she was being childish, but she had an insane desire to run away somewhere, to cry her eyes out.

It was indeed with an effort that she forced herself to talk with the Gentlemen on either side of her at dinner, and though she had no idea of what she said, she apparently charmed them by her sympathetic listening, for both at the end of the meal asked when they could see her again.

The Regent himself was a disappointment.

She had heard so often how handsome and attractive he was, but by now the dashing first Gentleman of Europe had become Falstaffian both in girth and in tonnage. He had left off his stays and his stomach was enormous.

At the same time His Royal Highness was obviously in an extremely genial mood. He went out of his way to compliment Caroline in quite an exaggerated way on her beauty, and to tell the Marquis, of whom he was particularly fond, that he intended to be the Best Man at their wedding.

All this took some time and when Orelia was presented to him the party was moving into the Dining-Room.

The Regent squeezed Orelia's fingers as she curtsied to him and his eyes flickered over her in an appreciative fashion.

'Charming! Charming!' he murmured.

Then Lady Hertford, simpering and playing flirtatiously with her fan, was drawing him towards the Dining-Room, whispering confidentially into his ear as she did so.

It was not a large party compared with many the Regent was accustomed to give, but over two hundred people were invited to join the dinner party of seventy later and to wander in the garden or dance in the Ballroom to a large orchestra.

Orelia found it was easy to slip away and she wandered through several of the Salons by herself, trying to take an interest in what she saw, but feeling that the heat was almost over-powering and that she felt un-accountably weary.

Nobody seemed to notice or be surprised that she was alone. People were standing in groups gossiping, the women glittering like the chandeliers with their sparkling jewels, and the Gentlemen's decorations attempting to outshine them.

The laughter, Orelia knew, was often spiteful. She had learnt from the Duchess that almost all the gossip in London emanated from Carlton House.

She would hear voices whispering and then a roar of laughter; she heard resplendent Admirals and Generals droning away about some real or imaginary grievance which they hoped eventually would reach the ears of the Regent. But noisiest of all were the sharp tongues of the Ladies.

Orelia heard Caroline's name mentioned once or twice and knew that people were discussing her engagement to the Marquis.

Not wishing to listen, she merely moved away and then, passing from one Salon to another, she came face to face with Lord Rotherton.

He was alone and for a moment they stood looking at each other.

Then, as Orelia would have turned away, he put out his hand and laid it on her arm.

'I wish to talk with you.'

'There is n . . . nothing to be . . . said, My Lord,' Orelia replied breathlessly.

'I think there is,' he answered.

There was something in his voice which made her eyes widen.

'You have been very clever,' he went on, speaking in a low tone so that they could not be overheard, 'but I have no intention of being cast aside in such a manner!'

'I do not . . . know what . . . you mean . . . My Lord,' Orelia stammered.

'You know full well,' he answered, 'but I promise you, my Lovely One, that I do not give up so easily! I always get what I want in life and I shall get you!'

Orelia drew in her breath, but her pride would not let her run away.

'You are . . . mistaken, My Lord,' she said, keeping her voice steady by sheer will-power. 'I tried to tell you when you first honoured me with your attentions that I could never become your . . . wife, but somehow it was impossible for me to be alone with you; so that is why I asked the . . . Marquis to speak on my . . . behalf.'

'He has spoken,' Lord Rotherton said grimly.

'Then please believe me, My Lord, that there is nothing more we can say to each other. I shall not change . . . my mind.'

'Do not be too sure about that,' Lord Rotherton replied; 'as I have already said, I never give up.'

Orelia dropped her eyes and would have moved away, but he still held her by the arm.

'I want you,' he said. 'I want you as I have never wanted a woman before! You will marry me or, if you prefer, you can become my mistress; but you will be mine! Sooner or later I shall hold you in my arms and then there will be no escape!'

There was so much passion in his voice that Orelia, frightened, stepped back from him, and then with a little twist of her arm, freed herself.

She had thought Sir Mortimer was bestial enough but she knew that Lord Rotherton was worse.

There was something about him that was almost fanatical; there was something lustful and obscenely horrible in the note in his voice, the expression in his eyes, and the movement of his lips.

She had felt ever since she had first met him that he reached out towards her and that she could not escape! It was like being pursued in a nightmare and being unable to run away!

He was overpowering, possessive, and compelling; so that she felt as if he sapped her will and that sooner or later if he did take her in his arms, she would be unable to struggle!

'No . . . My Lord! N . . . No!' she managed to gasp.

And then she saw his hand come out towards her to

touch her once again! But then she was suddenly aware
that the Duchess was approaching them.

'Good-evening, My Lord,' Her Grace said and Lord
Rotherton glanced round.

It seemed to Orelia in that moment that he set her
free and that she could escape him.

Without a word of explanation she turned and ran
swiftly away across the room, twisting in and out of
the other guests until she reached the far end of the
Salon.

Only then did she stop and look back to see that the
Duchess and Lord Rotherton were not watching her as
she had feared, but were seated close together on two
brocade chairs talking very intently.

Orelia watched them for a moment. She did not
know why, but she felt that what they said must be of
significance.

Then drawing in her breath she ran from the Salon
and down another Staircase which led her to the ground
floor.

She did not know where she was going, she only
wished to get away. She felt as if something evil was
entwining itself about her, encroaching upon her again
when she had thought herself free.

She had not thought of Lord Rotherton the last few
days, she had almost forgotten that he could still prove
a menace!

The Marquis had said that His Lordship would
trouble her no more, and she had believed him!

But she knew now the rebuff he had received had
merely enflamed his desire. This was not some transitory interest of a Gentleman of Fashion for an unfledged girl.

It was the passionate desire of an experienced so-
phisticate, and she knew instinctively that her desire to
escape from him and the Marquis's admonition that
he should leave her alone had fanned the flames which
burned in Lord Rotherton's breast into a conflagration
which would not easily be extinguished.

'What am I to do! What am I to do?' Orelia asked.

Then, finding herself in yet another crowded Reception Room, she saw an open window leading into the garden. She went towards it gratefully.

Perhaps, she thought, she could sit quietly out of sight until it was time to go home.

She was well aware that to ask to leave Carlton House at such an early hour would only arouse surprise and the accusation that she was ungrateful.

To most young girls it was the summit of their ambition to be entertained by the Regent. She had been, Orelia knew, the youngest guest at dinner.

How could she possibly let anyone think that she was not appreciative of such an honour?

But Carlton House had suddenly become a place of danger. Lord Rotherton was there and Orelia knew that, although for the moment he might be held in conversation by the Duchess, there was every likelihood that in a few minutes he would come in search of her once again!

She stepped out into the cool air and felt a sudden relief from the stifling atmosphere of the house.

It was a warm night, with a breath of wind and the enormous chandeliers with their thousands of candles generated heat.

The garden was lit by fairy lights and Chinese lanterns. Couples were moving amongst the scented shrubs seeking little hidden arbours or the shadows under the boughs of the great trees.

Then Orelia looked about her and saw a figure standing at the end of the terrace. There was no mistaking the height, the broad shoulders, the elegance of the Marquis.

He stood alone, staring up at the stars as if he asked a question of them!

Without thinking, without even remembering that she was incensed with him, aware only that he meant security and a momentary relief of her fear, Orelia walked towards him.

Her satin slippers made no sound on the paved terrace and when she reached him she thought that he had not heard her approach.

He did not look in her direction but merely stood

motionless, his face still raised towards the heavens.
Then he asked very quietly:

'Who has frightened you?'

She did not wonder how he knew, or how without
even looking at her he was aware that her eyes were
dark with fear and her breath came quickly between
her parted lips.

She only knew that suddenly she was no longer
afraid. He was there and that was enough!

The terror that Lord Rotherton had evoked in her
faded, the menace he had constituted in touching and
threatening her seemed suddenly to sink into insignifi-
cance.

'I am . . . all right . . . now,' Orelia replied.

Then without realising she did so, she moved still
closer to the Marquis.

There was a balustrade in front of them. Orelia put
out her hands to hold on it as if for support; and now
for the first time he turned his head to look down at
her.

'It is not like you to be afraid.'

'I cannot . . . help it,' she answered in a breathless
little voice.

'You are brave enough where I am concerned,' the
Marquis said, and now she heard the mocking note in
his voice.

There was a pause before he asked very gently:

'Am I forgiven, or shall I go down on my knees?
I want your forgiveness, Orelia. I want it desperately!'

There was something in his voice which made her
feel as if her heart had moved into her throat and
she could not reply. She wanted to look at him but
somehow it was impossible.

'Shall I tell you what I was thinking when you
joined me?' he enquired after a moment.

'What were you . . . thinking?' she asked.

'I was wondering,' he answered, 'what jewels would
become you. Then I knew the answer. There is no
jewel in the world perfect enough to encircle your neck;
so I was thinking that I should take a moonbeam and

twist it into a strand with which I could halo your hair!'

Orelia looked up at him in astonishment. She had never heard him speak in such a manner or indeed with so much gentleness and charm in his voice.

Then as their eyes met he said:

'You look like moonlight tonight, Orelia, and who can describe in mere words anything so lovely?'

As he spoke Orelia felt a strange pain shoot through her like forked lightning. It was a sensation such that she had never known before! Then she knew the truth —she loved him!

She loved the Marquis and had done so for a long time!

7

For a moment Orelia could only feel a kind of radiance seep over her. It was an ecstasy such as she had never known before in her whole life. This was love!

This was what she had been searching for, this was what she had always known was waiting for her somewhere in the world!

Then swiftly, like a blow, she remembered that the Marquis belonged to Caroline, and she felt humiliated and ashamed that she should be so disloyal to her cousin.

And yet it was impossible to deny the wonder in herself, the feeling of security and of joy because he was beside her.

She understood now why she had turned to him in her fear, and why because they had quarrelled earlier in the day the whole world had seemed dark and without hope.

Caroline was her special charge, Caroline had been left to her by her uncle! She was to be her Conscience!

How could she do anything so despicable, so shaming, as to love the man that Caroline was to marry?

And then, almost as if the answer came from outside herself, Orelia knew that love such as she felt for the Marquis could hurt no one unless she allowed it to do so.

It was her secret. It was deep within her heart, and, loving him, she must not in any way spoil that love by making it anything less than the spiritual ecstasy it was at this moment.

Because she loved both Caroline and the Marquis, she must help them.

Her love must make her more understanding of their difficulties. Because she wanted their happiness above all things, she must forget herself in trying to bring them together, in drawing them closer to one another, in giving them for each other some of the golden radiance that she felt at this moment with herself.

Orelia was not aware that she had stayed silent for a considerable time staring out of the garden, deep in her thoughts, until she heard the Marquis say:

'You have not yet answered my question!'

'What question?' she enquired.

It seemed to her that so many questions had succeeded one after another in her mind, that she could not remember if he had spoken them or whether they had come from within herself.

'I asked you if you would forgive me,' he replied, 'but now I know that what I said and certainly what I thought was unforgivable. All I can ask, Orelia, is that you trust me again!'

'It was wrong of me to . . . speak as I . . . did,' she answered in a low voice. 'I do . . . trust you, My Lord, I have always trusted . . . you. It is only that I was . . . desperately hurt . . . that you should think such things of . . . me!'

There was a little pause. Then looking down at her he said:

'I can only pray that you will also find it in your heart to forgive me. But there is one promise I would ask of you, Orelia.'

'What is that?' she enquired.

'That you will never again,' he answered, 'put yourself in such a dangerous position; that you will come to me for advice or help, however difficult it may seem. I swear to you that I will not abuse your trust and will try to help you in the way you wish—not necessarily as I think best.'

Orelia gave him a little smile.

'That is generous of you, My Lord, for I have a feel-

ing that you will disapprove of many of the things that
I wish to do.'

'Give me a chance to prove that your trust in me is
not misguided,' the Marquis pleaded, and there was a
sincerity in his voice that she could not misunderstand.

'I promise,' she said simply.

'And one other thing,' the Marquis went on. 'Always
tell me the truth, Orelia, never lie to me, for that I
could not bear.'

She looked up at him wide-eyed.

'I think I do always speak the truth.'

'I think you do,' he answered, 'and that is one of
the extraordinary things about you. Very few women
are truthful. Will you give me your promise?'

'Yes . . . of course!' Orelia answered quickly.

It seemed to her as if he gave a little sigh of relief.
Then as she waited for him to speak, there was a sudden interruption as Caroline came from the open window behind them onto the terrace.

'Oh, here you are, Darius!' she exclaimed. 'I was
wondering where you could have hidden yourself. His
Excellency and I have been searching the whole of
Carlton House for you!'

Orelia knew even as Caroline spoke that she was lying. She had lived with her cousin for far too long
not to understand every intonation of her voice.

When Caroline was trying to hide something, she
assumed a gay inconsequential manner and a lilting
note to her speech which Orelia recognised instantly as a
signal that she had something to conceal.

No one else, she thought—least of all the Marquis—
would be suspicious, but when she looked first at Caroline and then at the man who accompanied her, she
knew only too well what Caroline had been about!

Her eyes were too bright, there was a flush on her
cheeks, and there was no doubt that her mouth had
been kissed! There was that soft, smudged look about
her lips which Orelia had seen before.

And then as Caroline presented the Gentleman who
accompanied her, she knew she was right, because he

was in fact extremely good-looking and exactly the type of man that Caroline found most attractive.

'Your Excellency,' Caroline was saying, 'may I present my cousin, Miss Orelia Stanyon! Orelia, this is His Excellency, Count Adelco di Savelli, the Italian Ambassador. And of course, Your Excellency, you and my fiancé know each other!'

'Indeed we do,' the Ambassador replied. 'How are you, My Lord?'

'Very well, I thank Your Excellency,' the Marquis replied, 'but I find it extremely hot indoors on a night like this!'

'I have been longing to get outside,' Caroline replied in a slightly affected voice.

Orelia could not help glancing down at the slipper peeping beneath the gauze of Caroline's dress. It was decidedly dusty at the edges as if Caroline had been walking along the garden paths.

'And now, Darius,' her cousin was saying, holding onto the Marquis's arm, 'you and I must either dance together or you must get me a glass of champagne! Shall it be in the Ballroom or the buffet?'

'Decidedly the buffet,' the Marquis replied.

'And His Excellency,' Caroline continued, 'is longing to dance with you, Orelia. You have been neglecting the dance-floor and I cannot believe it is because you have lacked partners!'

'I, too, found it very hot indoors,' Orelia said quickly.

'Then perhaps you are cool enough now, Miss Stanyon,' the Ambassador suggested, 'to venture to dance with me a slow and not too strenuous waltz!'

Orelia was longing to refuse, but before she could speak Caroline interposed:

'That you must do, Orelia, for His Excellency is a magnificent dancer, and how can you show off your new gown standing in the darkness of the terrace?'

She clapped her hands together and added:

'Run along, my children. Darius and I will behave like Dowagers, and having sipped our champagne, will come and watch you from the dais!'

There was nothing Orelia could do but agree and

allow the Ambassador to lead her back into the brilliantly-lit Salon and along the corridor to the Ballroom.

She was well aware that Caroline had some reason for wishing her to dance with His Excellency, although she could not quite understand what it was.

Slim-figured, dark-haired, with eloquent, almost black eyes, and a full mouth that could smile beguilingly, there was no doubt that the Italian Ambassador was an extremely attractive man!

He seemed almost too young for a post of such importance, and Orelia wondered about him as he swung her around the room, dancing with a grace and rhythm which proclaimed all too clearly that Caroline had been right when she said he was a magnificent dancer.

'Miss Stanyon,' he said at length in a low voice, 'I have something to ask you.'

He spoke English extremely well, but there was an unmistakable accent and there was also something very un-English in the manner in which he looked at her.

'What is it?' Orelia asked.

'Caroline and I want your help.'

'Caroline and . . . Your Excellency?'

'We are both depending on you,' he answered, 'that is why Caroline wished you to dance with me.'

'What do you want?' Orelia asked with a sudden sinking of her heart.

She could almost anticipate what he was going to say.

'Caroline has told me that I can trust you,' he replied. 'Would you be surprised to learn that I am very much in love with her?'

Orelia felt herself stiffen.

'Your Excellency must be well aware that my cousin is engaged to the Marquis of Ryde!'

'I know that,' the Ambassador answered, 'but in my country, Miss Stanyon, marriages are arranged by our families. It is a question of finding someone of a suitable position, with the right dowry, the right background, rather than anything which the French call an *affaire de cœur!*'

'In England things are very different.'

'You are not suggesting, Miss Stanyon,' the Ambassador asked, 'that your lovely cousin might be crazily in love with her fiancé?'

'I think, Your Excellency, that is entirely their business!' Orelia said coldly.

The Ambassador gave a little laugh.

'You are enchanting when you are being formal and trying to "set me down"! Is that not the right expression? But I promise you, Miss Stanyon, I have Caroline's permission to speak to you. She told me that you loved her.'

'That at least is true,' Orelia admitted.

'Then let me give her a little happiness,"' the Ambassador pleaded. 'All we need is your help!'

'What can I do?' Orelia asked, 'and besides, let me make it quite clear, Your Excellency, that I do not approve!'

Again he gave a little laugh.

'So young, so very censorious, so very strait-laced!' he remarked.

Then swinging her expertly round the room, he went on: 'I have a feeling that you are not as unsympathetic as you appear! Shall I tell you that the moment I saw Caroline I fell wildly in love with her?'

'But she belongs to someone else, Your Excellency!'

'Not yet,' the Ambassador said.

'You mean that you wish to marry Caroline?' Orelia enquired.

He gave a sigh and shook his head.

'That, alas, is an impossibility! My engagement to a sweet and very wealthy girl—which is essential for me in my position—has been arranged for years.'

'And what do you think she would feel if she knew you were in love with another woman?' Orelia enquired.

'Gianetta is still at a Convent School,' the Ambassador replied. 'In a year, or perhaps two years, she will be presented to Society and then our engagement will be announced.'

'I do not understand or like your foreign customs,' Orelia said, 'and I beg of Your Excellency not to try to entice Caroline into doing something foolish and dangerous which might destroy her whole future!'

'I would not hurt the lovely Caroline—that I assure you,' the Ambassador replied. 'I am well aware that there must be no scandal. It is something which would be not only very disagreeable and, as you say, perhaps dangerous for Caroline, but also for myself! And that, Miss Stanyon, is exactly why we need your help!'

'I am afraid I do not understand,' Orelia cried almost despairingly.

She felt as if he were leading her into some maze of difficulties from which she would find it very hard to escape.

She must talk to Caroline, she thought. She would plead with her, she would make her see how stupid, how irresponsible it would be for her to become involved in a love affair just at this moment.

And, she thought, it was unfair on the Marquis!

Even as she thought of him, she saw again that lonely little boy who had grown up without love, who had had no one to care for him, no one to whom he could turn in his problems and his difficulties.

'You cannot do this,' she said aloud. 'Your Excellency must be aware how easily you and Caroline could become the talk of the gossips! You are both too well-known to do anything which would not be noticed!'

'We have realised that,' the Ambassador answered, 'which is why, Miss Stanyon, you will understand when I ask you, because of your love for Caroline, to let it appear as if I were your suitor rather than hers!'

For one moment Orelia felt as if she could not have heard him aright or understood what he meant.

Then looking up at his face she saw his dark eyes pleading with her and realised she had not been mistaken.

'But of course I would do nothing of the sort!' she answered sharply. 'How could you suggest such a thing? Besides, it would be encouraging Caroline in this madness, which I am convinced will damage you both!'

'Not if we are clever,' the Ambassador replied, 'and

I assure you, Miss Stanyon, that I am very experienced in such matters!'

'That I can well believe,' Orelia said sarcastically. 'And may I say here and now, Your Excellency, that I do not wish to be involved in your plots and that I will do everything in my power to prevent Caroline behaving in such a ridiculous manner when she is officially engaged to someone as important as the Marquis of Ryde!'

'Bravely spoken!' said the Ambassador. 'I admire you, Miss Stanyon, for your principles, but because I know you love Caroline you would hate to see her suffer the sniggering insinuations of the *Beau Ton* or being hurt or defamed by a scandal such as you suggest. That is why I know you will help us both!'

'No, I will not!' Orelia protested.

'I think Caroline will persuade you,' the Ambassador answered.

At that moment the dance came to an end, and standing still in the middle of the dance-floor Orelia said:

'Please, Your Excellency, do not do this! It is wrong, it may have disastrous repercussions. I beg of you to go away and forget Caroline!'

'You are both so beautiful,' the Ambassador replied, 'that it would require a man with a heart of stone to refuse either of you anything. But I cannot renounce my own or Caroline's happiness.

'Therefore, Miss Stanyon, much as I should like to say yes to your plea, simply because you ask it of me, the answer is that I cannot agree to what you suggest. I can only believe that the love of your warm heart will prove stronger than the cool commonsense of your lovely little head.'

He smiled at Orelia beguilingly as he spoke and then raised her gloved hand to his lips.

It was a gesture that no Englishman would have made to an unmarried girl on a dance-floor, and Orelia, well aware that they were being watched, felt herself flush as she tried to take her hand away from his.

'You are enchanting,' His Excellency said in a voice

which could be heard by anyone standing close to them.

Orelia's eyes flashed at him, but she knew there was nothing she could say that would not make matters worse.

Then, as she glanced up, she saw standing in the doorway, as if he had just come into the Ballroom, the Marquis. And he was watching!

The rest of the evening seemed to Orelia to pass very slowly.

She danced with several young men whose names she hardly remembered; the Ambassador sought her out again, but they stood up for a 'country dance' and to Orelia's relief there was no chance of a private conversation.

Then at last she was driving home beside the Duchess, who was making malicious and disparaging remarks about nearly everyone at the party.

Orelia, immersed in her own thoughts, did not even trouble to listen.

She was worried about Caroline, and worried too by the persistent nagging of her conscience first about her love for the Marquis, and secondly about what he would think of the behaviour of the Italian Ambassador.

She reached her own bedroom at Ryde House thankfully, and was just taking off her gown when Caroline burst into the room.

'Dearest!' she exclaimed, 'what do you think of him? Is he not divine?'

'If you are speaking of His Excellency,' Orelia answered, 'I think he is behaving despicably, in a manner which is most unbecoming to a man in his position.'

'Fustian!' Caroline exclaimed. 'I knew you would be shocked, but, Orelia, you must help me! You must! We cannot do without you, and I have to see him! You must understand that! I find him completely irresistible!'

'Caroline, how can you be so foolish?' Orelia asked almost angrily. 'Can you not understand the scandal it

will cause if it becomes known—as of course it will be
—that a man as important as the Italian Ambassador
is infatuated with you?'

'That is the whole point,' Caroline urged, 'no one
will know! They will believe he is running after you!'

'No, Caroline, you cannot do this!'

'Orelia, you cannot refuse to help me to see him
sometimes. If you only knew what heaven it is to be in
his arms!'

'Caroline, you must not say such things,' Orelia said
wearily.

'But it is! It is!' Caroline answered. 'He kisses di-
vinely—even better than my other Italian beau—and
he is crazy about me, he is really! I am not a fool,
Orelia. I know when a man is flirting and when he is
really serious. Adelco is serious!'

'And where will that get you?' Orelia asked. 'He will
not marry you, he told me so today. He is engaged
to a rich girl!'

'If I had money he would jilt her tomorrow,' Caroline answered, 'he has told me that!'

'That is very easy to say when you are engaged to
be married and so is he!' Orelia said sharply.

'Oh, if I were rich enough he would marry me,'
Caroline answered, 'make no mistake about that!
And if he were rich enough I might marry him. But
neither of us can afford such fancies. We must just
take the gifts the gods have given us; and they are not
very generous gifts, Orelia, for we only have a week!'

'A week!' Orelia echoed. 'Why? Is His Excellency returning to Italy?'

'No,' Caroline answered, 'I am to be married.'

'In a week?' Orelia asked in surprise. 'But why
such haste? I thought you were waiting until the end
of June?'

'The Regent has offered to be best man and to let us
have our Reception at Carlton House,' Caroline answered. 'Naturally it is a great honour and the whole
Beau Monde will be gnashing their teeth with envy,
hatred and malice.'

She smiled at the thought.

'But His Royal Highness intends to remove to Windsor,' she continued, 'for Lady Hertford prefers Windsor Castle, where she will take her whole family. So we must be married before Ascot, when the Regent will be staying at Windsor, Afterwards he will not return to London.'

A week! Orelia felt as if a cold hand was squeezing her heart. When Caroline married she must leave Ryde House. She would not see the Marquis again except at very irregular intervals.

She felt a sudden sense of desolation, a feeling as if she saw ahead a barren desert, an emptiness that was almost too frightening to contemplate.

Then with the thought there returned her feeling of shame because she loved the man who was to marry Caroline!

'Only a week!' her cousin was repeating. 'Only a week, Orelia! After that, as you know, I shall have to behave with great discretion, not only with him, but with every other man! Darius would never allow there to be any scandal about his wife!'

She paused, then said slowly.

'He may be disreputable himself, he may have flouted the conventions, but when it comes to a question of his family honour, then I am well aware that he is exceeding proud!'

'And quite rightly so,' Orelia said warmly. 'Caroline, do not encourage the Ambassador! Send him away now! It will not make things any better for you to let yourself fall more and more in love with him.'

Caroline threw herself down on the bed, regardless of the damage to her gauze gown.

'Am I really in love with him?' she asked aloud. 'I ask myself that. Quite frankly, Orelia, I do not know the answer. When I am with him he excites me. I long for him to kiss me. I want to be in his arms. I thrill to the fascinating things he says; the way he touches me.'

She paused.

'But of one thing you can be quite certain, my dearest Conscience, I am not going to run away with him, or do anything as nonsensical as that! Even if he were to ask it—which he would not, for he is far too ambitious—I would say no!'

'Then you are not in love with him,' Orelia said. 'Not really.'

Real love would overcome all obstacles, she thought. Real love would not be confined by considerations of money.

'But I want him! I want him!' Caroline cried, staring up at the ceiling. 'At the same time I am too sensible, although you do not think so, Orelia, to jeopardise the position I shall hold as the Marchioness of Ryde, or to antagonise Darius, so do not look so worried! I will behave in an extremely circumspect manner—as long as you will help me.'

At her last words Orelia put her hands up to her cheeks.

'You are blackmailing me,' she complained. 'You know that is what you are doing, Caroline, and it is extremely unscrupulous!'

'Dearest, all I want is just a little fun before I settle down to married respectability. If I have a baby in the first year we are married, think how boring it will be, with nothing to amuse me except the Marquis's cynical remarks. I mean to enjoy myself for just this last week of freedom.'

'I do not really know what you are expecting me to do,' Orelia said.

Caroline sat up on the bed.

'That means that you will do it,' she exclaimed. 'Dearest, I love you! You are the most wonderful, perfect, sweetest cousin anyone could ever have!'

'I am making no promises,' Orelia said sternly, 'until I know what you expect of me.'

'It is so easy,' Caroline answered. 'Did Adelco not tell you? You will pretend he is paying court to you. I shall tell the Duchess that I consider him a very eligible suitor. He will invite you to meet him, but as he is a foreigner I shall chaperone you most strictly. That is why we are dining with him tomorrow night.'

'Alone?' Orelia asked.

'Well, he is not likely to ask the Marquis and his Grandmother!' Caroline replied with a grimace.

'They will think it strange,' Orelia said desperately.

'No, I have it all arranged,' Caroline answered. 'Just leave everything to me! You will receive an invitation tomorrow morning asking you to dine at the Italian Embassy.

'I shall tell the Duchess that His Excellency has spoken about it to me and that I agreed that you should go, as of course you are longing to do, as long as I accompany you.

'If Darius suggests that he should come too—which he will not—I shall say that I happened to know that the Ambasssador has already arranged his dinner-party and that another man would prove an embarrassment.'

'And you really think that the Duchess will not think it somewhat extraordinary behaviour?' Orelia asked.

'She must be used to men being infatuated with you by now,' Caroline answered. 'I saw Lord Rotherton pouring out his woes to her just before we left to-night.'

Orelia said nothing. She was thinking of the expression on the Marquis's face as he had seen the Ambassador kissing her hand in the Ballroom.

'Please, Caroline,' she said in a desperate voice, 'please do not make me do this!'

'If you do not,' Caroline answered, 'then I swear that I will see Adelco anyway. I cannot give him up! He is the most exciting thing that has come into my life for months! I shall dine with him at the Italian Embassy tomorrow night, and the Devil take the consequences!'

Orelia gave a deep sigh. She knew when Caroline spoke in that hard, obstinate voice that it would be impossible to make her change her mind. She had been the same ever since she was a child.

Once she had set her heart on something, a toy, or a treat, then nothing anyone could say or do could alter her.

'As I have said already,' Orelia answered quietly, 'you are blackmailing me! Very well, I will dine at the

Italian Embassy, but, Caroline, promise me that you will not go too far, that you will remember whom you are marrying, that you will try to behave in a circumspect manner.'

'I will try to do so in public,' Caroline promised, 'but what I do in private, Orelia, is something very different!'

'I do not want to hear about it,' Orelia cried angrily. 'I hate this pretence! This subterfuge! I loathe the whole idea of your being involved in an intrigue which has nothing beautiful and nothing genuine about it! It is just rather petty and sordid!'

Caroline rose from the bed.

'At least you are frank, Orelia!'

Her voice was cold and there was a hurt expression in her eyes which made Orelia turn to her immediately and put her arms round her.

'Oh, Caroline, dearest,' she said. 'I do not mean to be beastly to you, it is just that I am so worried, so frightened, that you will spoil your life by behaving in this outrageous manner.'

'I have to be outrageous sometimes,' Caroline replied. 'Can you not understand, Orelia, that there is something inside me that seeks excitement, which wants the thrill of being loved?'

'I think that is because you yourself do not love enough,' Orelia said. 'Could not you try, Caroline, to love . . . His Lordship?'

'I have tried,' Caroline answered. 'You know I am very fond of Darius, but, as I told you before, I always feel that he is criticising me. If only he would talk to me as Adelco does.'

She sighed.

'If only I could feel his heart beating fiercely,' she went on 'and know that his breath comes quicker because I am close to him, that I could excite him until he lost control of himself, then I might, I really might, find myself in love with him!'

'Perhaps when you are married . . .' Orelia began.

Caroline gave a little laugh. It was almost a harsh sound.

'Are you really such a romantic?' she asked. 'I assure you only in story books does love come after marriage! It is when a man is pursuing you, when he is not certain he will catch you, when he wants the unobtainable, that love burns most brightly—or would you call it infatuation?'

'I would call it passion or desire,' Orelia replied, 'but not love, Caroline, and you know in your heart that that is not the love that we both wanted when we were very young!'

Caroline laughed again.

'The Prince Charming, who was to discover me—a little beggar-maid—and would carry me away to his Castle where we would live happily ever after!'

Caroline's voice was bitter.

'Such tales are not true to life, Orelia. You know that as well as I do! One cannot have everything! Not a Prince, who is handsome and wealthy and at the same time madly in love!'

She paused.

'One does not get so much together in the same man. You can have a Prince or a pauper, one with love, one with money! Unless, of course, you are clever like me! I can contrive to have my cake and eat it!'

'Which is cheating!' Orelia flashed.

'Cheating or not, that is what I intend to do!' Caroline said lightly. 'And now I must go to bed because I want to look ravishing for Adelco tomorrow night.'

She put her arms around Orelia.

'Thank you, dearest,' she said. 'I knew you would not fail me. Just for the moment, pack up that tiresome little conscience of yours and put it away at the back of a dark drawer! You can take it out again on the day I am married!'

'Oh, Caroline! Caroline!' Orelia said, laughing, but with tears in her eyes. 'I do not know what to do about you!'

'Then just do what I want!' Caroline said irrepressibly, and went from the room.

Orelia undressed slowly and got into bed. She thought she would lie awake worrying over Caroline, afraid of what lay ahead, anxious of what tomorrow would bring; but instead she found herself thinking of the Marquis!

She knew now that she had been in love with him from that moment when he had first kissed her on Morden Green.

She had found it impossible to forget him. She had in fact thought of him every night. She had shied away like a frightened horse from indulging such thoughts, not realising how much they had become a part of her life.

Yet now she faced the truth! She loved him! She loved him!

He had been right when he had compared her with the Sleeping Princess—his kiss had awakened her!

She had never known before the touch of a man's lips, and yet long after he had held her unresisting in his arms she had felt the pressure of his mouth on hers and known that something strange and unaccountable had occurred in her heart!

Now she faced the fact that ever since she had been at Ryde House she had been acutely conscious of her host.

He had only to come into a room, she had only to catch a glimpse of him as she came downstairs, to know a strange constriction in her throat, to feel her heart turn over.

She had refused to acknowledge an irrepressible longing to see him again, to notice him walk across the room, to look at him at the end of the Dining-Room table, to watch him riding in the park, seemingly a part of his horse.

She loved him! She could feel the words repeating and repeating themselves over and over in her brain.

Then, as she said her prayers, she prayed with a passionate intensity that she might bring both him and Caroline happiness.

She must work towards this end, she must try to make their future life together hold some semblance of happiness even if they could not know the ecstasy of love.

Then she knew despairingly that while she might be helping Caroline to a momentary amusement, she was certainly not helping the Marquis in conniving to conceal the flirtation of his fiancée with the Italian Ambassador.

'It is wrong!' Orelia told herself.

Yet she could not see how she could prevent Caroline from seeing His Excellency!

If she did not agree to do what they wished, she knew that Caroline was far too self-willed and too spoilt not to spend her time with the man she fancied, whatever the consequences!

Caroline would believe, as people always did, that she would not be found out! She would think that the way she behaved would not be noticed by spiteful eyes and repeated by even more spiteful tongues.

Caroline, because it was her nature, would always respond to the call of her senses.

She was like a child who would go on greedily eating slice after slice of iced cake and who would never anticipate for a moment that it would make her sick!

Caroline was determined to be with the Ambassador, and there was nothing, Orelia thought with a deep sigh, that she could do about it except to try to protect her from the consequences of her own stupidity.

She thought of how she had promised the Marquis, that very night, that she would never lie to him—now she must act a lie in something which actively concerned his own life.

In sudden agony Orelia buried her face in the pillow.

Which was the worse, she asked herself, to let him be hurt by finding out the truth, or to lie to him despite her promise, in the hope that he would never know he was being deceived?

She had no choice she realised except to play the game that Caroline and the Ambassador had demanded of her.

While her mind told her that it was the lesser of two evils, her heart cried out that the only thing with which she was really concerned was to protect the Marquis because she loved him.

The next morning neither the Duchess nor Caroline appeared early.

Orelia, having been unable to sleep, was up and had done a lot of small things that were waiting for her attention, before Caroline appeared.

She came into their Sitting-Room looking extremely beautiful.

'Good-morning, Caroline,' Orelia said, 'did you sleep well?'

'Like a baby,' Caroline answered. 'I was tired and happy, Orelia. It is the perfect combination; besides, I went to sleep pretending I was in Adelco's arms!'

She saw the expression on Orelia's face and burst out laughing.

'Dearest, I am but teasing you,' she said. 'You never had any sense of humour where I was concerned.'

'Not when you talk like that!' Orelia said ruefully. 'Oh, Caroline, do be careful, the very walls of this house have ears!'

'Then they must have plenty to talk about by now!' Caroline said irrepressibly. 'Come on, Orelia, let us go downstairs and see if there is anyone about to take us driving!'

Orelia glanced at her suspiciously, but Caroline had already run from the room and was hurrying down the Grand Staircase. She followed after her and saw as she reached the Hall an enormous basket of white orchids set on top of one of the gold tables.

'What lovely flowers!' she cried involuntarily.

'I wonder who they are from,' Caroline said, and then exclaimed: 'Why! They are for you, Orelia!'

'For me?' Orelia replied. 'But that is imposs . . . !'

As she spoke she saw Caroline's eyes and bit back the end of the word.

'There is a letter attached,' Caroline said meaningly.

Even as she spoke the Library door opened and the Marquis came into the Hall. Orelia was aware of his presence because it seemed to her that every nerve in her body tingled.

Almost without realising what she was doing, she

took the letter that Caroline put into her hands and opened it.

There was the huge, flamboyant crest of the Italian Embassy at the top of the paper, and then she read:

'Charming and Captivating Miss Stanyon,

May I Beg that you will Honour my Embassy with your Presence at Dinner tonight? I shall look forward very Greatly to your being my Guest and will Send a Carriage for You to Ryde House at Half after Seven.

You told me last Night that You were Disengaged and I cannot express in Words how eagerly I shall await your Arrival.

I remain Yours most Humbly and Admiringly,
                    Adelco di Savelli.'

'What a charming letter!' Caroline exclaimed, who had been looking over Orelia's shoulder. 'But, dearest, I do not think it will be at all correct for you to go alone! After all, one can never trust these foreigners, can one, Darius?'

She looked towards the Marquis as she spoke, who was staring with what Orelia thought was something like contempt on his face at the ornate basket of orchids.

'Of whom are you speaking, Caroline?' he asked in his most aloof voice.

'His Excellency the Ambassador to Italy has lost his heart to Orelia,' Caroline replied. 'I saw it in his eyes last night and indeed he begged my permission to invite her to dinner tonight. I have said that she can accept, but I am sure you will think I was right, Darius, when I suggested that I should accompany her.'

Orelia could not look at the Marquis. She stood staring stupidly at the letter which she still held in her hand.

She longed to tear it up, to throw it away, to announce that she had no intention of going to the Italian Embassy.

Then she heard the Marquis say:

'Orelia must, of course, do what she wishes; and if you think it your duty, Caroline, to protect your cousin's reputation, then naturally you should accompany her.'

There was something in the way he spoke which made Orelia feel with a frightened throb of her heart that he was not deceived.

Then she told herself she was just being imaginative! Why should he suspect for one moment that the Italian Ambassador was really interested in Caroline?

'The orchids are quite glorious!' Caroline said, 'and now, dearest, you must go upstairs and write the Ambassador a short note saying that we are both delighted to accept his invitation to dinner.'

'Are you coming driving, Caroline?' the Marquis asked sharply, 'or have you other plans for this morning?'

There was something in the way he said 'other plans' which made Orelia suspicious.

Then, because she dared not meet his eyes and was afraid to speak to him, she ran swiftly up the stairs as if all the devils in hell were running behind at her heels.

Only as she reached the landing at the top did she hear Caroline say:

'You know, Darius, I think that the Ambassador would make a very suitable match for Orelia.'

She did not hear the Marquis's reply because she ran into the Sitting-Room and slammed the door behind her.

It was intolerable, she thought! Intolerable that Caroline should put her in such a position!

And then, miserably, humbly, she told herself that the Marquis's opinion of her was not of the least consequence.

He had been kind to her, it was true, but she was only the cousin of his fiancée, the girl who was under his protection; someone who he knew was so ignorant of the ways of Society that he felt almost unnecessarily responsible for her.

She remembered his kindness last night, the manner in which he had told her he thought she looked like moonlight. It was all words, she thought.

He might have a slight admiration for her, as any

man might admire a woman's looks and not be interested in her as a person.

She remembered the Marquis had once compared her with a painting by Botticelli. That was what she was to him—an object he admired, but no more!

She had infuriated him yesterday by her indiscreet action, but his anger was, she felt now, based on his disgust and what he imagined was her depravity.

And yet she would never forget the note in his voice when he asked her forgiveness.

Alone in the Sitting-Room Orelia buried her face in her hands. She had thought last night that she was entering a maze. She knew now it was far worse!

It was like being caught in the web of a giant spider. Every time she moved she became more entangled.

She wanted to run away, to hide, and yet she knew she must stay; she must help Caroline and must deceive the Marquis. She wanted desperately to help them both.

But, she thought, despairingly, there was every likelihood of her crucifying herself in the process.

8

The Italian Embassy was almost as magnificent as Carlton House!

There were fabulous pictures which had been brought from Rome to decorate the walls, and everywhere Orelia looked there seemed to be carved mirrors, gilt tables and marble statues.

The flunkeys, dressed in an ornate livery plentifully bespeckled with gold braid, looked slightly theatrical as they escorted Caroline and Orelia along what seemed miles of red carpet to the private apartments of the Ambassador.

Here they were greeted by the Count looking extremely elegant in a room which was furnished with so many *objets d'art* and priceless Italian Masters that it was like a Museum.

'What words can I find to welcome you?' His Excellency asked, bending to take both Caroline's hands in his and raising them one after another to his lips.

Then as he greeted Orelia with a twinkle in his eye he said:

'I am glad Caroline has a more persuasive tongue than mine, Miss Stanyon!'

Orelia wished to look severely at him but instead she found herself smiling. There was something almost boyish about his gaiety and his undoubted sincerity where Caroline was concerned.

But she could not help worrying as she watched the familiar way in which the Ambassador led Caroline across the room, looking at her with deep burning eyes, and whispering passionate compliments which Orelia could not help overhearing.

It was all very bad for Caroline, she thought with a sigh, and as the evening progressed she was to think this again and again.

A friend and colleague of the Ambassador, who worked in the Embassy, was produced to make them a foursome.

They dined in the Ambassador's private Dining-Room, and although Orelia felt she should be stiff and make plain her disapproval of his behaviour, she found herself laughing and being incessantly amused by the wit and repartee of the two Italians.

In fact without the somewhat repressive presence of the Duchess, it was quite the most enjoyable dinner-party she had attended since she had been in London.

But at the same time there was no mistaking the burning desire in the Ambassador's eyes as he looked at Caroline, nor the fact that with flushed cheeks and sparkling eyes, Caroline was making every effort to encourage him!

Count Carlos Ferranda, the Gentleman who had been invited to join them, was about the same age as the Ambassador.

Orelia fancied that sometimes there was a twinkle of amusement in his eyes as he watched his friend exerting himself to be fascinating.

She was not surprised—indeed she had feared it might happen—that when dinner was over and they had moved into the Salon, Caroline and the Ambassador, on the flimsiest pretext, disappeared from the room, leaving her alone with Count Carlos.

The Count saw Orelia watch them go with a worried expression on her face, and he said with a smile on his lips:

'You are too young, Miss Stanyon, to look like an anxious chaperone!'

'But I am anxious,' she replied frankly.

The Count shrugged his shoulders expressively.

'What can one do?' he asked. 'When people are in

love they always forget that while the whole world loves a lover, it still enjoys gossiping about them!'

Orelia felt he was sympathetic, and bending towards him she said:

'Please ask the Ambassador, who I gather is a close friend of yours, not to endanger Caroline's reputation. He must realise that it was in fact very indiscreet for us to come here alone this evening to such a small dinner-party.'

'Do you really imagine that the Ambassador will listen to me?' the Count enquired. 'As I have already said, people in love are a law unto themselves.'

'They should not be in love!' Orelia protested. 'You must know, Sir, that my cousin is to be married in a week's time, and if it should become known that we were dining here tonight in such very intimate circumstances, do you suppose that the Social world would not put a very censorious construction on it?'

'Of course, I agree!' the Count replied, 'and that is why, Miss Stanyon, though you may think it indiscreet for us to dine here with but four of us present, how much more indiscreet would it have been had there been half a dozen additional guests who would inevitably have talked about their evening at the Italian Embassy!'

'Yes, perhaps you are right,' Orelia said with a little sigh. 'But it must not happen again.'

'And I am hoping that it will,' the Count said. 'Let us forget that pair of miscreants, Miss Stanyon, and enjoy ourselves. May I tell you that you are the most beautiful woman I have seen since I came to London?'

'Thank you,' Orelia answered, 'but please do not pay me compliments!'

'Why not?' he asked.

'Because they make me shy and embarrassed,' Orelia replied truthfully. 'Englishmen seldom pay compliments, and therefore when we hear the flattery which comes so naturally from foreign lips we always suspect it of being insincere.'

The Count threw back his head and laughed.

'You are not only the most beautiful woman I have ever met,' he said, 'but one of the most original! But shall we not enjoy ourselves since we are thrust together through—shall we say—no fault of our own?'

There was no mistaking the bold look in his eyes and Orelia turned her head away.

'Could we not play a game of piquet or some other card game?' she asked.

'So I am really embarrassing you?' the Count said. 'I detest games of that sort! May we not talk?'

'If it can be of any subject except me,' Orelia replied.

'I cannot believe that there is another woman in the world who would make such a remark,' the Count said. 'Everyone is interested in themselves, and who has more right to that than a beautiful woman?'

'You may think it strange,' Orelia answered, 'but I am really not interested in myself. Instead, can we not talk about you?'

He looked at her for a moment as if he doubted the sincerity of her words, and then settling himself comfortably on the sofa beside her, he said:

'Very well, I will tell you about my life in Italy, and why I am delighted to be in London at this particular time.'

He talked interestingly and amusingly. Orelia learnt he was married but his wife had some wasting disease which kept her almost permanently in bed. She could not travel with him to London and Orelia gathered that, as theirs had been a marriage of convenience, the Count was quite happy to be on his own.

She asked him questions about his interests, about his future.

Time passed quite pleasantly until it was almost a shock to Orelia to find that it was eleven o'clock and there was still no sign of Caroline and the Ambassador.

'I think we should be going home,' she said anxiously.

'Am I boring you?' he enquired.

'No, it is not that,' she said hastily, 'you know I

have enjoyed our talk enormously. But as there has been no dancing tonight at the Embassy, the Duchess will be expecting our return about this time.'

'What do you expect me to do?' the Count asked. 'Go and find out if our protégés have eloped together? Or interrupt them at what perhaps might be a most intimate moment?'

He was smiling, but Orelia said sharply:

'Please do not joke about it. It is serious to me and I feel a responsibility for my cousin.'

'Surely,' the Count asked, 'she is older than you?'

'Only in years,' Orelia answered. 'Sometimes I feel when I am with Caroline that she is nothing more than a naughty child and that I am as old as her mother or her grandmother.'

The Count laughed, and reaching out took Orelia's hand in his.

'I assure you, *mia bella,* that you are not the least like anyone's grandmother. You look like Spring itself. Perhaps really you are an impersonation of Persephone!'

His words recalled to Orelia the Marquis telling her she was like the beautiful creature that Botticelli had painted in 'Primavera'. She prayed that he might never know of Caroline's escapade this evening.

Then she remembered that she was the one who was supposed to have attracted the Ambassador.

Would the Marquis really be deceived by such a weak subterfuge? Would he really credit that Caroline would go anywhere to chaperone her if she was not personally interested in the entertainment provided?

Although Orelia hardly dared admit it to herself, she knew that what she really minded was having to lie to the Marquis when she had given him her word of honour that she would not do so!

He had trusted her, and now by being here tonight, by pretending that the flowers that the Ambassador had sent to Ryde House were genuinely for herself, by acquiescing in Caroline's demands, she was in fact lying to him—lying and deceiving!

She looked again at the clock. Now it was ten minutes past eleven and the hands seemed to move more and more slowly until finally they reached twenty past.

'We must do something!' she said in an agitated manner to the Count.

'If you are really worried,' he said quietly, 'I will go and see what I can do.'

'Please, please do that,' Orelia pleaded. 'I would not ask you to do anything so embarrassing if I were not really perturbed about the lateness of the hour.'

'Very well,' he said good-humouredly. 'But if my Ambassador dismisses me for impertinence, then, Miss Stanyon, the responsibility will be entirely yours!'

Orelia tried to smile at his words but she failed, and as he left the room she could only walk around restlessly, growing more and more anxious.

Finally, when she felt almost in despair, Caroline arrived looking radiant and extremely happy, but at the same time showing all too clearly by her dishevelled hair, crumpled gown and the softness of her mouth, how she had passed the time since dinner.

'Count Carlos says that you are in a fidget, my dearest,' she said to Orelia. 'After all, the night is still young!'

'We must go home,' Orelia said in a quiet voice. 'You know as well as I do, Caroline, that we shall have no reasonable explanation as to why we stayed so late! Please hurry!'

'Oh dear! Oh dear!' Caroline cried in mock dismay. 'What a nuisance it is to have one's conscience permanently in attendance!'

'I am sorry,' Orelia said in a contrite tone, 'but you must be sensible, Caroline.'

'Why is it always so unpleasant to be sensible?' Caroline asked petulantly.

The Ambassador came forward to take Orelia's hand in his and raised it to his lips.

'You are right, Miss Stanyon,' he said, 'and you must forgive me for being so irresponsible, but there is no counting of time in Paradise and that is where I have been this evening.'

Count Carlos helped Orelia into her cloak and the Ambassador slipped Caroline's wrap over her shoulders, looking down into her eyes as he did so.

Then after what seemed to Orelia an interminable delay and far too many effusive compliments, they were finally driving homewards in the carriage belonging to the Embassy.

Caroline lay back in her corner of the carriage and closed her eyes.

'It was wonderful! Wonderful!' she murmured.

'For Heaven's sake!' Orelia snapped, her patience exhausted. 'Try to look as if you were bored! If you arrive at Ryde House looking as you are now, no one will believe for one moment that it is I with whom the Ambassador is supposed to be infatuated!'

'How you nag me!' Caroline complained.

Nevertheless she made an effort to look more demure as they stepped into the Hall at Ryde House. To Orelia's relief there seemed to be no one about.

'Her Grace has retired, My Lady,' Willand said to Caroline, 'and His Lordship went out soon after dinner. He has not yet returned.'

Orelia drew a deep breath of relief, but when Caroline reached the top of the stairs she said angrily:

'You made me come away early! I could easily have stayed another hour or so!'

'How could we have taken the risk?' Orelia asked. 'How would you have explained our lateness if both the Duchess and His Lordship had been waiting for us?'

'I would have thought of something,' Caroline said airily. 'I shall not listen to you another time, Orelia.'

She went into her bedroom and shut the door.

The following day Orelia went driving in the morning with Caroline and the Duchess. They took the open landau and met innumerable friends in Rotten Row before they returned to Ryde House.

Orelia had learnt that there was to be a Luncheon Party to which the Duchess said a number of politicians had been invited.

'Is this your doing, Caroline?' she enquired as they drove homewards. 'I have never known Darius take the slightest interest in politics until now.'

'No indeed,' Caroline replied. 'I find all these arguments for and against the Whigs, or for and against the Tories, extremely tedious! Besides, I can never remember who belongs to which party, which results in endless confusion!'

There were twelve guests for lunch and to Orelia most of them were just names, until Willand announced:

'The Honourable Henry Grey Bennett, M'Lord.'

A tall man with an interesting face and a high forehead came into the room. He greeted the Marquis, saying:

'You remember last night, Ryde, when we were talking about my Bill to make illegal the use of Climbing Boys, I told you how little interest the public took in such cruelties? Well, to my amazement, this small book has come into my hands!'

As he spoke Henry Grey Bennett held out a green leather volume. Orelia drew in her breath. She felt for a moment as if she had been turned to stone.

'What is it?' She heard the Marquis ask, and another guest remarked:

'I saw that book yesterday. I am told it is causing a sensation! God knows who has written it! One of those damned reformers, I believe!'

'Whoever he may be, God bless him!' Henry Grey Bennett said. 'I must read you this rhyme, it will have, I am convinced, a tremendous recruiting value in support of my Bill.'

He paused for a moment to kiss the Duchess's hand, and then opening the book, began to read. A sudden hush fell on the assembled guests.

'Drunken fops in St. James's Street,
Buy little girls with painted eyes,
While climbing boys with bleeding feet
Choke in the soot their piteous cries.'

'What do you think of that?' he asked. 'And the Society which has been demanding the abolition of Climbing Boys for seventeen years has asked me to find out if they can have that verse printed and distributed in a pamphlet!'

'What is the book?' Orelia heard the Marquis ask.

Henry Grey Bennett handed him the slim leather volume, and as His Lordship turned the pages she edged a little further away into a corner by the fireplace where she thought she would not be observed.

How could she have ever imagined, she asked herself, that her book of verse would command the attention of such a man as the Honourable Henry Grey Bennett?

She knew all about him and about his fight on behalf of the wretched Climbing Boys, sometimes only four or five years old, who were forced up the chimneys.

Two years earlier, when Henry Grey Bennett had presented a Petition to forbid the practice to the House with hundreds of signatures, the Earl of Morden had been one of the first members of the House of Lords to sign.

He had after that a long correspondence with Henry Grey Bennett and Orelia had not only read all the letters but had helped her Uncle with many of his replies.

She had hoped that perhaps her verse would bring to a few people's attention the horrors that were taking place in London and the country, but now that she was actually hearing her work discussed she felt frightened.

The only consolation was of course that no one would suspect her. In fact Lord Worcester was saying:

'Who is the author? Do you know, Henry?'

'No indeed, although I would indeed like to meet him,' Henry Grey Bennett replied.

'If the man is not careful he will find himself in prison for sedition,' an elderly Peer remarked.

'Sedition?' the Marquis queried.

'I have seen the book already, Ryde,' the Peer replied. 'Read "The Cry of the Protester", and that will tell you the sort of firebrand with whom we are deal-

ing. If you ask me these chaps will get us all strung
up on lampposts before they are finished!'

The Marquis looked down at the book, but Henry
Grey Bennett took it from him.

'I will read it to you,' he said. 'I thought it an excellent poem, if you wish to know.'

'You would!' the Peer remarked. 'Personally, I think
this sort of talk is extremely dangerous.'

'What does it say?' the Duchess enquired. 'Let us
hear it!'

'Yes indeed, read it,' the Marquis said. 'You have
made us curious, Henry!'

The Honourable Henry turned the pages.

'It is called "The Cry of the Protester",' he said,
and then in a quiet cultured voice he read:

'How pleasant for the starving hordes to learn
Of thirty entrées served at Carlton House,
Of champagne flowing—"Keep the wheel a-turn,
You're nigh on six, you lazy little louse!"'

Old sewing-women working twenty hours
Are thrilled to know My Lady's jewels are fine.
While children drag the coal hewn for her fire
Half naked through a dark and filthy mine.

Where can we go? What is the end
To cruelty, hate, disease and ceaseless pain?
Another Government or King? God send
Our brave protesters have not died in vain!'

For a moment there was silence as Henry Grey Bennett finished, and then the Peer who had spoken before exclaimed:

'There you are, what more do you want? The sooner such traitors to the State are sent to the Tower, the
better! It is anarchy, that is what it is, and they will
have poor Prinny off the Throne before he even gets
there!'

'You seem to be very sure in your mind what sort
of person the author is,' the Marquis said slowly.

'All I know is that this sort of drivel does more harm than those filthy cartoons!' the elderly Peer snarled. 'Remember it was cartoons and lampoons which were partially responsible for the French Revolution! If you Gentlemen want to keep your heads and your Estates you had better crush such rebels as soon as possible!'

'On the contrary,' Henry Grey Bennett said firmly. 'I think the more such criticisms as we read of here are aired in public the more likely we shall get legislation to put an end to such abominations.'

'I do not mind wagering a monkey that you will not get your Bill through Parliament,' the Peer remarked. 'It will be laughed out of the Chamber, especially if Lauderdale has anything to do with it.'

He laughed scornfully.

'He has already declared that you are nothing but an old woman weeping crocodile tears over small boys who are far better employed cleaning chimneys than picking pockets in the streets!'

The Honourable Henry was about to make an angry response when Willand announced Lunch.

'Now stop quarrelling, Gentlemen!' the Duchess admonished them. 'That is always the trouble with politicians. You ask them to what you hope will be a congenial, friendly meal, and they instantly get themselves worked up on matters which should be kept for the House of Commons.'

'You are right, Ma'am,' Lord Worcester said. 'Personally I find politics a bore! I much prefer women and horses!'

The Duchess laughed, as he offered her his arm to lead her into the Dining-Room.

Orelia followed behind, conscious that her heart was beating uncomfortably and that her hands were trembling. It was stupid to be afraid, she told herself sternly. No one would ever connect her with the verses which people would naturally suppose to have been written by a man.

And yet, when she remembered her conversation with the Marquis, she felt uneasy! In the heat of her

anger she had said too much: she had betrayed to him
her knowledge of the Flash Houses.

Fortunately these were not mentioned in the poems,
but she had spoken of the child prostitutes and the
Climbing Boys.

However the latter were quite a general topic of
conversation.

She had even heard an elderly Lady at one of the
tea-parties to which the Duchess had taken her declare that Henry Grey Bennett was a crank, and that
the sooner Lord Tankeville directed his second son to
stop making a fool of himself, the better it would be
for everyone!

'If it were not for the small boys, how would we get
our chimneys cleaned?' the Dowager had asked, and
no one had appeared to have an answer to the question!

Nevertheless, Orelia was glad that she was not sitting
next to Henry Grey Bennett at Luncheon; for she
knew it would have been impossible not to discuss his
Bill with him or to wish him luck in bringing it before Parliament.

She was surprised to learn that the Marquis had
spoken to him the night before.

Could she possibly have aroused His Lordship's interest? Or had it just been a coincidence that he had
met the Honourable Henry and that the conversation
had naturally veered towards his favourite topic?

Luncheon seemed interminable and Orelia, seated
between two Gentlemen who appeared to be more interested in their food and drink than in her, was thankful when at last the Duchess rose to her feet and with-
drew the Ladies from the table.

'What are you going to do this afternoon, Caroline?'
she enquired, as they walked towards the Salon.

'I promised to go driving with a friend,' Caroline answered. 'He wants to show me a new pair of chestnuts he has purchased for his High Perch Phaeton.'

'Who is it?' the Duchess enquired curiously. 'Do I
know him?'

'It is the Count Carlos Ferranda,' Caroline answered

casually. 'I do not think he has had the pleasure of making Your Grace's acquaintance.'

Orelia gave a little start. She knew quite well that Caroline was going to meet the Ambassador and that the Count was merely conveying her to him in his High Perch Phaeton.

The Phaeton only held two passengers, so there was no question of anyone travelling with them; but Orelia knew that somewhere, somehow, they would encounter the Ambassador and Caroline would be alone with him again.

She wanted to protest, to beg Caroline to be more circumspect, but somehow she felt weary of the whole subject. What was the point of arguing? Caroline would go her own way, whatever she might say to her. She would do exactly what she wished to do!

The Ladies who had been present at the Luncheon were now taking their leave. Most of them were not prepared to wait for the Gentlemen to leave the Dining-Room.

Caroline slipped away and a few minutes later Orelia went upstairs.

She knew that if she were to do what was right she would go to Caroline's bedroom, where she was changing to go driving, and argue with her once again. But somehow it seemed just a waste of time and energy.

Caroline had made up her mind and Orelia knew that however much she pleaded with her nothing she could say would make any difference.

When Caroline wanted something she went at it bald-headed, like a greedy small boy at a pot of jam!

Orelia went into the Sitting-Room and took from a drawer of the desk a locked leather case in which she kept her private papers.

Although she had been frightened when Henry Grey Bennett had read her poems aloud, she knew now that she could think about it more coolly, that she had done the right thing in getting them published.

It was what her Uncle would have wished.

His work for the last three years against the horrors

perpetrated on children in the Flash Houses, in the mills, in the mines and in the lowest stews in the East End, would always remain unfinished.

But she must make her tiny effort to continue his crusade. She might be only a very small voice and it might indeed be crying in the wilderness, but at least she could try.

Her book had caused some stir, even if only because it annoyed the more conservative members of Society!

She opened the leather case and drew out several other poems she had written. She thought she would revise them and perhaps write some others; then take them along to Watkins and Rufus for their approval.

They had in fact asked her for another book. She had made up her mind now that she would offer them one.

She put the papers on the table and then suddenly some words came to her. She wrote them down quickly, without hesitation, almost as if they were being dictated by someone else.

They were there complete and formed in her mind. Then below the four lines she had written, she inscribed the date.

Like all creative artists she had forgotten time and place and everything else as she wrote. There came a knock at the door. Absently, hardly realising that she spoke, she said:

'Come in.'

'Some flowers for you, Miss,' she heard one of the footmen say.

'Leave them there.'

She heard the door close and started to read through her poem again. Then a voice, cynical and mocking, said:

'Your new Beau, Orelia, is certainly over eloquent when it comes to flowers!'

Orelia gave a little cry and started to her feet. Standing in the room beside an outsize basket of purple orchids was the Marquis.

Without realising she did so, she hastily turned over the piece of paper on which she had been writing and put both her hands on it as if to hold it down on the desk.

'You seem surprised to see me,' the Marquis said accusingly.

'No . . . My Lord,' Orelia stammered. 'I mean . . . yes! I thought . . . you would have . . . gone out.'

'Caroline preferred to make other arrangements for the afternoon rather than spend the time in my company,' the Marquis said, still with that cynical note in his voice. 'And I came to ask you, Orelia, if you would care to come driving with me; but I see you are otherwise engaged.'

'It is . . . kind of . . . Your Lordship,' Orelia faltered. 'I was just . . . writing . . . something.'

'A love-letter?' the Marquis queried. 'Is the Gentleman in question as extravagant with his protestations of love as he is with his flowers?'

'No, My Lord, I mean . . . I was not writing to the Ambassador . . . if that is what you are . . . inferring.'

'Who then is to be honoured by your confidence?' the Marquis asked.

'No one, it is not a . . . letter.'

The Marquis drew nearer until he was standing beside her at the desk.

'Not a letter?' he queried, 'and not to your latest and most ardent admirer?'

'No, My Lord.'

'Then why is it so secret?'

'It is not,' Orelia answered. 'It is . . . something . . . personal but not . . .'

Her voice trailed away. The colour had risen in her cheeks and she was unable to meet the Marquis's eyes.

'What are you hiding from me?' the Marquis asked, and there was a fierceness behind the question which was frightening.

'I am not . . . hiding anything,' Orelia protested. 'It is just that I . . . do not wish you to . . . see what I have . . . written.'

'Why should you suspect that I should wish to do so?' the Marquis enquired.

She could not answer this, knowing that she had

become involved into this uncomfortable position simply because she had so foolishly turned over the page
surreptitiously in front of him and in her shyness held
it down.

'What can you have written that I may not see?' the
Marquis enquired.

'It is . . . nothing,' Orelia said. 'You have no . . .
right to . . . question me.'

'I have the right,' he asserted, 'because you gave me
your promise that in future you would trust me, that
you would not involve yourself in any more dangerous
adventures and, what is more, that you would tell me
the truth! I am holding you to both your promises,
Orelia!'

'No! No! This does not concern . . . you, My Lord!'
Orelia said desperately. 'I swear to you this is . . . something quite . . . different, something I must . . . I must
keep to . . . myself!'

'I do not believe you,' the Marquis said harshly.

Orelia looked up at him in astonishment. She saw that
he was glaring down at her, his eyes filled with suspicion
and with some other emotion to which she could not
put a name.

She only knew that he was once again incensed with
her, that he seemed large and overpowering, and she
felt as if she could not resist him.

'P . . please,' she stammered, 'please . . . understand
. . . I cannot s . . . show it to . . . you!'

'Why not?'

'I cannot . . . explain, it is just that . . . I do not wish
. . . you to see . . . what I have . . . written!'

'And if I insist?'

'You cannot . . . you must . . . not!'

'Because I know that you are ashamed of what you
are doing; because the expression on your face gave
you away as I entered the room; because I know you
are deceiving me, and because I will not allow you to
do so, Orelia, I intend to read what you are trying to
hide from me!'

The Marquis reached out as he spoke and took the

paper from the table. Orelia's hands fluttered in protest and then she realised it was hopeless.

Making an inarticulate sound she ran away from him to stand at the window staring out blindly into the sunshine.

9

Orelia heard the rustle of the paper. Then slowly as if every word surprised him the Marquis in his deep voice read aloud:

> 'A kiss—to you a little thing!
> Yet I heard the angels sing.
> The stars all fell from out the sky,
> We cannot forget—my heart and I!
> *Morden Green* 1818.'

As he finished speaking there was silence, before in a tone she had never heard him use before, he said:

'Do you really believe it was but a little thing to me —but I knew then! I told myself it was a trick of the fading light, that I had drunk too much punch at the Inn, that I was tired after a long day's hunting. But I knew! Of course I knew!'

Because she was curious, but almost against her will, Orelia turned round, her eyes wide and still a little frightened.

"What . . . did you . . . know?"

She looked at him across the room and it seemed to her that she had never seen a man's expression so sharply etched, the lines in his face deep and harsh.

'I knew,' he answered, 'that something had happened to me that had never happened in my life before. I had fallen in love!'

'No!' she whispered. 'No . . . it cannot be . . . true!'

'Of course it is true,' he answered almost roughly.

164

'Do you think that I have not remembered the softness of your lips? That wonder when I touched them is stamped on my memory in letters of fire! I knew I loved you even as I kissed you, but because I had grown so cynical concerning life and women, my brain persuaded me that I was mistaken!'

He looked down at the paper he held in his hands.

'I love you, Orelia; and you know I am speaking the truth!'

'We . . . must not . . . speak of . . . it,' Orelia murmured.

Yet something within her leapt at the sheer wonder of knowing that he loved her as she loved him.

'I so nearly came back the next day,' the Marquis went on. 'I lay awake all night thinking of you, and then two things prevented me.'

She did not ask the question but he knew she waited for the answer.

'I did not think I could—offer you marriage,' he said, 'and I did not wish to spoil something so utterly perfect by offering you anything else.'

He paused, then continued:

'The other reason was that I felt I could not bear to be disillusioned once again!'

Orelia twisted her fingers together. She could not endure hearing the pain in his voice, the bitterness which told her all too clearly how much he was suffering. Then he said and it was a cry:

'It is the only good thing I have ever done in my life! And they try to pretend there is a merciful God!'

'No, you must not . . . think of it like . . . that!' Orelia pleaded. 'It was wonderful . . . perfect . . . we must not spoil it!'

He looked at her, standing silhouetted against the window, the sunlight on her fair hair. There was a kind of radiance about her face and yet her eyes were troubled. And he knew that she was thinking of him rather than herself.

'Oh, my sweet darling!' he exclaimed and his voice broke. 'What can we do?'

Instinctively Orelia stiffened.

'There is . . . nothing we can . . . do,' she answered.
'You are promised to . . . Caroline.'

'Suppose I go to her,' the Marquis suggested, 'suppose I tell her the truth and beg her to help us?'

'No, you could not do that!' Orelia exclaimed. 'If Caroline released you no one would believe for one second that you had not jilted her! She would be laughed at, pitied, and that I could never allow!'

'You know my nickname,' the Marquis said. 'All my life I have been disreputable and socially outrageous. I have been bad, wicked, utterly irresponsible—but I have never broken my word, I have never behaved in a manner which other men would consider dishonourable.'

I know that,' Orelia answered softly, 'and do you think I would permit you to do anything now which would hurt Caroline unbearably and also . . . defame our . . . love?'

She barely murmured the last words but the Marquis heard them.

'Oh, my sweet, my perfect little Primavera,' he ejaculated. 'You drive me wild with jealousy. Sometimes when I think of other men approaching you, of other men being able to say the things I cannot say, of other men offering you what I cannot offer you, then I believe I shall go insane!'

His voice deepened.

'How can I go through life without you? How can I live without seeing your beauty, knowing your sweetness and hearing the music of your voice?'

'We have . . . to be . . . brave,' Orelia faltered.

'It is all so unnecessary, so cruel!' the Marquis cried angrily. 'I had determined never to marry. I thought I would never find a woman who would give me what I needed, who would love me with a pure, unspoilt love, for myself—not for my title or my possessions.'

He paused. Then asked:

'Is that how you love me, Orelia?'

'You know it . . . is,' she answered.

For a moment he looked at her and she knew that it

was only by a tremendous effort of will that he did not move towards her and take her in his arms.

Then as if he forced himself to continue, the Marquis went on:

'I was still thinking about you when I went abroad. In Paris I became involved in one of my usual unsavoury scandals. I am not pretending, Orelia, that it was not entirely my own fault. I deliberately invited danger, and when I had realised I had gone too far and that my behaviour might cause an international incident, I asked Caroline to marry me.'

He drew a deep breath.

'It was the easy way out, but I never pretended to her—and this you must believe—that I loved her or that our marriage would be anything but an amicable arrangement between two people who both had something to gain from the union!'

'Caroline is . . . fond of you,' Orelia managed to say, feeling that she must defend her cousin.

'Do you believe that Caroline would marry me if I were poor and had no social position?' the Marquis asked.

Orelia knew there was no answer to this.

'We both entered into the engagement with our eyes open,' he continued, 'and then the day you arrived, when I saw you standing beside Caroline in the Salon, I knew as clearly as if the Devil himself had spoken that this was my punishment! This was how I would pay for my sins—not once, but for the rest of my life!'

'No, please . . . no! It cannot be like . . . that!' Orelia pleaded. 'It is so . . . wonderful for me . . . to love you . . . a wonder beyond words . . . and to know that you . . . care for . . . me!'

'I love you—why not say the word?' the Marquis asked. 'I love you! I love you more than I thought it possible for any man to love a woman!'

He walked across the room as if he could not bear to look at her before he said:

'I have laughed at love in the past, I thought it merely a figment of the imagination—a romanticised fairy

tale for adolescents and nitwits! How could I know that
I could feel as I feel now—humble yet proud, suffering
the agonies of the damned, and yet at the same time
lifted into the Heavens with a divine emotion I did not
know I was capable of feeling.'

'We must . . . do what is . . . right,' Orelia murmured.

'And my dearest heart, what will happen to you?' he
asked.

Then before she could answer he said roughly:

'You will marry, of course, but I do not know that
I can bear to think of it!'

'I shall never marry,' Orelia said.

'That is nonsensical and you know it!' the Marquis
replied harshly.

She shook her head.

'When I realised that I loved you and admitted it to
myself,' she said softly, 'I knew why all . . . other men
paled . . . in comparison. I think I am one of those people who can only love once in their lives, and I shall
go on loving you . . . wherever you may be . . . whoever you are with!'

'How can you say such things?' the Marquis asked.
'You are so beautiful that you are every man's dream
of what a woman should be. Can you not see that you
must marry: that you must have children? Besides, my
darling, let us be practical, you cannot live alone, and
you have not enough money!'

'I will earn some,' Orelia said.

She saw a smile touch his lips.

'Another volume from *The Watcher?*' he asked.

She started.

'Did you guess?'

'My sweet, even if the words had not been almost
identical to the ones with which you raged at me, after
I had seen you come from Wrotham's lodgings, then
your face would have betrayed you when Henry started
to read your verses aloud.'

'Are you . . . shocked that I should have written . . .
them?' Orelia asked anxiously.

'Shocked!' the Marquis answered. 'No! Only proud,

exceedingly proud. But at the same time, bewildered—how could you know so much about the sufferings of the poor?'

'Has Caroline never told you about her father's book?' Orelia asked.

The Marquis shook his head.

'I had no idea the Earl was a writer!'

'He was not until he became interested in the horrifying conditions in the coalmines,' Orelia answered. 'Then he became acquainted with William Cobbett.'

'Do you mean the Reformer, the man who was imprisoned a few years ago by the Government for denouncing the flogging of mutineers?'

'Yes, that is who I mean,' Orelia answered, 'and when my Uncle and I came to London in 1817 we spent a great deal of time with Mr. Cobbett. It was he who told us about the Flash Houses and showed us the one in St. Giles. I could not go inside, of course, but I waited in the carriage and saw those miserable children going in and out.'

'Cobbett took you to St. Giles?' the Marquis ejaculated. 'He must have been demented!'

Orelia smiled.

'I think he hardly noticed that I existed. He was so intent in converting my Uncle to his way of thinking! After that we had letters from him, from Mr. Henry Grey Bennett, and many other Radicals, Reformers and Protesters, who were all interested in helping my Uncle collect material for the book he was writing.'

She gave a little sigh.

'It will now never be finished, and that is why I thought I could perhaps help the causes he championed so wholeheartedly by writing a few verses which would be easy for people to read and understand.'

'They have already caused quite a stir in the House of Commons and the House of Lords,' the Marquis said.

'Have they really?' Orelia cried.

'But it must never be known that you are the author,' the Marquis said sternly. 'You would be ostracised, my darling, because people would be horrified that you know so much and have dared to denounce the Government's idle indifference to such social injustices!'

'Yes, I can see that,' Orelia said. 'But I can go on writing?'

She did not realise that already she was giving him the right to direct her life, asking his permission, anxious to do only what he wished her to do.

'As long as you do not concern yourself too closely or become involved personally in such unsavoury matters,' the Marquis replied. 'Because you are so beautiful, so innocent, so unspoilt, it is sacrilege to think of your coming close to anything that is bestial or criminal!'

'I will live in the country!' Orelia promised.

'So that I shall never see you?' he asked. 'God above! Can you imagine what it will be like when I have not even the solace of seeing your face, of hearing your voice, of knowing that even if I must not touch you, that you are near to me!'

'It would be wiser for us not to see each . . . other,' Orelia said gently. 'Sooner or later we might break under the strain or . . . betray ourselves. I must never hurt Caroline.'

'Caroline! Caroline! She stands between us like an angel with a flaming sword,' the Marquis said, 'and I have no one to blame but myself!'

'There is no point in . . . regrets,' Orelia said, 'and, My Lord, I want you to know that I shall always be grateful because we met and because I know that you . . . love me a . . . little. That will sustain and help me through the rest of my life.'

'It may be enough for you,' the Marquis said, 'but I assure you, my precious darling, it is not enough for me. All I can think is, that life as far as I am concerned will be a desolate empty wilderness. And I can only pray that I shall not live too long!'

'No! No, you must not say that!' Orelia cried.

Without thinking of what she was doing, she moved towards him and put out her hands. He looked at her and then he said harshly:

'Do not drive me too far, Orelia. I am only human,

and where you are concerned I am suffering in a hell so dark, so utterly without hope, that the only thing I shall pray for is oblivion!'

Orelia's hands dropped to her sides. Then as she looked up at him, the tears coming to her eyes because she could not bear to hear the agony in his voice, he turned and went from the room, slamming the door behind him.

For some moments she sat where he had left her, staring at the closed door, trying to realise what had happened.

Then slowly she sank down by the side of a chair and laid her face against the soft brocade of the seat.

He loved her! Somehow everything else seemed to disappear but this one overwhelming thought. He loved her! As he had never loved a woman before . . .

It was later that day that Orelia learnt from Caroline that the Marquis had been called to the country on matters requiring his immediate attention.

She was well aware that he had gone away because he must fight for control of himself, and that for the moment he felt that he could face neither her nor Caroline.

She found it extremely difficult to behave normally; to listen to Caroline eulogising the attractions of the Ambassador; to chatter to the Duchess on social matters; and take care that no one should suspect that she was any different from the girl they had met earlier in the day.

But Orelia knew she was different. It seemed to her that her whole life had changed.

Before she had felt alone—afraid and a little apart from other people. Now, even though she could not see him, even though she knew they must not so much as touch each other's hands, she felt she was close to the Marquis.

Their love made them one—a man and a woman who each had found the other half of themselves and who were complete in the glory and perfection of their love!

She thought of him all the time, moving about as if she were in a dream. She did in fact dream of him that night.

The whole world seemed to hold nothing but him: the sound of his voice; the words in which he had spoken to her of his love; the expression on his face, and the look in his eyes.

'I love him,' she whispered, over and over again into her pillow, and felt herself thrill and thrill again because she knew he loved her in return.

The following day the Marquis had not returned and Caroline with glee went off to spend her time with the Ambassador.

There were now only two whole days left before she was to be married in St. George's Church, Hanover Square.

On Tuesday morning Orelia learnt that the Marquis had returned late on the previous night after they had all gone to bed. She felt herself quiver at the thought of seeing him again!

Then she told herself sternly that she must be the stronger of the two.

She must contrive somehow to make the Marquis feel that he could be happy with Caroline even though they could not know the ecstasy and wonder of perfect love.

'I must not think of myself!' Orelia thought over and over again.

But it was hard not to start at every opening of the door, not to listen for the sound of one voice speaking in that great house, not to yearn with an almost inexpressible longing for a sight of the Marquis's broad shoulders and of his face, on which she felt she knew every line, every expression.

But there was no sign of His Lordship when she came downstairs.

Then as she waited alone in the Salon for the Duchess to appear, Caroline came hurrying towards her wearing her prettiest bonnet.

'Dearest, I have just learnt that His Lordship has left for Epsom,' she said in a low voice. 'He will be away all day inspecting the horses that he has there in training! I too shall be out, so keep Her Grace from being curious!'

'I need not ask where you are going, Caroline!' Orelia replied. 'But do you realise you are being married the day after tomorrow?'

'Yes, I know,' Caroline answered. 'And that is why it is such a wonderful opportunity for me to be with Adelco—perhaps for the last time!'

'Caroline, be careful!' Orelia begged.

'We shall be very careful,' Caroline answered. 'Adelco has a friend who lives in Chelsea. He has lent us his lodgings for the day. He is away and his servants have been given the time off. There will be nobody there and Adelco and I can be alone together!'

'Caroline, this is madness!' Orelia exclaimed.

'On the contrary, it is exciting, adventurous, and something I want to do very much,' Caroline smiled.

She kissed Orelia and added:

'Keep the old Dragon amused. I am leaving now before she can ask me too many questions!'

Before Orelia could protest further, Caroline had gone, leaving behind only a fleeting vision of an entrancing, mischievous face and the fragrance of gardenias.

The Duchess was not surprisingly extremely curious as to where Caroline was spending the day.

'She said she had some appointments,' Orelia said evasively. 'But perhaps she has accompanied His Lordship.'

'Really, I might be told what is happening!' the Duchess said sourly. 'A whole coachload of wedding presents has arrived and although the secretaries are listing them, Caroline should at least look at what she has been given! You would think she would be interested!'

'I think she is, Ma'am,' Orelia replied, 'but it seems that there are always a great number of things to do before a wedding.'

'And how would you know?' the Duchess asked sarcastically.

Her Grace continued to carp and be querulous and

disagreeable all through the morning. She and Orelia
had an early, light luncheon as Her Grace said she
wished in the afternoon to visit a friend who lived in
Hampstead.

Orelia was therefore ready and waiting in the Hall by
one o'clock, wearing a new driving-coat of very pale
turquoise blue crêpe.

Her bonnet was trimmed with ribbons of the same
colour and had a lace insert inside the brim which
framed her face and gave her an almost childlike look.

The Duchess came downstairs arrayed in violet satin,
a large number of ostrich plumes of the same hue on
her bonnet and wearing a sable-trimmed wrap. She
was carrying a small parcel.

It looked like a book and idly Orelia speculated as to
what present she might be taking her friend.

The carriage was drawn up at the front door; Willand was in attendance and the footman had rolled out
the red carpet on which they would step across the
pavement.

Orelia followed the Duchess, then, as they reached
the door, Her Grace stopped.

'I see over there,' she said in a low voice so that only
Orelia could hear, 'the landau belonging to my old
friend, the Countess of Berrington. I wonder, Orelia, if
you would be kind enough to take this present and give
it to her.'

She pointed her finger.

'As you see, her carriage has stopped a little way
down the road. She has quarrelled with His Lordship
and will not enter the house. Tell her how much I am
looking forward to seeing her at the wedding.'

As she spoke the Duchess pressed the parcel into
Orelia's hands, and obediently she hurried down the
pavement to where she saw a landau had drawn up at
the side of the road.

There was a footman in a high cockaded hat and
wearing a dark livery standing with his hand on a
silver handle; and at Orelia's approach he opened the
door wide.

She bent forward to look into the landau, and speak

to the Countess. But the blinds were drawn and the carriage was in darkness. She tried to peer through the gloom, beginning:

"Her Grace has sent . . ."

Then as she spoke she suddenly felt herself propelled violently forward into the carriage.

The door was slammed and even as she cried out, startled and breathless from the ruthlessness with which she had been handled, the horses started up and the carriage moved away.

For a moment Orelia could hardly realise what was happening.

'Stop! There is some mistake . . .' she began.

She realised she was alone in the carriage. She was sprawled half across the floor, half across the seat, and picking herself up, she sat for a moment to try to get her breath.

Then she banged on the front of the carriage which backed onto the box on which the Coachmen were sitting.

'Stop! Stop!' she called again.

The horses seemed merely to move faster and Orelia shouted: 'Help! Stop! Stop! Help!'

The swaying coach made her put out her hands to steady herself and it was then, in the faint light, that she saw a candle-lantern and realised there was a large crest emblazoned on its silver surface.

Holding on to the top of the seat because the coach was moving at an unprecedented speed, she reached up and lifted up one of the blinds.

As the sunlight entered the carriage she saw the crest only too clearly, and knew to whom it belonged.

With a start of sheer terror and breathless with a rising panic Orelia realised what was happening! She had been abducted! And by Lord Rotherton!

'Stop! Stop!' she cried again desperately and realised how ineffective her voice was.

Indeed, above the sounds of the hooves and the noise of the wheels moving over the cobbled streets, it was doubtful that she would be heard even by anyone who wished to listen!

She reached out to try the handles of the door. They were travelling so fast that she felt that if she did fling herself out through an open door, there was every chance of her being badly damaged.

But anything was better than being in the power of Lord Rotherton!

The handles would not move, and as she tried them both she knew that the doors were locked. She lifted up the blind on the other window.

They had already passed Hyde Park Corner and were now journeying down side-streets in which there seemed few passers-by.

Orelia lifted up her clenched hands to hammer on the window, then dropped them again.

What was the point? Even if she did attract the attention of some Lady or Gentleman walking on the pavement, what could they do?

And at the speed at which the landau was travelling, before anyone could realise what was happening, the horses would be almost out of sight. Besides, who was likely to interfere with a carriage belonging to a member of the Quality?

She sat back on the seat and tried to think calmly and sensibly about her predicament.

She could hardly credit that any Gentleman of Lord Rotherton's standing actually meant to harm her or to carry her away where she would eventually be able to get in touch with the Duchess or Caroline.

Yet with a sinking heart she remembered the fanatical look in his face at Carlton House. He had told her that night that he intended to make her his wife, or, if she preferred, his mistress!

With a tremor of fear Orelia wondered now if that was to be her fate!

She had always feared him. She had always hated him and the evil that she felt exuded from him, and now she knew that her instinct had been right—he was evil! And the feeling that she could not escape him had not been unfounded.

The landau was travelling so fast that Orelia wondered how any coachman dared to push his horses so brutally.

Then she knew that it was no ordinary coachman who was driving—it was Lord Rotherton himself!

He was known as a Nonpareil when it came to tooling a four-in-hand, and Orelia bit back a little cry of horror as she realised on looking out of the window that they were already outside the City and were travelling along country roads.

'Where can he be taking me?' she wondered.

How, if he were conveying her to the depths of the country, was she to escape?

She put her hands up to her face and now she was trembling violently. Then she took a deep breath and told herself that her only hope was to be brave.

If she panicked it would get her nowhere—she was far too small and weak to fight him physically.

She must keep all her wits about her! She must think how she could get away before he could ravish her! If not she would be his for ever!

She thought of the Marquis and it gave her courage. Then she remembered Caroline telling her that Lord Rotherton had a fine Estate near Guildford. That was where he would be taking her, to Guildford!

But Guildford was some way from London and one thing was certain, that at the rate he was driving they would have to change horses somewhere along the route.

That stoppage, Orelia thought, would offer her only chance of escape.

Yet with a shudder she had a vision of herself running away and Lord Rotherton sending his servants to catch her, and carrying her back forcibly to the carriage!

She gave a little sob although her eyes were dry. Then she saw lying on the floor of the carriage the parcel she had been carrying in her hands when she had been thrown so unceremoniously in through the open door.

The parcel the Duchess had asked her to give to her friend!

She knew now that it was the Duchess who had intrigued with Lord Rotherton! He must have asked her for her help that night at Carlton House, when she had looked back and seen them sitting together, side by side, talking so intently.

It was the Duchess who had arranged the exact time when they would leave Ryde House and Lord Rotherton's landau would be waiting.

Angry at the realisation of such perfidy, Orelia picked up the parcel on the floor and tore it open. Inside there was nothing, only some folded writing paper neatly parcelled together to make a package.

'How dare she do such a thing?' Orelia asked aloud, and wondered what explanation the Duchess would make for her absence to Caroline and the Marquis.

She knew the answer! The Dowager would tell them that she had deliberately run away with Lord Rotherton.

She would say that she had changed her mind and had decided after all to accept Lord Rotherton's offer. Not wishing to spoil or diminish the excitement of Caroline's wedding on Thursday, she had agreed to be married secretly and quietly without anyone being present.

She could almost hear the Duchess relating such a tale. Caroline would be surprised, but perhaps not suspicious.

Only the Marquis would know it was not true, and yet what could he do? Even if he came in search of her he would be too late.

By the time she was rescued she would have had no alternative but to agree to marry Lord Rotherton, provided he still made her the offer!

'I would rather die!' Orelia whispered to herself, and knew that if indeed there was no escape, then she must kill herself.

But somehow she could not yet give way to despair. She could not believe that there was not some way in which she could outwit Lord Rotherton, even though for the moment he appeared to hold every card in his hand.

Quite simply, like a child who is frightened of the dark, Orelia prayed for help.

She had never in the past prayed in sheer desperation, but she had always found comfort and been given some answer to what she had asked of her God.

'Help me!' she prayed now. 'Help me to escape from this man. Even if my love for the Marquis is wrong, this would be a degradation beyond words! This would make a mockery of everything that is beautiful and good and holy in love. Help me, please God, help me!'

The landau was swaying from side to side as they sped down the main road. The ground was dry and they were, Orelia knew, raising great clouds of dust behind them.

She looked out of the carriage wondering how long it would take to reach the place where they would change horses. Perhaps Lord Rotherton would speak to her there. Perhaps he would reveal where he was taking her!

She leaned forward to look out of the carriage. Perhaps Guildford would be marked on a signpost and she would know how much longer they would have to drive at this mad pace!

They passed a milestone and as they did so Orelia's heart gave a sudden leap, for written on it quite clearly was—'Epsom 5 miles'.

She gave a cry. Epsom! That was where the Marquis was! That was where Caroline said he was spending the day, inspecting his horses! Epsom! And she had the feeling that it was there that Lord Rotherton would change horses.

"Help me! Oh, God, help me!" she prayed again.

Idea after idea of what she could say, what she should do, ran through her mind. She had to have a plan! She had to find some way in which she could be free of the carriage and be given an opportunity to find the Marquis!

His stables must be well-known to everyone at Epsom; but there was Lord Rotherton and another man on the box to prevent her from escaping!

She wondered why His Lordship had driven the horses himself rather than sit beside her in the landau?

Then she thought it was because he was driven by an urgency to convey her as speedily as possible to his house, to waste no time in journeying to a place where he could take of her what he desired. And perhaps in some obscure manner he wished to impress her with his driving.

There was no doubt that he was a Corinthian. Few men could have driven with such speed or handled the ribbons so skilfully as he was doing now!

At the same time, Orelia thought, it was only a madman who would lock a woman he pretended to love alone in a swaying carriage for a journey that would take nearly two hours!

Surely he must realise that a woman of any sensibility would be in a state of agitation, if not hysteria, at such treatment?

And then Orelia thought that perhaps that was what he intended! He wanted to frighten her! He wanted her to feel that she could not escape, that he was the master, and that in his power she was as helpless as any slave in an Eastern market-place!

'He is bestial!' she told herself.

But she thought it was no use wasting time on recriminations. She had to have a plan of escape! She must think of one!

'Oh God help me!' she prayed again. 'Help me to think of something I can say; anything which will help me to escape! If not, wrong though it may be to take one's life, I must die! For I could not live with such a man or survive having been touched by him!'

She shivered at the thought. She could already see Lord Rotherton's dark eyes blazing into hers, the thickness of his lips as he sought her mouth, the greedy brutality of his hands.

Sternly, with an effort of will that was almost superhuman, Orelia stopped the rising panic within herself. Such thoughts, she knew, would get her nowhere! She had to think! They were getting near to Epsom!

If only she could reach the Marquis!

She thought of the sense of peace and security that had come to her that night at Carlton House when she had run away from Lord Rotherton and seen the Marquis standing on the terrace looking up at the sky!

He had seemed to her then like a quiet haven after a tumultuous tempest at sea. She had known as she reached him that she was safe; she had known that her terrors were dispelled and she was no longer afraid.

'Think of me now! I want you! I want you!' she called from her heart.

She felt her whole being reach out towards him, as if she sent her heart winging towards his. She tried to pretend that he was near her, that he was talking to her, calming her fears and telling her what to do.

'What shall I do?' she whispered aloud. 'Oh my love, tell me! Tell me!'

She shut her eyes and imagined he was beside her. She could see his face, the twist of his lips, and felt herself quiver because he was so close.

The horses began to slow their pace. Orelia opened her eyes. They were on the outskirts of Epsom. There were houses and traffic in the narrow streets.

They were going slower still, and a moment later they turned under the archway of a Coaching House Yard. Orelia could see the name on the swinging sign board—'The Spread Eagle'.

It was then, like a sudden light illuminating the darkness, that she knew what she must do.

10

Lord Rotherton stepped down from the box of his carriage with a smile of satisfaction on his face.

He was convinced that he had beaten the record from London to Epsom, and he also knew triumphantly that he had outwitted the Marquis of Ryde and that Orelia would be his wife in a few hours' time.

He had every intention of marrying her, because once she was legally his no power on earth, including that of the Marquis, could take her away from him.

Everything had gone according to plan; he watched his sweating horses being removed from the shafts by his own grooms and knew that four equally fine bloodstock from his stables were waiting to take their place.

He nodded to the footman who had descended from the box at the same time as himself, the man unlocked the carriage door and Lord Rotherton opened it.

For one incredulous moment he thought that Orelia had escaped, and then he saw that she was lying on the floor, her head back against the seat, her eyes closed.

'Are you ill?' he asked.

She opened her eyes slowly, as if with an effort.

'It is . . . the swaying . . . of the . . . coach,' she answered in a voice that was hardly audible. 'I am . . . sick. Please . . . can I lie . . . down for . . . a few . . . moments?'

'Carriage-sick!' he ejaculated, 'that is something I had not anticipated!'

Then as he looked at her white face and limp body he seemed to come to a decision.

'Very well!' he said. 'I will give you ten minutes. A little brandy should revive you!'

He put out his hands and pulled her to her feet. Although she had to prevent herself from shuddering at his touch, she allowed him to help her stagger the few steps to the door of the Inn.

The landlord was waiting for them, bowing obsequiously.

'The Lady is indisposed,' Lord Rotherton said sharply. 'Have her shown to the best bedchamber and send up a glass of your finest brandy immediately.'

'Very good, M'Lord, at once, M'Lord,' the Innkeeper replied, and looking over his shoulder he shouted: 'Moll!'

Almost immediately a young, rosy-cheeked girl appeared wearing a mob-cap and a spotless white apron over her print dress.

She put her arm round Orelia, helped her up the narrow oak staircase and opened the door into a pleasant bedroom with windows looking out into the garden.

No sooner were they inside than Orelia freed herself from Moll's arm and turning round moved quickly to lock the door behind them.

'Listen,' she said. 'I need your help!'

The girl looked at her in surprise.

'I am being abducted by this Gentleman against my will,' Orelia explained, 'and I want you to find someone who will take a note to the stables of the Marquis of Ryde. Do you know where they are?'

'Nay, Ma'am,' Moll replied, 'but Jim'll know!'

'Who is Jim?' Orelia asked, at the same time moving across the room to sit down at the dressing-table.

Here she drew from her reticule and smoothed out a piece of the writing paper which the Duchess had enclosed in the false parcel. Then she took out a small painted box that Caroline had given her as a present.

It was a beauty box such as Ladies of Fashion

carried to repair their complexions during the day or at a dance.

It contained a small mirror besides a place for rouge and another for face-powder. And more important than those, as far as Orelia was now concerned, there was a tiny pencil with which to darken an arched eyebrow.

Quickly she wrote on the paper:

'Lord Rotherton is conveying me to his House near Guildford. I am at the Moment at the Spread Eagle Inn. Please Save me, My Lord.'

She signed her name, folded the paper, and wrote on the outside in block capitals: 'The Most Noble Marquis of Ryde.'

She handed it to Moll, who was watching her with astonishment. Then opening her purse, Orelia took out a sovereign.

'Give this to Jim,' she said, 'and tell him that there will be another sovereign waiting for him if he is quick enough to reach the Marquis before he returns to London.'

'He'll find 'is Lordship,' Moll said confidently. 'That be a lot o' money to Jim!'

'And here is the same amount for yourself,' Orelia said, placing a gold coin in the girl's hand.

'Oh, Ma'am! 'Tis more than I expects t'earn in months,' Moll cried and turned towards the door.

'Wait a moment,' Orelia said. 'You must impress on Jim that on no account must he let anyone see that note or tell any of the men in the yard where he is going. And tell him to hurry, hurry! It is of the utmost import!'

'I'll tell 'im,' Moll answered.

'And if the Gentleman down below asks any questions,' Orelia said, 'inform him that I am extremely ill.'

'I'll do as ye says, Ma'am,' Moll replied and hurried from the room, leaving Orelia alone.

She crossed to the basin to wash her hands and face, feeling that somehow she must be unclean from having been in close proximity to Lord Rotherton. Then as she lay down on the bed, she prayed that Jim might find the Marquis.

She was sure in her heart that he would save her. She felt that her cry of help must have winged its way towards him and that intuitively he would be aware that something was amiss. But would he be prepared to trust his instinct?

She only knew that loving him as she did, to be touched by any other man, especially Lord Rotherton, was a humiliation so vile, so beastly, that she felt almost as if she might lose her sanity at the thought.

She heard voices at the bottom of the stairs and realised that Lord Rotherton was speaking to Moll. She heard the girl reply, although she could not quite hear what they were saying. A moment later Moll came into the room carrying a glass of brandy.

Orelia waited until the door was shut before she asked in a whisper:

"Is it all right? Did Jim understand?"

' 'E knows th' Ryde Stables,' Moll replied, 'and as there be a need for 'urry 'e's a taken 'is 'orse, though it be not far to walk!'

'Thank you,' Orelia said with a sigh of relief.

'Th' Gentleman below says ye must be a leaving,' Moll continued.

'Go downstairs and tell him that I am so ill you think it would be wise to send for a Doctor,' Orelia said.

'I'll tell 'im,' Moll answered, 'though I doubts, Ma'am, if 'e'll a listen to I.'

She went obediently down the stairs and Orelia lay back. As she feared, a few moments later she heard Lord Rotherton's footsteps. He knocked perfunctorily, opening the door at the same time.

'What is the matter with you?' he demanded. 'A little carriage-sickness has never hurt anyone! Come along, Orelia, the Parson is waiting to marry us!'

Orelia opened her eyes slowly.

'The . . . Parson?' she questioned in a hesitating voice.

'That is what I said,' Lord Rotherton answered.
'And I have never met a woman who did not feel better
at the sight of a wedding-ring on her finger!'

'You are well aware I have no wish to . . . marry
you, My Lord,' Orelia answered.

'But I wish to marry you,' he said. 'Come along,
Orelia. There will be plenty of time to rest after the
ceremony!'

He paused for a moment, his eyes flickering over her
body lying on the bed in front of him. They did not
miss the sweet swelling of her breasts or the soft curve
of her hips.

'That is—if I let you,' he added almost beneath
his breath.

Orelia's eyes were closed. She could feel the evil
emanating from him and knew that the lust of his
desire possessed him.

'Are you going to walk to the carriage?' he asked.
'Or would you prefer that I carry you in my arms?'

Almost instinctively she shrank from the idea and
said quickly, too quickly:

'I will walk!'

He laughed, as if he sensed that her sickness was
more of a pretence than the reality.

'Still running away, Orelia?' he asked softly. 'It is
too late! I told you that I always get what I want!'

Orelia rose from the bed and picked up her bonnet.

'I have nothing to say to you, My Lord,' she said,
'except that I did not believe that any so-called Gentleman could behave in such a despicable manner to a
woman alone and defenceless.'

'You forget,' he said jeeringly, 'that I am prepared to
marry you. Other men might not offer you that!'

'If you expect me to acquiesce in becoming your
wife at any ceremony or in front of any clergyman,
you are mistaken!' Orelia retorted.

'I doubt that you will say that in a few hours' time,'
Lord Rotherton answered.

There was something in the way he spoke, in the
narrowing of his eyes, which made her shrink away

from him as if he were a poisonous reptile. Then, as
he saw the fear on her face, he laughed.

'You will be grateful to me for making an honest
woman of you,' he mocked, and taking her arm he
led her towards the door.

There was nothing Orelia could do but step into the
carriage.

She had a quick glance at the fresh horses, then
saw with a sinking of her heart that there was a
Coachman holding the reins.

As she had anticipated, Lord Rotherton got into the
carriage and sat down beside her. The footman jumped
up on the box, and the Coachman drove the horses out
of the yard and onto the main road.

Orelia shrank back in the corner of the landau, apprehensive and fearful, wondering desperately how
long it would take Jim to find the Marquis, and if perhaps by some cruel stroke of fate he had in fact already left Epsom for London.

She was acutely conscious of Lord Rotherton's presence.

He sat watching her with that look in his eyes which
always made her afraid—until, as the horses quickened
their pace, he reached out his arms and drew her close
to him.

'Do not dare touch me!' Orelia cried. She tried to
fight him off with her hands, and realised how utterly
helpless she was against his superior strength and the
hunger of his lips.

She twisted and turned, but slowly and relentlessly
he drew her close. One hand was imprisoned against
his body, the other held immobile by the arm which
encircled her, leaving His Lordship's right hand free.

He took her chin between his fingers and turned
her face up to his.

'So valiant, but so utterly ineffective,' he smiled.

Then his lips came down on hers and she felt a
shudder of horror go through her. She felt as if he
dragged her down into the depths of darkness and
degradation.

There was something horrible in the hot passion of
his lips; and then as she tried to move but found it
impossible, she felt his hand fumbling beneath her coat
at the soft muslin which covered her breasts.

She tried to fight herself free, tried despairingly to
move her lips from his, but she was powerless.

The horror of it, the feeling of his hands, the manner
in which he seemed to sap her strength and hold her
utterly and frighteningly captive, made her feel as if
she must faint.

Then as everything seemed to go dark, the horses
were suddenly drawn to a standstill, and there was a
sound of voices.

Lord Rotherton raised his lips from Orelia's, his hold
on her slackened, and in a second she had twisted herself free and shrank away from him to a corner of the
carriage. Even as she did so the door opened.

'What the devil is happening?' Lord Rotherton asked
furiously of the footman.

'There are two Gentlemen on horseback across the
road, M'Lord, and one of them wishes to speak with
Your Lordship.'

'Tell him to go to Hell!' Lord Rotherton said. 'I
will speak with no one! Drive on!'

'I think not, Rotherton,' a deep voice said, and
Orelia gave a little cry of joy.

It was the Marquis! He had come to save her as she
knew he would once he learnt of her predicament!

'Ryde!' she heard Lord Rotherton ejaculate.

'Come outside, I wish to speak to you!' the Marquis
said, and Orelia knew by the tone of his voice how incensed he was.

Just for a moment she thought Lord Rotherton would
refuse, and then he answered.

'Very well, I will hear what you have to say, Ryde.'

He rose as if he would get out of the landau. But as
he did so he tipped up the seat in front. Beneath it was
a deep box which Orelia remembered now was often
used by Gentlemen in which to hide their valuables
from Highwaymen.

Lord Rotherton put in his hand and drew out a pistol.

It was all done very quickly, and then as he transferred the pistol to his other hand, Orelia realised what he was about to do.

She gave a scream of sheer terror just as Lord Rotherton aimed the pistol at the Marquis.

'Take care! Take care!' she cried.

Swiftly the Marquis moved to one side just as Lord Rotherton fired. The shot went wide and then, before Lord Rotherton could fire again, the Marquis had seized his arm and twisted the pistol from him so it fell onto the road.

Then he dragged Lord Rotherton clear of the carriage and, with one terrific punch of his right hand, caught him on the chin.

Lord Rotherton half sprawled on his knees but he rose to his feet and rushed at the Marquis like an infuriated bull.

Once again the Marquis floored him with a tremendous punch, and now a long trickle of blood ran from Lord Rotherton's nose and down over his mouth.

White with rage, it was doubtful if he even felt the pain of it, as once again he rose to his feet. The Marquis in an expert fashion warded off his milling fists and floored him for the third time!

This time Lord Rotherton lay spread-eagled in the dust and did not move!

The Marquis seized him however and dragged him by the collar onto his feet.

'You will not get away with it as easy as that, you swine!' he scowled and he hit him again and yet again so that the blood was streaming down his face and both his eyes were closed.

It was only when Lord Rotherton finally fell face-forward and was obviously unconscious, that the Gentleman who had been sitting astride the other horse dismounted and touched the Marquis's arm.

'That is enough, Darius!'

'I want to kill the cur!' the Marquis replied, his words as grim as his face.

'There would be too much explaining to do,' his friend said, 'and besides, Rotherton is finished. He

drew a pistol on an unarmed man and that is unforgivable. I will see to it that no one will speak to him in
future.'

'If I ever set eyes on him again,' the Marquis said, 'I
will finish the job you are preventing me from com-
pleting at this moment.'

He drew his handkerchief from his pocket as he
spoke and wiped the blood from his knuckles.

As he did so there was a flurry of wheels and a
black and yellow Phaeton came speeding down the
road drawn by four well-matched chestnuts.

The Marquis glanced towards it and went to the door
of the landau. Orelia was standing on the step, her
eyes wide in her pale face, but with a light in them
that was almost indescribable.

'You . . . came!' she whispered softly as the Marquis
reached her side.

It seemed as if he hardly glanced at her.

'Are you well enough to travel in my Phaeton?' he
asked.

'But . . . of course,' she answered.

She picked up her bonnet as she spoke and hastily
put it on her head, tying the ribbons under her chin.
The Marquis assisted her from the carriage and led her
to the Phaeton, helping her up onto the high seat.

Then as he took the reins from his groom, he said:

'Ride Thunder home behind us, Harris.'

'Very good, M'Lord.'

The Marquis smiled at his friend.

'Thank you, Charlie. I am much obliged. I will do
the same for you one day!'

'I will hold you to that!' his friend grinned, and
turned to remount his horse.

The Marquis drove off. He never even glanced at the
body of Lord Rotherton lying face-downwards in the
road, or at the consternation on the faces of his servants.

Orelia found she was fighting for her breath, but
they had travelled for nearly a mile before the Marquis
said:

'Did he—hurt you?'

She understood what he asked, and replied:

'No, no . . . he drove the horses . . . himself until we reached . . . Epsom . . . it was only just now . . . that he . . .'

She paused, finding no words to express what had occurred.

The Marquis said nothing, and as they travelled onwards Orelia felt her agitation subsiding. Her fear had gone. She had known when she heard his voice that she was safe.

She had only been stricken by the horror of that moment when she thought Lord Rotherton would shoot him down.

But now she was beside him! He was there! He had come to save her as she had known he would do!

They passed through Epsom and then about two miles on the other side the Marquis drew up at a small black and white Inn standing in a hamlet of a few thatched cottages.

'I think we could both do with a glass of wine,' he said quietly.

An ostler ran to hold the chestnuts and the Marquis helped Orelia down from the Phaeton. Harris, coming behind them, swung himself from the black stallion that the Marquis had been riding.

They were shown into a small private parlour and the Marquis ordered wine and some cold meats. Then, as the door closed behind the Landlord, it seemed to Orelia that he looked at her for the first time.

She had taken off her bonnet and her driving-coat as he ordered the food and wine. In her turquoise-blue gown, which was a little torn at the neck by Lord Rotherton's rough fingers, she looked very small and very defenceless.

Their eyes met across the room. Without realising what she was doing, without conscious thought, Orelia moved towards the Marquis and hid her face against his shoulder.

'I thought . . . that he would . . . kill . . . you,' she whispered, and as his arms went round her, he felt her tremble.

'Your cry saved my life,' the Marquis answered. 'But I think, Orelia, that I was not meant to die, because you had need of me.'

'I prayed . . . that you . . . would come. I felt . . . that you must . . . know what was . . . happening to . . . me,' Orelia whispered.

'It is strange that you should say that,' the Marquis replied in his deep voice. 'I have been uneasy all day. I felt that something was wrong. I was in a hurry to return to London, perhaps to see you!'

'I knew it!' Orelia said. 'I knew . . . that I could not . . . want you so . . . desperately and . . . you not be . . . aware of it!'

His arms tightened round her and then he said quietly:

'Orelia, come away with me? We will be married abroad. People will talk for a short while, but by the time we return to England it will all be forgotten.'

He felt her draw in her breath, and as if she realised for the first time that she was close against him, she moved away.

He did not attempt to stop her and she stood holding on to the edge of the wooden mantelshelf, staring into the empty fireplace.

'Caro . . . line!' she said almost inaudibly.

'Caroline's pride will be hurt,' the Marquis answered, 'but doubtless she will continue to console herself with the Ambassador or someone like him.'

Orelia's eyes went to his face.

'You knew?' she asked.

'Do you really think that I am such a fool, so corkbrained, that the amateurish theatricals enacted by Caroline and Savelli for my benefit could deceive me?'

'You are not . . . angry with . . . Caroline?' Orelia asked anxiously.

'Angry?' the Marquis questioned. 'Who am I to sit in judgement on Caroline? She may give her lips and her body to the Ambassador, but I, my darling, have given you my heart and soul.'

His voice was bitter as he added:

'Not that they are of any great value!'

'To me . . . they mean . . . everything in the . . . world,' Orelia replied very softly.

The Marquis's arms went out towards her, but at that moment the door opened and the Landlord came in with wine and a trayful of cold meats. He set it down on the table, opened the wine, and looked towards the Marquis.

'We will wait on ourselves,' the Marquis said. 'We do not wish to be disturbed.'

'Very good, M'Lord.'

The man went from the room and shut the door behind him. Orelia moved into the bow-window which looked out onto a garden bright with flowers. The bees were buzzing among the blossom; otherwise it was very quiet.

The Marquis did not speak, and after a moment she turned to face him.

'This will be the first time, My Lord,' she said, 'that we have ever had a meal together . . . alone. Could we not pretend just for a short time that we are two ordinary people who have met each other and who have . . . an affection for . . . each other?'

He did not answer and she went on:

'Let us pretend that there are no . . . horrors behind us and no . . . unhappiness ahead. There is just today and . . . us.'

There was a note of pleading in her voice and the Marquis capitulated to it.

'Just today, just this moment,' he said. 'And two people—very much in love, Orelia!'

He took her hand as he spoke and she thought that he would kiss it, but instead he looked down at it, holding it in his.

'Such a little hand,' he said softly, 'and yet it holds everything that for me is worth having.'

She moved away from him towards the table. They sat down and then, as if he entered into the game which she had asked of him, the Marquis began to talk of his horses, and the races he hoped to win at Ascot; or his Stable's prospects for next year.

Orelia told him how the publishers had asked her for

another book, and how she was considering on what subjects she might write.

But all the time they were talking, as their eyes met each other's, there were sudden pauses, moments when it did not seem to matter what they said while their hearts were listening to a very different conversation taking place between them.

Neither of them managed to eat much and finally the Marquis leant back in his chair, a glass of wine in his hand.

He looked so elegant, so at ease, just as he did at the head of his dining-table, that Orelia felt her heart turn over at the sight of him.

'And now, my darling,' he said, 'I have to hear what happened. I know you do not wish to speak of it, but I must know.'

'Can we not . . . forget it?' Orelia asked, thinking how embarrassing it would be to tell the Marquis what part his Grandmother had played.

And yet how without relating the truth could she explain why she had entered the landau in the first place?

'I have to know,' the Marquis repeated.

Hesitatingly, stumbling over the words, Orelia told him what had happened. She knew that with his pride in the family honour the knowledge would humiliate him.

Then she went on quickly to say how she had deceived Lord Rotherton by pretending to be carriage-sick, how she had written the note in the bedroom and asked that it should be taken to his stables.

'Oh, I forgot!' she exclaimed. 'I promised Jim that he should have another sovereign if he found you quickly!'

'Do not worry,' the Marquis said. 'I gave him a sovereign. I would have given him a thousand sovereigns if I had had them with me! I just threw him the first coin that came into my hand and galloped across country with Charles following me!'

He drew a deep breath.

'You were safe, my sweet, from the moment I received the note. If we had not seen the carriage travelling along the road, I would have come to Rotherton's house and killed him before he could force you to marry him.'

Orelia drew in a deep breath. The fury in the Marquis's voice was very moving. Then he said:

'I have managed to save you this time, Orelia, but what of the future? What will become of you, my little love? For you cannot live alone! Even a companion, such as I made up my mind to find for you, will not be protection enough!'

His voice sharpened.

'There will always be men who will be maddened by your beauty, who will be determined to make you theirs in one way or another!'

'I shall be safe in the country, where everyone knows me,' Orelia announced. 'And I shall not see many strangers—it is very quiet at Morden Green.'

She tried to smile as she spoke but her eyes met the Marquis's and she could only stare at him spellbound by the expression in his eyes.

'And do you imagine for one moment that I shall be able to think of you in possible danger alone, perhaps unhappy, and not go insane because I cannot be with you?' he asked harshly. 'How can I sleep at night, wondering if you are safe? How can I get through the day when all I want, all I ask of life, is that you should be beside me?'

Orelia's eyes fell before his and her fingers locked and unlocked themselves as she felt herself vibrate to the passion in his voice. Then he went on:

'We said we would behave like two people in love. Very well, Orelia, let me tell you that I am in love, crazily, wildly in love with you! I cannot leave you and know that my only memories are of the miracle when I once touched your lips and when, a few moments ago, I held you in my arms.'

He paused.

'Do you not realise that what I want, more than my

hope of Heaven, is to kiss you as you were meant to be kissed, to feel your lips respond to mine; to kiss your eyes, your cheeks, your neck?'

His voice deepened as he continued.

'And then when I feel you thrill perhaps a little at my touch—to kiss you from the top of your precious, wonderful head, to the soles of your tiny feet! That is what I want, Orelia, and I think that in your heart you want it too.'

His voice died away and now Orelia looked up at him. She saw the fire in his eyes and she felt herself thrill and tremble with the wonder of it.

'I want you,' the Marquis said hoarsely. 'I want you unbearably, Orelia. I cannot leave you. Come away with me!'

He saw as he spoke her hands move upwards to her breasts as if to quell the tumult of her heart. He saw her lips quiver as if they already felt the passion of his kisses, and he saw deep in her wide eyes a sudden flickering flame which reflected the fire in his.

They sat looking at each other, and it seemed to Orelia as if she was already one with him, close against him, surrendering herself utterly to his demands.

'Will you come with me?' the Marquis asked, and his voice was so unsteady she hardly recognised it.

'Please,' she whispered, as if the words burst from her lips, 'please do not make . . . me answer you. I cannot think . . . any more! I can only feel how deeply . . . how tremendously . . . I love you! I am not strong and good where you are concerned . . . I am weak, and I no longer know what is . . . wrong or what is . . . right! I only know that I love you and that . . . nothing else seems to . . . matter in the . . . world . . . !'

She paused for a moment and there were tears behind her voice as she continued.

'I cannot answer you because . . . I do not know what the . . . answer should be! I only want to be with you . . . to make you happy . . . and therefore you must decide for us . . . both! You must do what is . . . best for . . . yourself and for . . . me.'

Her voice died away for a moment and then, almost pathetically, she added:

'I cannot fight . . . you and my . . . heart any . . . longer!'

'Are you asking me, my darling,' the Marquis enquired incredulously, 'to protect you against yourself?'

'I do not know what . . . I am asking,' Orelia replied in a whisper. 'But I will . . . . do what you . . . tell me to . . . do.'

For a long, long moment he stared at her. Then suddenly he rose to his feet so roughly that his chair fell over backwards and crashed to the floor.

'Come!' he said loudly, and his voice was raw, 'I will take you back to London!'

They drove back in silence, the Marquis driving almost as swiftly as Lord Rotherton had driven on the outward journey, save that he had greater expertise and handled his horseflesh more gently.

It was only as they turned down Park Lane and Ryde House lay just ahead of them, that Orelia looked up at him and said softly:

'I love you . . . I will love you all my life . . . but I also . . . respect and . . . honour you.'

He did not answer. She saw his face was grim and set, like a man who faces the Executioner! Then he drew up his horses outside Ryde House. Orelia stepped down and walked into the Hall.

'I have a headache, Willand,' she said to the Butler. 'Will you please inform Her Grace and Lady Caroline that I have retired and that I do not wish to be disturbed under any circumstances.'

'Very good, Miss!'

Orelia walked up the Grand Staircase. At the top she fought back an inclination to turn and look down at the Marquis, who must have entered the Hall behind her.

With a considerable effort of will-power she went straight into her bedroom, closed the door and locked it.

She stood forlornly for a moment inside the room, before she drew off her coat and her bonnet and put them down on a chair.

Then it seemed that something cracked inside her and she ran across to the bed to fling herself face downwards and hide her face in the pillow.

After a moment she began to cry desperately, despairingly, agonisingly, and without hope.

11

'Hell! I look as pale as a ghost!' Caroline ejaculated. 'Give me the rouge-pot, Martha!'

Her maid gave it into her hand as Orelia said:

'You look lovely and very magnificent!'

It was true. Caroline's wedding-gown was white, but as she was a widow, the neck, sleeves and hem were all deeply embroidered with sparkling gold paillettes.

The long train which fell from her shoulders, to be carried by four page-boys, was embroidered all over and edged with white ermine.

On her head she wore the most magnificent tiara in the Ryde collection.

It was almost like a crown and sparkled and glittered with every movement which she made, as did the diamonds which encircled her neck and her wrists.

Her veil, of Brussels lace, framed the darkness of her hair, and waiting for her on a side-table was a bouquet of yellow lilies tied with gold ribbons.

'What I really need is a glass of champagne,' Caroline said. 'Martha, go and order some for me. I cannot think why nobody thinks that I might be in need of something to sustain me in the ordeal which lies ahead!'

'You have very little time,' Orelia said as Martha left the room. 'You must not be late and keep the Marquis waiting.'

'It will do him good!' Caroline retorted.

There was silence and then Orelia said:

'You will be . . . kind to him, will you not, Caroline? He needs kindness and . . . understanding.'

Caroline laughed—it was not a pretty sound.

'Darius needs kindness and understanding!' she mocked. 'And what about me? His Lordship was exceedingly disagreeable to me all yesterday. In fact he was like a bear with a sore head. No one would think that he was an ardent, impatient bridegroom!'

There was no mistaking the sarcastic note in her voice and Orelia said hesitatingly:

'Caroline, you are not . . . unhappy?'

There was a little pause.

'No, of course I am not!' Caroline said defiantly. 'Besides, the honeymoon will not take long and Adelco will be waiting for me on my return. He has sworn to be faithful until he sees me again, and strangely enough I think he will keep his promise.'

'Caroline, you promised me that you would behave properly after you were married,' Orelia cried.

'And what do you call properly?' Caroline asked. 'Besides, I am extremely desirous of seeing Adelco again. That is, if the Beau I left in Paris does not prove more attractive. Remember, we are spending several weeks in the Gay City.'

'What am I to say to you?' Orelia asked.

As if she could not bear the pain that Caroline's words had evoked, she rose to stand behind her cousin looking at her reflection in the mirror.

'I do so want you . . . both to be happy,' she said, almost as if she said it to herself.

'When you and I talk of happiness,' Caroline said, 'we talk of something quite different. For goodness' sake, Orelia, stop sermonising and find out what has happened to the champagne!'

'I will do that,' Orelia answered.

She turned towards the door, but she heard voices outside and turned back again towards Caroline.

'Here it comes,' she said. 'But you really will have to leave for the Church in three minutes' time.'

Even as she spoke the voices outside the door grew louder as if two men were arguing with each other.

Then the door was flung open and a Gentleman stepped into the room, pushing aside a flunkey who was trying to prevent him from doing so.

He was looking somewhat dishevelled; his hair untidy against his sunburnt face, his boots and breeches splashed with mud, his coat grey with dust.

He stood for a moment, saying nothing. Then with a shrill cry which seemed to echo round the room Caroline rose from the dressing-table.

'George! George!' she cried, and ran towards him.

'Caroline!' he exclaimed, catching her in his arms. 'Am I in time? I heard you were to be married.'

'You have come back. Oh, George, you have come back!'

Caroline was half crying, half sobbing, and now, looking down into her face, he was holding her crushingly in his arms.

'My ship docked at Southampton yesterday,' he said, 'and I was told you were to be married. I have ridden all night! Caroline, my dear one, you cannot do this!'

'I thought you were dead!' Caroline sobbed. 'Oh, George, where have you been?'

'Making my fortune!' he answered. 'I am a rich man now, my sweetheart.'

'It does not matter! It is not of the least consequence!' she answered wildly. 'It is you whom I want! I have always loved you, George. I have never loved anyone else!'

'Oh, Caroline, Caroline!' he spoke her name against her lips.

Then he was kissing her wildly and she was clinging to him as if she had been drowning and he had saved her from extinction.

With a start, Orelia, who had been staring in astonishment and frozen into immobility, realised that the Marquis would be leaving for the Church.

Caroline and Lord Faringham locked in each other's arms were quite oblivious of her presence. She hurried past them, pulled open the door and left the room.

She ran to the top of the stairs. Below her, just passing across the marble Hall, was the Marquis.

His carriage was outside—a State Coach which the Ryde family used for the opening of Parliament and all important occasions.

'My . . . Lord!' Orelia called.

The words were choked in her throat and she could not make him hear.

'My Lord!' she managed to say again, and this time, just as he reached the front door, he looked up.

His face was grim and stern, and there was no light in his eyes as he stared at her.

'Caroline would . . . speak with Your . . . Lordship,' Orelia managed to say.

She thought he was about to refuse, and added quickly:

'It is of the utmost import!'

With a gesture of impatience, as if he resented that his plans to leave the house had been disrupted, the Marquis turned and came slowly up the stairs.

He was looking more than usually magnificent, a dozen decorations glittering on his satin coat.

He reached the top of the staircase, and not even looking at Orelia, he passed her by, the lines on his face sharply etched as he went to the door of Caroline's bedroom.

He knocked and turned the handle as he did so. The door opened to reveal Caroline with her arms round Lord Faringham's neck. They were kissing each other passionately!

For a moment it seemed to Orelia as if the Marquis was turned to stone. Then Caroline looked up and saw him.

Her face was radiant. Her eyes, wet with tears, were shining like a thousand candles.

'Darius, forgive me!' she cried, and her voice was a paean of happiness. 'Forgive me, but I cannot marry you!'

It was then that Orelia felt she could not bear to listen anymore, and stepping forward she shut the door behind the Marquis.

It was too poignant! She was too deeply involved to

stand by and know that her whole happiness, her whole future, hung on the Marquis's reply.

She heard a sound behind her, and turning round she saw a footman carrying a silver tray on which reposed a bottle of champagne in an ice-cooler and several crystal glasses.

'Her Ladyship cannot be disturbed at the moment,' Orelia said quickly. 'Put the champagne on the table.'

She indicated a side-table on the landing and as the footman did as he was told, she said:

'I have to journey to the country. Kindly order a travelling landau immediately and tell the Coachman to wait at the back entrance in Park Street.'

The footman was too accustomed to the strange behaviour of the Quality to question why anyone should wish to leave for the country just before the wedding. He merely replied:

'Very good, Miss,' and went to carry out his orders.

Orelia ran to her bedroom. She knew she could not stay, could not wait to see the disruption of the wedding, the commotion it would cause, or alternatively to learn that things had gone too far and that Caroline must marry the Marquis as had been arranged.

After all, the Regent was waiting at the Church; the Reception was already prepared at Carlton House.

She snatched up the cloak she had worn at Morden Green the first time the Marquis had kissed her. She pulled out the bag she had carried the night he had prevented her from running away.

Into it she tumbled, hardly realising what she was doing, her books of poetry, a gown, one or two things that were lying on her dressing-table.

Then remembering that many of her clothes had been left behind at Morden Green, she ran from her bedchamber and down the twisting passages and narrow stairways which led to the servants' quarters.

She saw no one as most of the staff had already left for the Church. Seats in the gallery at St. George's, Hanover Square, had been allotted to them.

Everyone had wished to see their Master married,

and to have the privilege of beholding the glittering Personages of the *Beau Ton,* who would be present at such a fashionable ceremony.

The landau was waiting but there was no one to see Orelia off.

Having told the Coachmen where to go, she lay back against the cushions, her hands clasped together, her eyes closed as she tried to still the tumult of her brain and the excitement which raged over the whole of her body.

'Please, God,' she found herself praying, 'whatever happens, let it be for his happiness! That is what I want above all else—that he should be happy.'

It was the fourth day since Orelia had come to Morden Park.

She walked across the garden carrying in her hands some writing-paper, an ink pot and a quill pen. The sun was warm on her hair and she felt it penetrating her thin muslin dress. And yet she felt cold.

She did not see the flowers rioting in the unkempt but beautiful garden, nor did she notice the profusion of butterflies floating from bloom to bloom, or hear the songs of the birds.

She was conscious only of a terrible loneliness which seemed to strike chill and freeze her heart so that it lay heavy in her breast like a continual pain from which there was no relief.

At the end of the flower-garden there was a small replica of a Grecian temple where Lord Morden had always worked.

There Orelia found, as she expected, a writing-desk besides a sofa and some comfortable chairs, now somewhat dilapidated and dusty.

She put her paper and ink pot on the desk and sitting down told herself sternly that it was time she began to earn her living. The Marquis had not come for her!

She knew now that she had lost him. She did not know whether he had married Caroline or if he was just no longer interested in her.

She only knew that she had lived for a moment in a miraculous world of fantasy, she had dreamt a dream that would never come true, and now she had awoken to reality.

How foolish she had been, she told herself, looking at a blank sheet of paper.

How could she suppose that he could really have wanted, even for a moment, anyone as insignificant as herself for his wife?

She had grown so used to thinking of him as first a lonely little boy and now as an unhappy man, she had forgotten how important he was!

She had omitted to consider his vast possessions, the position he held at Court, his consequence in the social world.

How childish, how absurdly presumptuous it had been of her to think that she could be anything to him but a passing interest—something that he had briefly desired simply because it was out of reach.

She picked up her pen and strove to concentrate her mind on composing a poem.

Should she write of the Flash Houses, of the children working in the mills, of babies that were stolen or borrowed from their mothers so that they could be used by begging women to evoke sympathy?

How often had she felt herself angry and deeply distressed by such suffering. But now she could think of nothing but the Marquis.

She could not see children, maimed and starving, but his handsome face, twisted smile, and his eyes looking down into hers. She loved him! Dear God, how she loved him!

A tear fell from her eyes and splashed onto the white paper. She must have been staring at it for a long time, but she had not written a single word.

The tear was followed by another, and then suddenly a deep voice said:

'Crying? And I had the conceit, my darling, to imagine that you would be pleased to see me!'

Orelia gave a startled cry and sprang to her feet; the quill pen splashed ink over the paper; but she had eyes only for the Marquis, who had come quietly across the grass so that she had not heard his approach.

He was wearing riding-breeches and polished boots, and he looked exceedingly elegant with his yellow waistcoat and a close fitting cutaway coat of grey whipcord.

He was carrying his high hat and his gloves in one hand, and now he threw them down to stand looking at her as she watched him wide-eyed, holding onto the back of a chair as if for support.

'You have . . . come!'

She said the words wonderingly, almost as if she spoke them to herself.

'Did you not expect me?' he enquired. 'If it has seemed a long time, my darling Heart, you must forgive me, but I had some important plans to make.'

Orelia felt a breathless happiness creeping over her and with an effort she said in a low voice:

'There is . . . something I would say to . . . you, My Lord.'

'I am listening,' he answered.

He made no attempt to draw nearer to her, but leant back against one of the pillars, unhurried and at his ease.

Orelia looked away from him across the garden. After a moment, as she did not speak, he said gently:

'I am waiting.'

'It is difficult . . . to put into . . . words,' Orelia hesitated. 'It is just . . . that . . . you said certain things . . . to me, the day you . . . rescued me from . . . Lord Rotherton. You were not . . . free . . . and perhaps you would not have . . . spoken . . . in different circumstances.'

She paused and then with an effort continued:

"I would not like you . . . now to feel . . . to feel tied.'

'Suppose I tell you that I do not feel tied,' the Marquis said. 'I am tied, irrevocably, Orelia.'

'It is not only that,' she murmured, her lips trembling. 'It is also . . . that I am not . . . suitable.'

'Not suitable for what?' he enquired.

'For such . . . an important, grand . . . position,' she managed to reply.

'The position I am offering you,' the Marquis answered, 'is very simple. It is that of my wife.'

For a moment Orelia could only quiver with an ecstasy which could not be denied. Then she heard him say commandingly:

'Look at me, Orelia.'

A sudden shyness made her long to resist him, and yet she must obey. She turned her head and across the space between them their eyes met. She drew in her breath.

She had never seen him look so young, so happy, so carefree, and now, as if he mesmerised her, she moved towards him, her eyes held by his, her lips parted.

Only as she reached him did he move, and slowly, almost as if he savoured the moment and wished to prolong it, he drew her into his arms.

It was then that she gave an inarticulate little sound and hid her face against his shoulder.

He held her for a moment, his cheek against her hair, and then with the same gesture he had used the first time they had met, he put his fingers under her chin and turned her face up to his.

He looked down into her eyes.

'If you only knew how I have dreamt of this,' he said softly and kissed her.

It was a very gentle kiss, almost as if he were afraid to touch the softness and the sweetness of her mouth.

Then as Orelia felt her lips respond to his, his arms tightened and she knew a rapture and a wonder beyond anything she had ever imagined.

She was his, his at last! And she must surrender herself body, heart and soul because he demanded it of her!

It was a moment so wonderful, so perfect, so utterly spiritual, that Orelia felt they were no longer in the world, but man and woman touched by the Divine.

She was trembling, and she had the feeling that he

was trembling too as he raised his head and said in a voice curiously unsteady:

'Have the stars fallen down, my precious darling?'

'No,' she whispered. 'You have taken me . . . up to . . . them!'

Then he crushed her against him and was kissing her, wildly, passionately, frantically, like a man come back to life from the grave . . .

Later, very much later, Orelia found herself sitting on the old sofa at the back of the Temple with her head on the Marquis's shoulder.

'Is Caroline married?'

'I have never seen a more radiant bride,' the Marquis answered.

'When were they wed?' Orelia asked.

The Marquis smiled.

'I gave Faringham my clothes, my carriage, the wedding ring, and my position at the altar.'

Orelia looked at him in astonishment.

'You mean he was married in your place?'

'There was a slight delay,' the Marquis said with a grin, 'but only a very slight one. Faringham was taking no chance of losing Caroline. As he said himself, it was a narrow squeak, for his ship nearly foundered in the Bay of Biscay!'

'But what did the Regent say? And the congregation?' Orelia asked.

'Prinny saw the amusing side of it when I explained to him what had happened,' the Marquis answered. 'And he was greatly relieved that the wedding breakfast should not be wasted.'

His eyes twinkled as he went on:

'As for the congregation, it gave them something to talk about, and the satisfaction of believing that the disreputable Marquis of Ryde had received a set-down for the first time in his life and one that was undoubtedly overdue. That really delighted them!'

He laughed, and then said more seriously:

'That was why, my darling, I was determined that

they should not gossip about you. So I have made a plan, to which I hope you will agree.'

'You know I will do . . . anything that you . . . wish of me,' Orelia said. 'But I am so glad about Caroline. She never loved anyone but George.'

'She certainly loves him now,' the Marquis replied. 'When they left for their honeymoon Caroline was running round him, obeying his slightest wish as if she were one of the Eastern women he had left behind in India.'

'Has he really made his fortune?' Orelia asked.

'He assures me he is as rich as Croesus,' the Marquis replied, 'and even if not, I would willingly have given him half my own wealth.'

He drew in a deep breath.

'I had lost hope,' he said. 'I could not believe that as I turned up the very last card—I would win.'

'We have been lucky,' Orelia said. 'So lucky, that even now I can hardly believe it is not a dream!'

'It is reality, my precious,' the Marquis told her. 'And now can I tell you my plans?'

'What are they?' she asked.

'Early this morning,' he replied, 'I sent two horses to your stable, although you were not aware of it. If we ride across country, which is very much quicker than going by road, we can be at Ryde Park in under three hours. Tonight we can be married in my private Chapel.'

'Tonight!' Orelia exclaimed. 'Can we really be married so soon?'

'Nothing can prevent it,' he answered, 'unless you no longer love me.'

'You know I want only to be with . . . you for the rest of our . . . lives.'

He kissed her cheek, his lips lingering against the softness of her skin, before, with what was obviously an effort, he continued:

'Because I cannot allow anyone to gossip about you, my beloved, it will be a very secret wedding, and the day after tomorrow we will go abroad. I am taking you

first to Florence where you can see the portrait of yourself painted nearly four centuries ago by Botticelli.'

He kissed her hair.

'Afterwards we will explore in the canals of Venice
and perhaps visit Rome. Two months after we have
been away, it will be announced that our marriage has
taken place abroad. By the time we return people will
be tired of talking about us. Some other scandal will
prove far more interesting!'

'It sounds so . . . wonderful!' Orelia murmured.

'Then let us start now,' the Marquis said. 'I have an
urgent desire, Orelia, to show you my house, which will
be our home in the future.'

She let him draw her to her feet before she said:

'I have just remembered, I have no riding habit here.
I left it in London and I threw away my old one when
Caroline and I went to stay with you.'

'I brought your habit with me when I drove down
from London this morning,' the Marquis said.

'You think of everything!' she exclaimed.

'I think of you,' he answered. 'In fact it is impossible for me to think of anything else.'

She put her cheek with a little gesture of affection
against his arm as they walked across the garden.

It seemed to Orelia that never had the flowers seemed
so bright, the butterflies so colourful, the song of the
birds so joyful.

The old servants at Morden House provided them
with a light meal, and when it was over Orelia and the
Marquis mounted two magnificent horses with an Arab
strain in them, and rode away across country towards
Ryde Hall.

It was a sunkissed day with just a slight wind to
relieve the heat. There was a shimmering haze over the
river, and the fields yellow with buttercups were like
a golden carpet specially made for them in their happiness.

They did not hurry. They stopped at a small way-
side Inn where they drank home-brewed cider, and later
the Marquis insisted that they should rest for a short
while in the shade of a wood.

Orelia knew that he made the excuse because he wished to kiss her, and after they had dismounted and tied up the horses she melted into his arms as if they were a haven of security which she never need leave again.

They sat on a fallen tree covered with moss. There was a stream running through the wood and they watched the dragon-flies gliding iridescently over the clear water, and a kingfisher winging its brilliant flight to and from its nest in the bank.

'Happy, my darling?' the Marquis asked, his eyes on Orelia's face.

She looked at him and he saw the answer in her eyes before she spoke.

'I did not know it was possible to be so happy,' she answered. 'I only wish we could stay here for ever . . . alone . . . away from the world . . . just you and me!'

'There is no need to be frightened of anything now I am with you,' he said.

'I am not really frightened,' she answered, 'but just a trifle apprehensive. Suppose I fail you!'

'You could never do that,' he answered 'in a deep voice.

'And I think I am afraid,' she went on, 'that after a while you will find me dull. You have known so many beautiful and witty women with great talents, and I have nothing to give you except my love.'

'Do you think I want anything else?' the Marquis asked, and taking her hand he kissed her fingers one by one. 'You see, my beloved, a man, whether he admits it or not, is always searching for the woman who will be to him the other half of himself. When he finds her she seems to him to be perfect. But until they meet he must look for her amongst many other women, always to be disappointed.'

'Am I the other half of you?' Orelia asked.

'You know you are,' he answered, 'save that you are the better half. All that is good, perfect, and lovely, while I am wicked . . .'

She put up her fingers and laid them against his lips.

'You are never to say that again,' she said. 'It was a nickname given to you because you were defiant. But your defiance sprang not from evil or vice but from your loneliness—because you had to fight the world by yourself.'

Her voice was very soft.

'To me you have always been everything that is good, noble and kind. I will not have you spoken of in any other way!'

The Marquis pulled her into his arms so roughly that she gave a little cry. Then he buried his face in her neck.

'I love you!' he said. 'God, how I love you! Make me as you wish me to be! Make me the man in whom you believe!'

It was growing late when finally they reached Ryde Hall. They came upon it suddenly, as they rode over a top of a hill, and there below them lay the great house, its windows shimmering gold in the evening sun.

Orelia had known that it was one of the largest houses in England, and it had been restored and added to by the Marquis's Grandfather. Now that she saw it she felt a sudden tremor of fear because it was so huge and imposing.

Then she looked at the Marquis and saw that he was watching her.

'You will be there!' she said softly—it was a statement not a question.

'Always,' he promised.

'I would have wished for no more than a cottage,' she said, 'where I could work for you, cook for you, look after you.'

'But as it is, will you take me as I am?' the Marquis asked.

There was a deep tenderness behind his words. He knew no other woman of his acquaintance who would wish his home was only a cottage.

'Yes . . . please!' Orelia answered simply, and held out her hand.

He kissed her fingers and then with one impulse they spurred their horses as if they were both filled with a desire to reach the house and all that waited for them there.

The bedroom into which Orelia was shown was magnificent. It was known, she was told, as the Bride's Room, and she felt even as she entered through the door that it had a strange, almost unearthly happiness about it.

A bath was waiting for her, scented with the fragrance of roses. There were two maids to help her undress and then as she wondered for the first time what she should wear, the Housekeeper brought from the wardrobe a gown she had never seen before.

'His Lordship sent it down from London, Ma'am, with your other clothes,' she explained.

Orelia looked at the gown and realised that perhaps this was one of the reasons why the Marquis had been delayed. It was the loveliest gown she had ever seen, made of fragile white gauze, and embroidered all over with tiny stars.

When she was dressed in it, she found that there was a tiara of diamond stars for her to wear in her hair and a necklace of them to clasp round her throat.

The Marquis must have scoured London, she thought, for these jewels, which she knew were not in the family collection, and she felt an almost overwhelming happiness because his thought for her extended even to every detail.

'You make a very lovely bride, Ma'am!' the Housekeeper exclaimed, and the maids stared at her as if she were a Princess in a fairytale.

Finally Orelia was ready to go downstairs. She wore a family veil of lace so fine that it was like a cobweb. It enveloped her like a cloud and made her look strangely ethereal, almost as if she were but a figment of a man's imagination.

As she came down into the Hall where the Marquis was waiting for her, she heard him draw in his breath.

He had a bouquet for her and as she took it she knew

that it too was symbolic. It was not of lilies or exotic
orchids, it was only a posy of tiny white rosebuds not
yet open.

The Marquis raised her hand to his lips. He did not
speak; he only drew her arm through his and led her
down long winding corridors until finally they came to
the Chapel.

There was a sound of soft music played on an organ,
but there was no one in the carved pews, and only the
Chaplain standing at the Altar.

The evening sunshine—golden, crimson—shone
through the stained-glass windows and there was a scent
of roses and honeysuckle. It seemed to Orelia when
the service began as if the whole Chapel was filled with
the songs of angels.

The Marquis held Orelia's hand tightly in his as they
repeated the solemn vows in low grave voices.

Then they walked back the way they had come, until the Marquis drew her into a small, very beautiful
Salon overlooking the rose-garden at the side of the
house.

A flunkey closed the door behind them, and then
the Marquis stood for a moment looking down at Orelia
before he took her in his arms.

"My wife, my love, my life!' His voice was deep with
emotion.

How long they were together in the Salon, Orelia
could never afterwards remember. She only knew that
she thrilled at the touch of him, that she felt an enchantment and an ecstatic joy which she had never
known before.

Afterwards they went into another room where dinner was laid at a small oval table decorated with
white flowers.

'Our second meal together,' the Marquis said with a
smile.

What they ate neither of them noticed, but they sat
talking long after the servants had withdrawn.

There seemed to be so much to say, so much to re-
late, so much to get to know about each other, that it

was with a start as the clock chimed on the mantelpiece that Orelia realised how late it was.

Her voice died away. She looked at the Marquis and knew without words what he was asking of her.

She rose and they stood for a moment looking into each other's eyes. He did not touch her. Then she turned and went up the stairs to the Bride's Room.

The maids were waiting for her. They undid her gown and lifted the tiara of stars from her head and brushed her hair. Finally they blew out the candles, leaving only one alight at each side of the bed, and retired.

The great room was dark, full of shadows, and yet it seemed to Orelia that she was surrounded by love which was reflected down the centuries—the love of other brides, of other women who had come to this great house and made it a home for themselves, their husbands, and their children.

She knelt down beside the bed to say her prayers, and when she had prayed she opened her eyes and saw that, although she had not heard him enter, the Marquis was standing just inside the room.

He was wearing a long brocade robe with a high collar of velvet, and he was standing looking at Orelia with an expression she had not seen on his face before.

Then the joy that was in her heart made her rise to her feet and run across the room to him, eagerly like a child, forgetting that she was clad only in the soft transparent chiffon of her nightgown.

She threw herself into his arms, felt him hold her close and knew that his heart was beating violently against hers.

'Oh, Darius!'

She hardly breathed the words. He did not kiss her, he only looked down at her, still with that strange expression on his face.

'Were you praying for me?' he asked, and his voice was deep.

'No,' she answered, 'I was thanking God that we had found each other . . . that we were together. Oh dearest, I am so grateful for our love!'

'Listen, my precious darling, I have something to say to you.'

Because the Marquis's tone was serious, Orelia felt a sudden little tremor of fear in case anything should spoil their happiness.

'What is . . . it?' she asked.

'We have not known each other very long,' the Marquis said. 'We have actually been together such a short time, that I want you to consider what I have to say.'

Orelia's eyes searched his.

'Is something . . . wrong?' she asked.

'No, indeed,' he replied. 'Nothing could be wrong now that you are my wife, now that I can call you mine. But my sweet Dream, if you would rather wait a little while for me to—own you, not only by name, but in actual fact, then I will wait! I love you so desperately, Orelia, that I could not bear to frighten you in any way!'

He paused before he went on:

'You know that I desire you as a man desires a woman. It is indeed a consuming fire within me, but I also adore and worship you because of your goodness, your purity, your innocence! That is why if you wish, I will wait—even though it will be hard—until you are ready for me.'

Orelia knew in that moment how much he loved her. He was, she was aware, making the greatest sacrifice that any man could make at such a moment.

Once before the Marquis had deliberately turned aside from his own need because he had known that even though she would have gone with him into the Social wilderness, she would have thought it wrong and it would have been against her deepest instincts.

Now he was controlling his desire—he was offering her not only his heart, but his body to do with it as she would.

For a moment the immensity of the sacrifice he was making made it hard for her to find words, and then she said very very softly:

'I know that our love is Divine . . . I know it has

been blessed by God . . . But just as you want . . . me as a woman . . . I want . . . you as a . . . man.'

For a moment he stared at her, and then his arms tightened so fiercely that she almost cried out with the pain.

'Do you understand what you are saying?' he asked. 'Are you sure, my precious? Are you really sure?'

'I love . . . you,' she whispered. 'I want to belong to . . . you . . . completely and . . . absolutely . . . I want to be . . . yours . . . please Darius . . . make me your . . . wife.'

She could say no more for the Marquis's lips, triumphant, possessive and fiercely passionate, sought hers.

Then lost in a rapture that was beyond expression, he lifted her in his arms.

ABOUT THE AUTHOR

BARBARA CARTLAND, the celebrated romantic author, historian, playwright, lecturer, political speaker and television personality, has now written over 150 books. Miss Cartland has had a number of historical books published and several biographical ones, including that of her brother, Major Ronald Cartland, who was the first member of Parliament to be killed in the War. This book had a foreword by Sir Winston Churchill.

In private life, Barbara Cartland, who is a Dame of the Order of St. John of Jerusalem, has fought for better conditions and salaries for Midwives and Nurses. As President of the Royal College of Midwives (Hertfordshire Branch), she has been invested with the first Badge of Office ever given in Great Britain, which was subscribed to by the Midwives themselves. She has also championed the cause for old people and founded the first Romany Gypsy Camp in the world.

Barbara Cartland is deeply interested in Vitamin Therapy and is President of the British National Association for Health.